Alias Simon Hawkes
Further Adventures of Sherlock Holmes in New York

Based Upon the Lost Notebook of
John H. Watson, MD.

Detail of drawing for "The Adventure of the Copper Beeches" by Sidney Paget, 1892

Based Upon the Character Created by
A. Conan Doyle

by Philip J. Carraher

ISBN: 1-4033-6991-7 (e-book)
ISBN: 1-4033-6992-5 (Paperback)

Library of Congress Control Number: 2002094120

This book is printed on acid free paper.

Printed in the United States of America
Bloomington, IN

1stBooks - rev. 03/31/03

Introduction

Readers of *The Adventure of the Dead Rabbits Society, The Lost Reminiscence of John H. Watson* will be familiar with the circumstances surrounding the fortunate discovery of that manuscript by Cornelius J. Watson, a descendent of the good doctor who so famously chronicled many of the cases of Mr. Sherlock Holmes. What was not mentioned previously was the fact that, together with the completed manuscript discovered tucked away at the bottom of the old Watson steamer trunk, was found a notebook utilized by Doctor Watson during his many visits to his now retired long-time companion and friend.

While containing no completed works, that notebook stated in detail many facts and circumstances surrounding cases taken on by Sherlock Holmes while away from London and presumed dead following his battle with Professor Moriarty at the Reichenbach Falls. The notes were created as a result of the many conversations the good doctor had with his famous friend following the detective's retirement.

The discovery of that notebook is fortuitous for those who faithfully follow the life and cases of Sherlock Holmes. Based upon the notations contained therein it was possible to recreate with some great degree of accuracy the occurrences of criminal investigation in which the great detective took part while presumed dead and residing in New York City in the United States.

I have selected certain adventures from among those that appear in John H. Watson's notebook based upon the unusual details of each case and/or the skill exhibited by Holmes to resolve it. Having made my selections, I then expanded the good doctor's brief, written facts into the narratives that follow. I sincerely hope they will prove to be acceptable to all readers, especially those legions who have read the original adventures of Mr. Sherlock Holmes as put down to paper by Doctor Watson himself.

Philip J. Carraher, 2002

Contents

The Adventure of the Magic Alibi

Chapter One

The skeleton moved forward, its shimmering shinbone appearing first in the dim light afforded by the small sconce on the wall; then came the bones of the rest of it, moving out of the slant of shadow in which it previously stood.

"May I take your coat, sir?" it asked.

David Conroy smiled as he surrendered his overcoat. It was a nice touch for a Halloween Party, having the attendants wear traditional Halloween costumes, although he doubted the dignity of the attendants thought much of it.

"Straight ahead, sir," directed the skeleton. "Down the hall."

As he followed the sound of music down the corridor, Conroy continued to be amused by the servants' costumes, the women garbed as witches and the men as skeletons. His smile expanded as he envisioned the reaction of his own elderly man-servant should he, Conroy, ever request the extremely dignified man wear such a costume. He would be unnerved completely.

The costumes did add to the festive mood of the party. A nice touch. Clifford Greenleaf knew how to throw a party, that much at least could be said for the man. He was fast gaining a reputation for his imaginative affairs within the wealthy society in which he so doggedly sought acceptance. Each event was a kind of engineered and choreographed little marvel, planned to the slightest detail so as to maximize the pleasure of the guests. *Too bad,* thought Conroy as he went down the hall, *my wife is away visiting her mother. She would no doubt find the night enjoyable.* Her absence forced David to come alone.

He reached the small room at the corridor's end and was surprised to see it designed so as to resemble a graveyard. Imitation tombstones and mausoleum facades sat here and there. A large mechanical owl hooted a protest down to him from a crooked tree branch as he stepped past the iron gates of the make-believe graveyard entrance. The place looked like a Bowery stage-set designed for a play featuring the exploits of grave robbers.

Whatever his other shortcomings, Clifford Greenleaf did know how to throw a party, no doubt about it.

The Greenleaf home was a handsome place, a small mansion, sitting at the top of Manhattan overlooking the North River where it held a fine commanding view of the waters. The house was at least a century old and contained much architectural charm very much admired by Conroy. It had been in the Pontseele family since it was built and was still known widely as *The Pontseele House* despite Greenleaf's ownership. It had recently passed to Greenleaf by virtue of his marriage to the last surviving Pontseele sibling, Virginia Pontseele. The marriage took place despite the objections and much to the dismay of Virginia's parents. Subsequently, both parents perished in a boating accident occurring in the waters beneath the windows of their own mansion.

Entertainment wandered here and there, primarily in the form of hired magicians who, strolling about, paused now and then to perform an eye-popping bit of prestidigitation before a small appreciative circle of onlookers. In the main room, just through the graveyard, a large band played tunes while guests danced or simply sat at the various tables situated about the room. Sitting, they either conversed or listened to the music while sipping their drinks and enjoying the excellent food.

This Halloween gala was, as Conroy was well aware, Greenleaf's most enthusiastically planned celebration. Greenleaf held a great appreciation for magic (the man was himself a skilled amateur magician) and what better atmosphere was there to both entertain and be entertained by feats of wizardry and pretend-witchcraft? Magic and the supernatural might be the norm on this special night when the spirits themselves surged from their sepulchers to walk the material world once more.

A skeleton approached Conroy and extended a small card to him. "For you, sir," declared the servant as he waggled the small card before Conroy's eyes.

"What is this for?" asked a mystified Conroy as he accepted the card and studied it. Clifford Greenleaf's personal card. Flipping it over, he saw that on the back was written the number eighteen in blue ink.

"It's a ticket, sir," responded the skeletal servant. "It will allow you to participate in a feat of magic that will be performed by Mr. Greenleaf himself at precisely midnight tonight. Only twenty people will be allowed to attend the private showing, ten men and ten woman. Upon instructions from Mr. Greenleaf, they are all to be selected arbitrarily. Will you attend? If not, I must give the ticket to someone else."

"I'll attend with pleasure," replied Conroy with a smile. Immediately he pocketed the Greenleaf card.

"Good, you must go up the stairs to the second floor at ten minutes or so before midnight. To the third door on the left of the corridor. Will you do that, sir?"

Conroy said that he would and then, checking his watch, noted the time: eight-thirty-five. It would be almost three and a half hours before the magic feat would be performed by Greenleaf.

Unknown to Conroy and to all others present, or almost all, Mrs. Virginia Greenleaf had just that approximate amount of time of life remaining to her. Shortly following the stroke of midnight, the unfortunate woman would be dead, a victim of a violent and bloody murder.

A murder in which the woman's killer would then be under the protection of an unshakable "magic alibi" shielding him from arrest and justice.

Chapter Two

Ten minutes prior to the stroke of midnight, the twenty men and women receiving the twenty invitations were directed to the entrance of a medium-sized room in the rear of the Greenleaf home. The hall in which they stood was dimly lit and filled with shadows, so much so that it was almost difficult to see the face of any person who was not standing immediately next to you. The room was a rectangular box, large enough to serve as a small den but certainly not sufficient to entertain a large group. The size of the room, reasoned Conroy, peering inside from the hall in which he and the others stood, explained the need for the limited audience. Even the twenty would be straining the walls.

The room was, as Conroy was soon made aware, one with a single entrance, that was the door leading to the hall, the door through which he and the nineteen others would pass to gain entry inside. Heavy purple velvet drapes covered the entire wall opposite the door. Unseen behind the curtains was a single window, nailed shut that very morning. With the nailing of the window, the door became the sole means of passage in or out of the small chamber. Against the wall, very near the drapes, stood a brand-new graphophone for the playing of music. It was silent now. In front of the drapes was a long metal pole on which was attached three incandescent lights that remained unlit. The interior of the room was as dimly lit as the hall.

What is the purpose of that? wondered Conroy when his eyes fell upon the pole of lights, barely discernable in the shadows. *Incandescent lights? Why not have the room lit if you have lights?* Perhaps the incandescent lights were not working properly; that would explain why the room's interior was now dependent upon the feeble light thrown off by a sole and lonely gaslight on one wall.

Another guest, a New York City Chief Inspector named William "Big Bill" Devery, was specifically selected by Greenleaf's servants (acting on Greenleaf's orders) to serve as "gatekeeper" to the room. That is, while the first twenty selected as spectators were locked inside the small room with Clifford Greenleaf, Devery would stand outside the lone entrance to the room and make certain that no one, neither magician nor spectator, left or entered the room.

A few minutes before the midnight hour, Clifford Greenleaf made his appearance in the corridor accompanied by the chief inspector. Greenleaf was dressed in the revolutionary "tux" recently created by Pierre Lorelard IV. The other men were clad in formal black tie and tails.

Greenleaf, a small, slim man of no more than five and a half feet in height and weighing just short of one hundred and thirty pounds, seemed to Conroy to be little more than a young man playing grownup. Still there was a flair, a magnitude of the man's personality, which compensated well for the diminutive physical proportions. The overall youthfulness of Greenleaf's countenance was also offset, in part at least, by his wearing a very sophisticated manicured goatee. His facial hair was dark brown, as was the hair atop his head.

"Hello, all," he greeted the twenty-one present. "I have gathered you here to be witness to an occurrence of such miraculous portent that you will of course disbelieve its truth. To verify its truth as best we can is why I've outlined a specific procedure that I ask you all to follow to the letter."

All those in attendance, including Conroy, were immediately tantalized by the Greenleaf pronouncement. *Miraculous portent. Very good.*

"This is not," continued Greenleaf, "as previously told to you, merely a magic trick but rather something else. I have, after years of study into the occult, discovered the means by which humankind, living physical beings, may pass over into the realm of the spiritual. I have discovered the means by which the unseen bridge between this physical world and the world of departed souls may be utilized and I mean to cross that bridge this night. In short, tonight I will, for a time, depart this world, and walk among the spirits."

A murmur of appreciation and even some wonderment purred through the small group.

"Unfortunately," Greenleaf went on, "the actual crossing over cannot—for reasons best left unspoken for now—be physically witnessed by other eyes. I am therefore forced to gain my witnesses in another manner other than the mechanism of sight. In a moment I will enter this room in front of which we stand. The door will be locked behind me by Mr. Devery. I've asked him to join us as a kind of gatekeeper to persuade even the most cynical that all is indeed on the up and up. Two things: First, this door is the only way in or out of the room. Second, and both I and Mr. Devery will give you our assurances on this, the Chief Inspector is not acting as a secret confederate of mine in any way. He is here, as all of you are, only to verify the truth of what occurs."

"That's certainly true," spoke up Devery as all eyes shifted to him. "I don't know what's goin' on here any more than you do. I was just approached earlier and asked to serve as a sentry in front of the door. That's what I'm goin' to do."

"Precisely," beamed Greenleaf. "Here's what will happen. As I said, I will in a few moments enter the room. The door will be locked behind me by Mr. Devery. I've given him the sole key. In precisely one minute after I enter, he will again unlock and open the door. By that time, I will have passed over to the other side. All of you will then enter the room for the sole purpose of verifying that the room is empty. The door will be locked behind you just as it was locked behind me. You will then have a full fifteen minutes to verify that I am indeed not inside and that there is no other way out. By doing that you will offer proof to the world that I can be in only one other place, that is, among those who exist within the spiritual world.

"As an extra added precaution, each of you, upon entering the room, will surrender your numbered ticket to Mr. Devery. No one without a ticket will enter, Devery will remain outside to lock the door and you will be free to study the entire room to make certain I'm gone. After the quarter-hour passes, Mr. Devery will again open the door and request that you leave. At that time, as you leave, he will return your numbered card to you. Each of you should check to make certain you receive the same numbered card as you surrendered to him, the same as you have now. Is everything clear?"

All present nodded their heads and murmured that it was. One of the women giggled nervously.

"Then we're set to go," responded Greenleaf. "I will now enter the room. I must state that there involves some risk to myself in doing what I'm about to do. Mr. Devery has instructions to summon assistance immediately if, when you enter, you should find me unconscious or injured inside."

With that touch of danger added to the mix, Greenleaf motioned to Devery to get the key ready for use, then turned and walked through the door. Immediately, Devery closed the door and twisted the key in the lock. "My instructions," he said as he pocketed the key, "are to wait exactly sixty seconds an' then open the door to let you all inside." Lifting his arm, he lowered his gaze to his pocket watch which contained a second hand. "So now we wait."

The seconds ticked by as all stood silently in the hall, most straining their ears to hear any sounds that might emanate from behind the locked door.

Their attempts were met with nothing but silence. There was nothing to hear excepting the faraway music of the band music floating up the stairs from below.

Conroy stood and considered the situation. Despite the fanciful patter, when all was said and done, Greenleaf was performing a simple disappearing act. He decided that he would do his best to find the man inside. There had to be a place in the room in which the man could hide or another way out, pure and simple, and, standing in the hall and waiting, he vowed to do his best to discover it.

Thirty seconds had passed when there came from behind the door an eerie whine, the sound of the howl of spirits. *A nice touch.* Conroy smiled as he noticed the goose flesh rising on the flesh of the bare arm of the woman standing beside him. "Goodness..." she murmured softly, placing her fingertips to her lower lip.

"It's just a trick," he whispered to her.

"Time," declared Devery and immediately he was at the door with the key. He pushed it open wide. Conroy, peering through, as did some of the others with a view of the interior of the room, could see no sign of Greenleaf inside.

"Please enter one at a time," instructed Devery. "As you enter, let me have your invitation. Greenleaf told me to tell you that the first to enter should go to the rear of the room, so as to allow those enterin' behin' you adequate space to go in as well. Once you're inside you're to do nothin' until told to do so. You're to enter in the order of the numbers on the tickets. Who's got number one?"

Number One, a woman wearing rather thick spectacles, handed her ticket to Devery and then stepped inside, somewhat timidly, or so it seemed to Conroy. *Shame about the glasses,* he thought. *Rather attractive otherwise.* At least she appeared so in the dim light.

Conroy, holding number eighteen, stood and watched as the other lower numbers entered before him. At last, the bulk of the audience in the room, he handed his own card to Devery and he too went inside.

The shadow-filled room accepted them all into its murk. If not for the gaslight they'd all be standing in complete darkness. As it was, they were as near to that blackness as it was possible to be and not have people tripping over each other.

Darkness to hide the seams of a secret door, perhaps? mused Conroy as he dutifully joined the group huddled by the purple drapes. There he turned and faced the entrance, waiting, as did the others, for further instructions.

Numbers nineteen and twenty entered behind Conroy and stood nearby. With their entry, Devery, standing in the doorframe, made his announcement. "I'll now close and lock the door. It will remain locked for fifteen minutes. Durin' that time you're free to search and examine the room an' all its contents to verify Mr. Greenleaf is indeed not inside. After the time is up, I'll open the door again an' you'll exit the room. As you leave, I'll give you back your ticket. Greenleaf asked me to remin' you that the purpose of this is to verify with absolute certainty that he is not inside. That will be his proof to others that he has crossed over. He therefore requests that each of you perform the best search you can. That's it."

With that Devery pulled the door shut. Conroy could hear the key turning in the lock.

A moment later, the room was filled with a sudden flash of blinding light as the three incandescent lights on the pole suddenly sprang to life. The suddenness and brightness of the light caused the twenty to gasp and cover their eyes. At the same time, the nearby graphophone began to play a rather eerie tune. Unable to see, the recorded music for the moment dominated their senses. Both effects, the light and the music, were the result of inventions created by the genius of Thomas Edison less than twenty years earlier. This display could not have been possible two decades ago. A couple of seconds and the bright lights were once again turned off. A few members of the audience giggled at their own nervousness.

"Well, now we know why the lights were here," spoke up Conroy. "To scare the life out of us."

There came a few murmurings of agreement from about the room.

"Well, shall we get down to business?" spoke up someone in the crowd and Conroy found himself responding: "Yes, let's find him. Assuming he told us the truth about there being no other way out he's got to be concealed in here somewhere."

The furnishings in the room consisted of a straight-backed wooden chair, a rather thick cherrywood table, a desk on which an unlit green-shaded banker's lamp was sitting, a bookcase and, opposite the desk, a small comfortable appearing loveseat. The bookcase, immediately beside the desk, held a few leather and cloth-bound novels and reference works on its shelves. Above the loveseat was a small framed daguerreotype, a portrait of Edgar Allan Poe. Beneath the portrait, in the same frame, was the famous author's signature. Conroy, seeing them, took them both to be originals. Greenleaf must be an admirer of the author. In the center of the floor was a small Oriental style rug.

Everyone began to search the room, haphazardly for the most part, sometimes bumping into each other as they moved about for the room was not large enough to permit so many to wander about without some inevitably coming into contact with others.

Conroy, determined to find the hidden Greenleaf, performed his own search in a very ordered systematic manner as compared to the others. He began first with the window behind the drapes. Moving aside the heavy cloth, he examined the window thoroughly. It was indeed nailed shut as they were told. Looking outside, he saw that it led nowhere but to empty sky. Even if the window did open, it couldn't be used as an exit. If Greenleaf had a secret means in and out of the room, this window wasn't it.

Near the window was the light that had flashed shortly after they'd entered the room. Three incandescent lights attached to a long thin pole. Nothing to see there. Against the wall was the graphophone, now silent as the recording had run its course. It was much too small to conceal the man or anyone for that matter.

He tapped and probed the wall and then continued around the entire room, knocking on the walls, checking for a concealed door. The ceiling too appeared solid enough but Conroy was not one to accept simple appearances. In the middle drawer of the desk he found a long ruler. Grabbing the wooden chair he stepped up on it and stood and tapped the ruler against the ceiling. Doing this about the entire room, checking walls and ceiling, moving aside the furniture when necessary, yielded no hidden place of concealment nor revealed another means out of the room. A check of the floor, even lifting the small rug, revealed no clandestine trapdoor.

There's no secret means in or out, concluded Conroy. *So he's still in here, hiding somewhere.*

But where?

No closets in the room. That left only the furniture. *Did any piece of furniture offer the man room enough to hide?*

The desk was the largest piece of furniture in the room and Conroy, weaving his way between the wanderings of other searchers, went to it. It was a heavy piece of furniture, as Conroy had discovered when he'd earlier pushed it aside to check the wall behind it and the floor beneath. He'd succeeded in moving it but only with some real effort. Now he'd inspect the desk itself.

First the light. It suddenly dawned on Conroy that he could put on the incandescent banker's lamp and thus gain more light. Stupid not to think of it earlier. However when he tried to put it on, nothing happened. Broken? Or did Greenleaf make certain it wouldn't work, wanting shadows instead of illumination in the room?

Back to the desk. It appeared to be very ordinary. A businessman's desk. The middle where the legs went, was open on both sides. Conroy could see through to the wall. The top was inlaid with leather with a gold scroll design running around its edges. There were large, spacious-appearing drawers on either side and, across the middle, another much more shallow drawer. It was from this middle drawer that Conroy had earlier removed the ruler.

Two drawers on each side, four all together. He checked the top two first, right and left, and saw nothing inside but writing materials and a few reference books. The lower drawers were deeper, the size of small cabinets. A look in the lower left-hand side drawer revealed nothing of interest. When Conroy went to check the final drawer, the bottom one on the right, he was surprised to find it was not a drawer at all, but rather a camouflaged door concealing a small combination safe that was secreted in the desk.

A tug on the handle of the safe door revealed it was locked tight. Still, thought Conroy, there was no real reason to look inside, the safe was much too small to allow someone, even someone with the slight stature of Clifford Greenleaf, to conceal himself inside. The safe at least explained the troublesome weight of the desk and the effort he'd had to make in moving it away from the wall and back again.

Not the desk. The loveseat, perhaps?

Yes, if the loveseat was hollowed out beneath the cushions there would be plenty of space for the man to hide. A quick check of it however produced nothing but additional frustration. The loveseat was very ordinary and had not been tampered with so as create a place of concealment. What was left? The bookcase was out of the question, it was nothing more than a few pieces of wood. *But the table. Perhaps....*

Conroy stepped over to the table and studied it. It was a good five feet in length and three feet wide. A good stout piece of furniture with thick legs and top.

Could he hide in there? But a quick check of the table, begun with high expectations of success, offered him no triumph. There was no hidden latch that would allow the table top to be lifted and permit someone to lay down and disappear within its shallow depth. A few raps of the knuckles on the wood produced no echo but rather the deep sound of dense thickness. The table was apparently as solid as it appeared to be.

Conroy's bafflement was complete. Greenleaf, as far as he could determine, was no longer inside the room. "I'll be cursed," he muttered to himself. "Where is he?"

He checked his watch. The allotted fifteen minutes was just about up.

"Gone over," responded a woman who'd overheard his remark. "Gone over to the other side, just like he said."

Another minute and the door was opened once more. "It's time to leave," announced the police commissioner. "Please be advised that the experiment is not entirely over. As each of you leave, wait in the hall for further instructions."

Each person left the room as they entered, one at a time, this time the numbered ticket being handed back to each of them as they exited the room.

"Greenleaf has previously asked me to extend his thanks to you," said Devery once the twenty were again in the hall. "The experiment is however only partially complete. Greenleaf must make his way back from the spiritual world in which he (or so he told me) now exists. He will shortly reappear in the room. I will again lock the door. For the next ten minutes I must stan' guard outside to assure that no one goes in or out. I ask one of you to volunteer to stan' with me durin' that time. Greenleaf would like there to be two witnesses just in case you believe that I'm workin' with him."

"I'll stay," piped up Conroy, prodded by frustration over his failure to ferret out Greenleaf's hiding place. He had no intention of leaving in any case.

"Thank you, Mr—?"

"Conroy."

"Conroy. Thank you. In the meantime, the rest of you may return to the party proper. Or stay if you wish. If you leave, I ask that you respect Mr. Greenleaf's request and return here within ten minutes."

The others murmured common consent and most began to drift off.

It was five minutes afterward that a cry of thief was suddenly heard. *A Halloween prank?*

"Good God! She's dead! She's dead!" This time the shouts contained true horror and left no doubt as to their genuineness. This was no Halloween prank.

Conroy and Devery, as did the others nearby, went running toward the sound of the screams of brutal murder.

Chapter Three

"Excuse me. Mr. Hawkes."

Simon Hawks lifted his face from the newspaper on his lap to gaze at the speaker, immediately recognizing the face of Detective Cullen, the same detective he'd assisted in resolving the heinous murders chronicled by John H. Watson years later under the title *The Adventure of the Dead Rabbits Society*. Cullen was a large, thick man with a head of light hair, a pleasantly pugnacious face, a tenacious jaw and a good-sized blond-red moustache that now, following the contour of the detective's deep frown, seemed to droop with depression.

"Detective Cullen," said Hawkes by way of a greeting. "What brings you here to the Dead Rabbits?" Folding the newspaper he pointed its paper snout to the easy chair next to his, an invitation to Cullen to sit.

The referred to "Dead Rabbits" was The Dead Rabbits Society, a men's-only establishment located on Prince Street in New York City. Sherlock Holmes, under the name of Simon Hawks, obtained a room in this establishment and remained ensconced there for most of the time he remained incognito in America. He was seated now in its main room, very near the blazing hearth.

Cullen accepted the offer to sit. "The reason for my coming to you is in your hands, Mr. Hawkes," he replied, pointing a stubby finger to the folded newspaper held by Simon. "You saw the lead story, no doubt, telling of the murder of Mrs. Virginia Greenleaf. That's why I'm here."

"Oh? The news story is quite wanting I must say, just stating a few facts. Not very clearly either. More emotional than factual. The Pontseele family is very rich and very well known. The murder is quite shocking, to say the least." Hawkes' keen eyes sparkled. The reading of the case had clearly interested him in it and he was eager to hear what Cullen had to say.

It was an unusually agitated and clearly frustrated Detective Cullen who responded. "Shocking. And frustrating—"

"Ah, here comes my half-glass of cognac," broke in Hawkes as the drink he'd previously ordered was brought over to him. "Would you like anything?"

"A glass of water will do. I'm on duty. Thanks"

Hawkes took a sip of his cognac from the snifter, then placed it on the nearby side table and faced Cullen. "The tabloids," he said, "are filled with conflicting stories about suspects in the murder. One says it's Clifford Greenleaf and the next insists it's not. What do you say, Cullen? Do you indeed suspect the husband of killing his wife?"

"Mr. Hawkes, the woman herself named her husband as her killer," responded Cullen firmly. "In her own blood, as she lay dying and bleeding to death she wrote the words: *Cliff killed me*. A bloody sprawl on the wall of her bedroom. It doesn't get plainer than that in my opinion. I'm convinced the man's guilty as sin."

"I read of that message in the papers. So it's true. But I don't understand. If that's so, then why isn't he under arrest?"

The detective shook his head.

"He's got an alibi, Mr. Hawkes. A perfect alibi. In fact, the others, other detectives, I mean, are convinced the woman's dying declaration is nothing more than a forgery, written by the woman's true killer to try to pin blame on her husband. This despite the blood on her fingertip and her own fingerprint pressed onto the wall at the end of her declaration."

"That would seem sufficient to indicate she did indeed write the message."

"They say the murderer could have picked up her hand after she was dead, dipped her fingertip in her own blood and written the message by moving the victim's hand."

"It would indeed take a cold-blooded killer to do that. But cold-blooded killers do exist. However, despite this plausible explanation, you continue to believe it's her husband who murdered her?"

"I'm certain of it. I can read it in his eyes. I feel it in my bones."

Hawkes grunted derisively. "Please, Mr. Cullen, don't talk of feelings. You're a detective. Facts are what count. Feelings are irrelevant. What of the possibility that he had an accomplice? Someone else who killed his wife, while he built himself this unbreakable alibi?"

"Yes, I wondered that…but then why would Mrs. Greenleaf write specifically: 'Cliff killed me'?"

"Yes, quite correct. You cannot say the message is valid, that is, that Mrs. Greenleaf identified her killer as her husband and then declare that she was then murdered by someone else, even an accomplice. If the message in blood is true, her last living declaration, then it must have been Clifford Greenleaf who did the deed. But if he could not have done it then it must stand that the message is false."

"I know…but…" Here the detective's hand bunched into a fist. "Goddamn it, it's him! I know it! It's him!"

"What's the man's motive for killing his wife?"

"Motive?"

"Surely that's not a new concept, Cullen. Why did he kill her?"

"I-I don't know—for certain, that is. The money probably. She's rich and he—"

"There's a history of marital problems?"

"I-I don't know…"

"Still, Cullen, you have your *feelings*," said Hawkes with some sarcasm. "What then is this perfect alibi you mentioned? Perhaps it isn't as perfect as you think."

"If there's a hole in it I can't see it." Here Cullen pulled from his pocket his small black notebook, opened it and started turning pages. "May I tell you the facts of the case."

Hawkes replied that he was all ears and leaned back in his chair, prepared to sit and listen.

"The facts," said Cullen, "simply stated, are these: At approximately twenty minutes after midnight on the last night of October, the body of Virginia Greenleaf was discovered on the floor of her bedroom. She'd been stabbed three times in the back and died of the wounds she received within minutes of the attack.

"She bled profusely, one of the stab wounds slicing a major artery, but lived long enough to use her own blood and the forefinger of her right hand to print a dying declaration on the wall near the floor where she lay dying. Cliff killed me. We interpreted this—"

"Excuse me, but you said you'd state the facts. It's your *thought* that Virginia wrote this note, is it not? While others see it differently. It's therefore not yet a fact, but simply a conjecture on your part."

"It's a fact as far as I'm concerned."

"May I ask an obvious question? Was Virginia acquainted with another Cliff? Someone else with the same first name as her husband?"

"We did ask ourselves that same question. She knew one other Cliff."

Cullen turned a page in his notebook. "Here. A Clifford Clemens. He was miles away on Halloween night."

At that moment Cullen's water arrived. Cullen took a quick gulp and placed the glass on the table beside Hawkes' cognac.

"And why was Virginia in her bedroom? While the party was taking place? Why wasn't she with her guests?"

"I asked that too. It seems she's come to hate her husband's big parties. She's been refusing to attend them for a while now. She greets the guests just to be polite and then goes and stays in her room, to read usually."

Hawkes nodded his head and Cullen continued his narrative.

"A servant discovered the body. He went to Mrs. Greenleaf's bedroom driven there upon his hearing her screams. Screams 'that raised the hair on the back of my neck' is the way he put it. Thief! Thief! Help me! He's killing me! He's killing me! He ran to the room, entered and saw the woman lying on her stomach in a pool of blood, her right hand on the floor extended from her shoulder with the forefinger pointing to the bloody message sprawled on the wall just above the floorboard. No one else was in the room. Facts."

"She hollered thief? Why would she do that if it was her husband who attacked her?"

"I'm guessing she didn't know it was him right off. Maybe he was wearing a mask to disguise himself. She might have pulled it off if she struggled with him."

"More conjecture. Please go on."

"I arrived on the scene and looked about. After seeing the message on the wall, I of course directed my attention to the husband. It was then I ran into the brick wall of his rather astounding alibi. There are twenty people, twenty-one counting Chief Inspector Devery himself, who are prepared to swear with absolute certainty that Clifford Greenleaf could not have killed his wife."

"What is astounding about that? They were with him at the time the killing took place, were they not?"

"They believe they know where he was."

"What? What the devil does that mean? Either they were with him or they weren't."

"If only it was that simple. Greenleaf is an amateur magician. He performed a magic feat that night. That feat is now his alibi."

"A magic feat?"

"Greenleaf selected a few guests to be an audience for his little trick. Here are the basic steps of it as confirmed by all twenty-one people involved. During the course of the party, one of Greenleaf's servants went around handing out tickets arbitrarily to guests, that is, Greenleaf's own personal card with numbers written on the back, permitting those selected to view the trick. Twenty in all were selected.

"Each was given instructions to go up the stairs to the second floor just before midnight and stand in front of a specific room to meet Greenleaf. This each one did. At a few minutes before midnight Greenleaf too shows up with, get this, Chief Inspector Devery in tow. He declares to the group that he has discovered a means by which he's able to cross over to the spiritual world. He tells them all that he'll enter the small room in front of which they're all standing and will, once inside, cross over. That's all talk to build up the illusion. What he actually does is a disappearing act inside. He enters the room alone. The door is closed behind him. After a minute, the others are allowed to enter. All do so except the chief inspector who remains outside to lock and guard the door. Inside they find Greenleaf is gone from the room. They search for him, for a quarter-hour as per Greenleaf's own instructions to them, and fail to find him inside. He has apparently crossed over as he said he would."

"Now I'm confused," broke in Hawkes. "If Greenleaf was not in the room then where is his alibi?"

"That would be so," replied Cullen. "Except that everyone present is, in fact, prepared now to state that Greenleaf *was in the room*. Hence his alibi."

"Let me be certain," said Hawkes, his eyes glittering and leaning forward in his chair. "The room was searched. No Greenleaf was found. Yet all those who did *not* see the man are convinced he was there with them all the time?"

"That's it."

"And pray, how is that possible?"

"Because he *was* in the room," responded Cullen. "Or so he says. Despite them not finding him. It'll be clear in a moment. Just let me state what happened in the correct sequence."

"Please go on. This is getting extremely interesting," said Hawkes, once again leaning back in the easy chair. A slight smile appeared momentarily on his face.

"After the twenty searched the room," continued Cullen, "the door was unlocked by the chief inspector who was out in the hall. All inside were all asked to leave but to return within another ten minutes. During that time the door to the room would remain locked. When again the twenty and the chief inspector assembled, the door would be opened and Greenleaf would reappear inside. During the time the door was locked and the room vacated the chief inspector and one guest, a certain David Conroy—"

"David Conroy?" spoke up Hawkes. "I've met him. A member here."

"Yes, well, Devery and Conroy stayed outside the door the entire time, until the scream of murder went up, that is. Then, like many others, they went running toward the screams."

"If I understand it correctly, these two, Devery and Conroy, remained in front of the door to this room until the screams were heard. And no one went in or out during that time. In addition, the door was locked."

"That's right."

"And Greenleaf was in the room all this time?"

"Correct, again."

"Pray, go on. How was it possible that the man was inside the room yet no one could see him?"

Cullen nodded his head. "When I went to Greenleaf to question his whereabouts at the time of the murder, he revealed to me the secret of his so-called grand illusion. There was a desk in the room. It appears to be an ordinary desk of good quality but that ordinariness is in fact a deception.

"The desk was ordered and built upon instructions supplied by Greenleaf. There is what appears to be a small safe on the right-hand side where the lower drawer would be. It is a false safe with only a door and no sides or back to it. The upper drawer also on the right is deceptive too in that it goes back only half-way. But that wouldn't be apparent to anyone who didn't pull the drawer completely out of the desk. The result of all this is that there exists a space on the right-hand side of the desk quite sufficient to allow a man of Greenleaf's rather small stature—the man is a little less than five and a half feet tall and weighs about as much as one of my legs—to conceal himself. This is what he told me he did. That he was sitting knees to chest inside the desk the entire time the room was being searched and that he was therefore *inside* the locked room at the time his wife was killed."

"I begin to see," said Hawkes, chuckling, his eyes glittering. "He enters the room and conceals himself within his trick desk. The twenty others come in and search for him in vain. They're then asked to leave but to return in ten minutes to witness the return of Greenleaf in the supposedly empty room. During that time, the door to the room is locked and outside there is standing the chief inspector and Mr. David Conroy to verify that it remained locked throughout—or at least until after the cries of murder were heard."

"Right, Greenleaf said that during that time, he simply exited the desk and waited inside the room for Devery to open the door so that he could complete his illusion."

"And being locked inside the room, he couldn't possibly be in his bedroom killing his wife."

"Precisely."

"If you are to be proven right, Cullen, in your *feelings*, then, for Greenleaf to have murdered Virginia, it must stand to reason that there is another way in and out of that room."

"Yes, that's what I thought right off and me and my men went over the whole room myself searching for it. Another way in and out. But it isn't there! There is no other way in or out of that infernal room! The walls, ceiling and floor are solid as iron. There's a window behind some drapes, but it's nailed permanently shut. It couldn't have been used. The nails are solid and haven't been disturbed at all."

"You're certain? There's no other way in or out except the door?"

"Certain."

"And you find no fault with the statements of Conroy or Devery? They remained outside the door and the door was locked throughout?"

"No and yes."

"Then the man is innocent and your feelings are wrong," responded Hawkes with a shrug.

Cullen bristled as though receiving a personal insult. "No, the man's guilty. He did it. I've interviewed enough criminals to know when I'm being lied to. I'm right ninety percent of the time and I'm right now. When I talked to him I got the sense of a man *pretending* to be a distraught husband, pretending and nothing more. He's a man secretly gloating over his own cleverness. I see through him—I do—and what I see is a man enjoying the fact he's getting away with murder. And—there was something else…"

"Something else?"

"Don't laugh at me, Mr. Hawkes, but when I went into that bedroom and saw that body, I-I felt something…a woman's presence. It was as if Mrs. Greenleaf herself was talking to me. Her spirit anyway. She told me—I swear it was she telling me!—It was her husband stabbed her to death. A woman's voice it was, whispering a secret into my ear. I heard it clear as day."

Simon Hawkes, the man who'd moments ago insisted Cullen be specific as to the facts, responded with a sneer. "You insist the man is guilty because the spirit of the murder victim told you so?"

Cullen lowered his eyes. "I know how foolish that sounds. I do."

Hawkes leaned back in his chair, lazily took another swallow of his cognac and asked Cullen if the detective had any objection if he, Hawkes, spoke to David Conroy.

Cullen lifted his head, his eyes filled immediately with appreciation. "Of course not. That's why I've come. To plead for your help. Do you see a way that Greenleaf could have done this?" he asked, his voice now edged with optimism.

Hawkes shook his head. "Not right off. If what you're saying is true and Clifford Greenleaf did indeed murder his poor wife, then there must exist a means, a mechanism of sorts, by which he got out of that room undetected to perform the deed. If that's so, and if you did your search as diligently as you say, then it is a means extremely clever, perhaps even ingenious, since no one has yet detected it. If you're right in your *feelings* and he is the killer of his wife then it is indeed a very interesting and tangled knot we must unravel. I'd like to talk to Conroy to get an eyewitness account of what exactly occurred. Maybe something he says will offer some insight." With that he drained the last of the cognac from the goblet. "But," he added as he put the empty snifter down, "It is equally likely, right now at least, that he will convince me of nothing more than Clifford Greenleaf's innocence."

Cullen rose up out of his chair, gratitude resting on his weary features. "Thank you, Mr. Hawkes. Thank you. I'm certain that if *you* give it a look you'll see the way to the truth of it. The man is as guilty as Satan himself. I'm certain of it." He took Hawkes' hand and shook it heartily. "Thank you," he said once more, then he turned and strode out of the room.

Hawkes watched the detective's back until the man was out of the room. A good man. A detective who, unlike many, strove for justice albeit with very limited abilities. A man with a club foot attempting to run a long race.

Still, even the desire for justice was more than many other detectives working on the city police force held. Hawkes had been in New York City long enough to become aware of how detectives were, all too often, appointed here. Corruption more than ability served to create the New York City detective force. Little wonder then that so many were so inept.

Until appointments were made based on talent rather than payment of funds, little more than ineptness could be expected. Cullen was better than most.

The chief inspector mentioned by Cullen was a case in point. "Big Bill" Devery was corrupt to the core, and thought little of his own corruption, considering it the norm. When queried on it, he often admitted the fact readily. He was an East Side clubhouse man intimately involved in both the hiring and promotional opportunities of the police. It cost a man approximately $300 to become a patrolman, $1,400 to be promoted to sergeant and a bit more than that to make detective. Whether or not Cullen was one who rose to his current position through payment or through ability Hawkes did not know, and had no desire to discover.

Devery's payoffs came to him through his tailor. Anyone who wanted to buy an opportunity simply went to Devery's tailor and ordered a suit, a very expensive suit that cost much more than the material used or the labor expended in its making warranted. Corruption well known to many, but still able to flourish. For the time at least. There were voices in the city beginning to be raised against it.

The Greenleaf murder. One thing was clear, the woman had been murdered. If not by her husband then by someone else. She deserved justice in either case.

But if by her husband.... Hawkes' eyes gleamed at the thought. If Greenleaf was guilty as Cullen suspected, then here was a crime of great interest. Unique even in Sherlock Holmes' vast experience. If Virginia Greenleaf was indeed killed by her husband, then he was being presented with a murder quite unlike any that had previously come before his eyes. He rubbed his hands together in anticipation of that very real possibility.

Chapter Four

David Conroy shook hands with Hawkes as he entered the room. "Come on in, Mr. Hawkes. Bit of a while since I've been to the Rabbits. "Good to see you again."

"Thanks for seeing me," responded Hawkes, offering Conroy a fleeting smile.

"Can I get you anything? Scotch?"

"No, thank you. How's the latest book?"

Conroy, a part-time writer, chuckled. "In terms of execution, it's fine. In terms of sales, moribund and losing what little pulse exists. But I can't say I'm disappointed. I never expect my books to sell well. One thing I apparently don't have is my finger on the collective pulse of the masses. A *Nights with Uncle Remus*, it's not."

"I'm sorry, Nights with—?"

"A collection of tales by Joel Harris. Quite nice, but not the sort of thing I'm interested in. It's selling well for him."

Conroy prepared a scotch for himself for himself and the two men went to a set of armchairs that stood facing each other before the hearth in the parlor. The fire was burning steady and bright. Except for one sconce on an opposing wall containing a wan electrical light, the fire was the sole illumination in the shadowy room. Drapes pulled stubbornly across the windows kept all daylight from entering. Once the men were seated, the flames of the hearth glowed yellow-orange on the sides of their faces, as though the last rays of light from a setting sun were shining upon them despite the opposition of the heavy drapes.

"I understand from our last talk that you are an art collector," said Hawkes. "I happened to talk to someone recently who wishes to sell a small drawing by Degas. Would you be interested?"

Conroy, a connoisseur of the new Impressionists school of art, both the American and French variants, now gaining in prominence and notoriety, smiled at the news. "Certainly. A Degas? That'd be great. I have a drawing by him now. It is one of the loves of my life. Another would be wonderful."

Hawkes, who had little interest in art, simply nodded his head. "The man happened to mention he was looking to sell it and I thought of you. Here's his card." Hawkes produced a business card and handed it over to Conroy.

Conroy accepted it as though it was gold.

"Virginia Greenleaf," said Hawkes, as Conroy tucked the card away into the breast pocket of his suit jacket, "what can you tell me of her murder?" He wanted to get straight down to business.

"Virginia...a good person. We were friends for a long time, you know. She spoke to me over the telephone just the night before..." Conroy's eyes filled with genuine sadness.

"You spoke to her the night before? May I ask what about? Did she mention her husband at all?"

"Well, yes, in a manner of speaking. Virginia is not normally overly status conscious yet she did complain to me about being left off the list of 'the 400'. She thought it was quite possibly because she married Cliff. Married beneath her status, you see. But she wasn't bitter, I don't think."

"I'm sorry. You mentioned 'the 400'?"

"You don't know of it? Well, why should you? It's pompous silliness really. It's a term coined recently by Ward McAllister, who fancies himself the city's social arbiter. It evolved from the fact that the Astor ballroom can hold only 400 people. Hence they invite only that number to their affairs. McAllister remarked something to the effect that there are only 400 persons worth inviting in all of New York society. A slap in the face to those who are not invited, those not on the Astor list. Virginia was, quite rightly, insulted, for her family as well as for herself. They're excluded now from the Astor affairs. Her marriage. It came up in our talk. We chattered about some other things as well. Nothing important."

"I see. But you're not aware of any other—friction shall we say—between Mrs. Greenleaf and her husband?"

"Not at all. That detective who was here. What's his name—"

"Cullen?"

"Yes, that's him. He asked me the same thing, evidently looking for a motive for the murder. Suspected Clifford. That can't be right though. The man couldn't have done it. And the motive must have been robbery. Virginia was after all screaming thief when she was killed. But this Cullen is not so sure it's that simple, for some reason. There was some desperation in his coming to me, I think. He was trying to find something, anything, to support his theory. He's convinced robbery was not the motive. That it was deliberate premeditated murder. Unfortunately, nothing I could tell him was of any use to him. He questioned me for more than an hour. It seemed to me he was trying to poke holes in Greenleaf's alibi. He was almost insistent that I, and the others there, had to be wrong when we told him that Greenleaf was locked inside that little room at the time Virginia was killed."

"And you cannot be wrong about that?" asked Hawkes.

"Ah, he's got you thinking Greenleaf did in his wife, too. No way. It's impossible."

"Yet an accusation was written in blood by her own hand."

"Yes, and a good little frame-up that would have been, if the man didn't have us there to prove he couldn't have done it."

"Still, it is strange. If it was a thief caught in the act of stealing, why would he stop in his flight to print such a message? Especially after the woman screamed so loudly. Thief! she shouted. Loud enough for others to hear. How could a thief expect such a ruse to work under those circumstances? It's much more natural that a thief, certainly under those conditions, having just been forced to kill, would simply rush from the house, isn't it?"

"Um, yes, I suppose, now that you say it…."

"It would also have to be a thief familiar with the names of those living in the house, since the name of Cliff was written."

"Well, that could be."

"Yes, could you tell me, please, exactly how Greenleaf performed his illusion? Down to the smallest detail. Perhaps there is a way he could have gotten out of that room, without you and the others realizing."

"Well, let's see. We, the twenty of us selected to participate, and Chief Inspector Devery, stood outside the room as Greenleaf, after building up the trick with some talk of crossing over to the spirit world, went inside. The door was locked by that Devery fellow. After a minute or two, the time needed, I now assume, to allow Greenleaf to hide in his trick desk, we, the twenty, were let in. We filed in one at a time, handing over our tickets to Chief Inspector Devery as we went in—"

"Handing over your tickets. Please tell me precisely how that was done."

"Yes, well, it was done for control reasons. Each ticket was numbered, one to twenty. The chief inspector collected them in numerical order until he had all twenty cards. This way he knew that only those who were supposed to enter, did."

"I see. Now you're all inside."

"The room was empty. Or at least Greenleaf was by then out of sight. We were all told to stand before the drapes at the back of the room which we did. Then, after everybody had entered, Devery told us we had fifteen minutes to search the room, to verify that beyond a doubt Greenleaf was indeed gone. Devery closed the door and locked it. I heard the key turn. Then we all started to search—no, wait, I remember, first there was this flash of bright light. It was sudden, made us all jump a bit. Which is I guess what it was supposed to do. It was a Halloween party after all and so a little fright was appropriate. Then there was that spooky music playing in the room which added to the mood, and we began to search."

"Music?"

"Yes, one of those new-fanged recording cylinders playing on those new graphophones put out by Bell's cousin. Cliff Greenleaf loves all the new gadgets and he got one for his little display. They're quite amazing. Sound from a machine. Sound comes from nowhere seems like. Like magic."

"That light you mentioned. Was it bright enough to blind you?" asked Hawkes.

"Yes, it was quite blinding. Came on all of a sudden and the room was dark previously, just one gaslight to give us light. So the flash of bright light did blind us all. For a few seconds we couldn't see. At least I couldn't. I found out later that it was part of Devery's instructions. There was a switch in the hall. After we were in the room he was told to put it on, wait a second or two and put it off again. That's what he did."

"Interesting."

"Well, we began to search. I took it seriously. More so than most. I was determined to find the man. I checked the floor, the ceiling, the window, banged on the walls looking for a secret door. Nothing. I remember going over the furniture, including the desk, looking for a place he could hide. It fooled me. It didn't occur to me that the safe in the desk was a fake and half the drawers were cut away. Looking at it then, I didn't think the man had enough room in it to hide. But that's where he was all the time, as it turns out.

"After the time was up, Devery again opened the door. We left in the same order as we entered and he handed each of us our card back. Twenty in, twenty out. He then told us to come back in ten minutes, at which time he would open the door and we would see Greenleaf again inside, supposedly having returned from the other dimension into which he slid. To make certain no one either entered or left by the door during that time, Devery and I stood outside, standing guard. The door was locked all the time, right up until the time we heard the screams."

"Hum, the idea of taking the cards from each person as they went inside, was that Devery's idea, or was he acting on Greenleaf's instructions?"

"I asked him that same question, as we were waiting together. It was Greenleaf's instructions that it be done that way."

"I suppose it served as a guarantee that no one would remain hiding in the room, after the fifteen minutes had passed, and so see him climbing out from the desk."

"Didn't think about it. But that does make sense. It seemed at the time to add a sense of—of scientific certainty—to the whole stunt, which was after all presented as a kind of experiment to us. Made the thing that much more impressive."

"You and Devery never left the door while you both stood guard? Not even for a moment?"

"Never. Not until we heard the screams. I'm telling you, Simon. There's no way Greenleaf left that room before then. He went in and never went out. There's no way he could have killed his wife. No way."

Simon Hawkes pursed his lips. "It would seem so," he murmured. "It would certainly seem so. But you never saw Greenleaf 'reappear' if I understand you correctly. You never saw him walk *out* of the room after he walked in."

"No, that's so. When we heard the screams we all went running, or at least I think we all went running. I stopped paying attention of course, so we never saw Greenleaf finish his illusion. But it makes no difference, does it? He entered the room and then we, twenty of us, went in after him. The door was locked. Then twenty of us went out and the door locked again. Greenleaf *had* to be in that room simply because he had no opportunity to leave. He had to be in that room when Virginia was murdered. There is no other possibility."

"Do you know if Greenleaf and Devery are friends? Could he have been a participant in the illusion? Working with Greenleaf?"

"I don't know. But even if he was, what means could he have used to help Greenleaf get out of that room? I tell you it's an impossibility. And even if Devery was willing to help him with his illusion I seriously doubt he would continue to keep that knowledge secret after what happened. He is on the police force, after all."

"Yes, still, I'd like a word or two with him. I think I know where I can find him. One more thing, do you know any of the others who went with you into that room? Can you give me their names?"

"Only one, a Mrs. Durbin, an older lady and friend of my wife's. No one else was familiar to me."

"Well, I thank you, both for your time and your clear statement of what occurred at the Greenleaf house." Hawkes rose up from his chair. "I wish you luck in obtaining your drawing. I do believe it can be had for a good price given my observation of the man who wishes to sell it. He is in need of funds unless I miss my guess."

Chapter Five

Hawkes knew where the greatest likelihood of finding Chief Inspector Devery lay on any given day when the time approached the noon hour.

Cullen had told him that it was Devery's habit to eat at Steve Brodie's saloon on the Bowery near Grand Street. There Devery would accept the offer of a free lunch each day and it was to Brodie's saloon that Hawks was walking now after leaving the Conroy home.

David Conroy was certainly adamant that Greenleaf could not have gotten out of that room to kill his wife, thought Hawkes as he strolled past the standing horses and wagons that lined Grand Street. Given the apparent thoroughness of Conroy's search of the room and the fact that he remained outside what he believed to be the only exit to the room, the man appeared to have very good reason to be so fixed in his belief.

Still…

There are unusual aspects to the situation. The accusation written on the wall in the victim's own blood pointed to Greenleaf as the killer, that was certain. Explained away by the police (all but Cullen) who declared it to be a ruse by the real killer. A rather weak explanation, concluded Hawkes. The only reason the police doubted the veracity of the message was that the force of Greenleaf's alibi seemed to make it impossible that he could be his wife's murderer. *Accepting the alibi, the police had to conclude the message was false. But what if it was not?*

Hawkes couldn't help but smile as he walked the streets of lower Manhattan. He was the same Sherlock Holmes who more than once complained that the criminal element in London was too often without imagination, offering a man of his abilities little challenge. Here at least was an astounding exception to that lament. An exception if Cullen was correct in his suspicions. How delicious was it? The man has a score of witnesses prepared to testify that he was inside that room although not one of those witnesses *actually saw him the entire time*. To their collective mind, there was no way for him to leave the room, so it must stand to reason he had to be inside.

If the man did kill his wife, it's a very unique alibi, thought Hawkes. *Quite an admirable feat in its own way. A story for good old Watson's pen for certain, if Greenleaf indeed proved to be the murderer of his wife.*

Up ahead Hawkes saw his destination, Brodie's saloon, and his thoughts turned back in time, to a few weeks prior, back to the image of the bruised and bloated body of the young girl he'd viewed after she was pulled from the rushing river beneath the Brooklyn Bridge. She was a suicide, a jumper off the gigantic span, her death a prelude, although Hawkes didn't know it at the time, to a case of multiple murder that would eventually, years later, be penned by Dr. Watson under the title *The Adventure of the Dead Rabbits Society*.

Brodie too was a jumper off the famous bridge, or so he claimed. Brodie's history was well known to the locals. A former newsboy who'd begun boasting that he would jump off the bridge and live to talk of it.

A friend of his, with connections to the newspapers, began to spread the word of what was no doubt, at first, a foolish bit of verbal bluster and bravado by a boastful young man. Not meant to be taken seriously.

But it was taken seriously enough that a liquor dealer named Moritz Herzberg came forward to tell the young Brodie to "put up or shut up". He offered to buy Brodie his own saloon if he ever actually did the jump.

In July of 1886, prodded by either the dare or by the offer of the saloon, Brodie jumped, or so he alleged. No one, other than the friends of Brodie, actually saw him do it. It was thought by many that it was not Brodie at all but rather a weighted dummy that took the fall into the river, Brodie was, some believed, hiding beneath a pier in a rowboat waiting for the dummy to hit the water so that he could swim to where it landed.

No doubt, opined Hawkes, that was the truth of it. It would be a miracle for anyone to survive a jump off that great span. Brodie's success was quite likely a lie, and perhaps many knew it but said they believed it anyway, simply because they wanted to believe it.

The story made the man a legend. He went on to stage other jumps from great heights that, again, no one ever really saw. But it wasn't until 1890 that he finally opened his saloon. Whether or not it was Herzberg's promised payoff that ultimately paid for the place Hawkes wasn't certain, as those telling him of Brodie's feat of daring could not say it was so with any confidence.

Brodie's saloon was a three-room affair, but the majority of patrons never got to see the rear two rooms, those reserved for Brodie's friends, which list consisted primarily of professional fighters and, of course, of the news reporters who merrily printed whatever Brodie declared to be true.

Above the bar there were many signs. The one that may have inadvertently, yet most blatantly, captured the saloon owner's theory of life, immediately caught Hawkes' eye. "If You Don't See What You Want, Steal It" said the sign.

Beneath the sign, sitting at the bar and consuming his free lunch, sat William Devery, his broad back to Hawkes.

"Chief Inspector Devery," said Hawkes as he stepped up to the bar beside the sitting man. "May I have a few moments of your time?"

Devery's eyes narrowed to slits as he looked Hawkes up and down waist to crown.

"An' who might you be?" he asked. His mouth was filled with half-chewed food.

"My name is Simon Hawkes. I've been asked to work with the police regarding the investigation the murder of Virginia Greenleaf. I'd like to ask you a few questions about that night."

"Ah, yes, I've heared of you, Mr. Hawkes. Helped Cullen out with that Hammond thing. Good job that. An' from the word aroun' the station you've pulled the commissioner's chestnuts out of a fire as well. Sit. Harvey, a pint for me frien' here."

"Thanks, that's good of you," said Hawkes as he placed himself on the stool beside Devery. Harvey, the bartender, shuffled off to get Hawkes' pint.

"'Tis nothin'" responded Devery. "So Cullen's got you lookin' at this Greenleaf thin'. Le' me say flat out he's way off base with this crazy idea of his, that Cliff Greenleaf did it. No way, I can vouch for that." He stabbed a piece of potato with his fork and brought it up to his mouth by way of punctuating his sentence.

"That's my understanding," returned Hawkes. "Are you a personal friend of his? Of Clifford Greenleaf, I mean?"

"Frien'? No, why would you think it?"

"You were at his affair."

"Ah, well, touchin' upon that, I can say that the Fancies often invite us lowly servants of the people. Never know whe' they might need our services, you see. They tolerate us an', at the same time, we tolerate them. Don't like the Fancy Dan's but I like their big bashes so's I go whenever I get an invite."

"I see. How is it that you were selected to be the, ah, shall we say, the ticket-taker that night?"

Devery shrugged. "Well, touchin' upon that, I can say it was just me being there when he needed somebody. I ran into Cliff Greenleaf. He told me he was goin' to do his stunt in a few minutes and asked if I'd help him out. Saw no reason not to, so's I did."

"Tell me exactly what happened, in the order in which events occurred."

Devery did so, his account of events agreeing perfectly with the facts as described by David Conroy.

"No one came in or out of that door other than the twenty ticket holders while you were posted there, is that right?"

"Right. As I say, I took the tickets from them in number order and handed them back the same way as they came out. No one else wen' in or came out."

"He asked you to throw a light switch, I understand?"

"Touchin' upon the light switch, I will say I was asked to put the light on inside the room after countin' to ten when I closed the door with the twenty inside. Then turn it off again after a couple of seconds. I did as Greenleaf asked."

"Did you ask him what the purpose of it was?"

"Did as a matter of fact. Seein' as how there's a light in the room why put on another is what I asked. He said it was just a stunt to frighten them a bit. Get them in the right spirit so to speak. It did that I wager. I heard them all scream a bit when I did it. Heard them through the door."

Hawkes' pint appeared on the bar and he took a swallow of it. "After the twenty exited the room, the door was immediately locked again?"

"I locked it meself. And me an' another fellow stayed in front of the door in any case, so it didn't matter if it was locked or not, did it?"

"Quite so. You and this other fellow—his name is Conroy by the way—stayed in front of the door the entire time? Until the screams were heard?"

"That's it. So Greenleaf couldn't have done it. I watched the man go into that room and I'm ready to say for certain he didn't come out of it until after his wife was dead, until we heard the screams that is. No way the man could've done it, locked up inside that desk inside that room."

"It would seem so," responded Hawkes, repeating the words he'd said to David Conroy earlier when he'd listened to him state essentially the same story. "Well, thank you, Chief Inspector, for your time and"—Hawkes grabbed up the pint and swallowed down what was left in the glass—"for the beer."

"Touchin' upon that, let me say it was a pleasure, Mr. Hawkes. Hope to see you again." The words were sincere and friendly enough, the large man seemed to have taken a legitimate liking to Simon. "Listen, I'd wish you luck, but I want Cullen to find this killer and it's clear both you and him are dogs barkin' up the wrong tree. It's a thief did in the Greenleaf woman. I told Cullen to stop goin' after Cliff Greenleaf an' I'd tell you too except you don't have to listen to me. We'll find him eventually, the killer, out there on the streets, even while Cullen has you nippin' on the heels of the wrong man."

"That may very well prove to be correct," replied Hawkes, in a somber tone. "Enjoy the rest of your lunch. Good day."

Devery nodded his large head and stabbed another potato as Hawkes went out of the Brodie saloon. On a stage at the end of the bar, a trio of newsboys got up and began to sing a song to entertain the customers. The last sound Hawkes heard as the door of the saloon closed behind him was the blend of youthful voices raised in harmony singing "Three Blind Mice." They complemented their song by stepping about with their eyes very nearly shut and bumping into each other and anything else nearby. This for the most part delighted the noon-time patrons, many of whom threw the boys nickels and dimes as reward for their song and their touch of vaudeville-like comedy.

Chapter Six

Hawkes walked away from Brodie's saloon with the simple tune sung by the newsboys repeating itself in his head. Fearing that it might eventually find its way to his violin he mentally attempted to shake it off. Still, it remained stubbornly with him for the time, like a stray dog that had attached itself to a potential new owner and would not let itself be chased away.

He had an hour before his scheduled meeting with Cullen at the Greenleaf house where he would examine the crime scene, and it was a good, sunny day, so he decided against hailing a cab and instead walked uptown.

A few of the avenues in lower Manhattan were becoming thick with places of entertainment, especially the "museums" that offered the odd and unusual to be viewed for payment of a nickel or a dime. Reaching Fourteenth Street, Hawkes strolled past one such establishment, the Dime Museum, offering potential patrons the sight of the "dog-faced boy" and the "human horse" among other such wonders. A barker, a large man with a handlebar mustache, described in a sing-song voice the nature of the wonders just inside.

A few doors down the avenue from the Dime Museum stood a theater advertising the appearance of the magician, Servais Le Roy, appearing with his wife, Mary Ann, billed as the "Queen of Coins". Hawkes stopped in his stride to gaze at the colorful poster standing before the theater entrance telling of the talents appearing inside, the show to occur later that evening.

Then, acting on a thought, he stepped forward to enter the theater, desirous of speaking with the magician. Magic, the art and practice of it, was, after all, a key element of the mystery of the death of Virginia Greenleaf. With a little luck, Servais Le Roy would be inside.

Cullen was busy pacing outside the Greenleaf home nervously waiting for Hawkes' arrival and fairly bounded over to Hawkes as he descended from the landau he'd taken from the East Side. "I'm glad you're here," he said. "I thought something had happened to keep you from coming."

"I did stop off somewhere—but I'm only five minutes late," said Hawkes, surprised by the man's anxiousness. Perhaps it was explained by the fact that Cullen alone, of all the police involved, was unwilling to accept the casual truth of Greenleaf's innocence and was being subtly mocked because of it. Perhaps he was counting too much on Hawkes being able to find the hidden evidence that would justify his position.

"This way, Mr. Hawkes," he said. "Greenleaf is threatening to enter his 'magic room'—I'll call it that for lack of something better—and move things about. I've made certain nothing was changed too much as of yet, but he's becoming quite insistent that he wants the police out of his home and out of his hair. And he's rich enough to get some to pay attention to him. They think his innocence is plain as a pikestaff. I'm being told by my bosses to let him be, to start looking for the killer elsewhere. It's a thief, they say." Here he shook his head grimly before adding, "I'll take you upstairs."

Cullen led the way up the entrance steps lined with polished brass railings, through the black-painted front door and the large entrance hall, to the stairs that curled elegantly up to the second story. "Quite a home," murmured Hawkes, his gaze taking in the opulence of the rich furniture and decorations.

"It's not a tenement cellar, that's certain," said Cullen, throwing the statement over the shoulder of his overcoat as he went up the stairs. Cellars were the lowest form of habitation then available under a roof in the city. Below the first floors of the tenements lay two lower levels, one, a basement, that permitted a degree of light and air to enter since it was at least partially above ground, and, beneath the basement, the cellar, which was completely lightless and without any natural ventilation. Rooms were erected within these caves and rented to those who could afford no better. In truth, the street gutters might have been healthier for the residents.

Cullen led Hawkes down the hall to the room in which resided the unassailable alibi of Clifford Greenleaf. Outside the door stood a uniformed patrolman who nodded at Cullen as he drew near. "That'll do it, Baker. There'll be no need for you to stand here after Hawkes looks about." The patrolman took this as his dismissal and, acknowledging it as such with another nod of his head, stepped away and went down the hall past Cullen and Hawkes. Cullen opened the door to the room and he and Hawkes stepped inside.

It was exactly as described by Conroy, a smallish room with heavy drapes opposite the door. In front of the drapes stood the pole of lights, three incandescent bulbs attached to the vertical rod that held them. Nearby, against a wall, was the graphophone that had played the music that had accompanied Greenleaf's demonstration. A table, a sofa, a bookcase, the deception of an ordinary desk and a small chair completed the furnishings. On the wall was the photographic portrait and autograph of Edgar Allan Poe.

Hawkes stepped across the length of the room, pulled back the drapes and drew out his lens. After a few moments, he announced, "I see no marks of interest. The window is tightly nailed, as I was told. It is highly unlikely it was used as a means to get in or out of the room. Hum, what's this?" He reached out and plucked something that had attached itself to the fabric of the back of the drapes.

"You see something?" asked Cullen.

Holmes extended his hand, thumb and forefinger touching, holding what appeared to Cullen's eyes to be little more than a bit of fluff.

"What's that?" he asked Hawkes.

"A bit of ostrich feather," said Hawkes. "Unless I miss my guess it's off the trim of a woman's dress, the jabot."

Cullen blinked, and then shrugged his shoulders. "And…and what does that mean to us?"

"Perhaps…nothing," responded Hawkes, placing the bit of feather into a small brown envelope he withdrew from his pocket. Noting Cullen's gaze as he placed the bit of feather into the envelope, he stated, "I've taken to carrying a few of these for just such a purpose whenever I'm called upon to investigate a case. I also carry a few matchsafes as well for the same purpose, for other types of objects."

Hawkes continued his examination. "No false walls," he announced. "No way in or out through the floor or ceiling. The graphophone is what it appears to be as is the sofa and table. Let's have a look at that desk."

It was a quite ordinary piece of furniture in its outward appearance, a simple desk with drawers on either side, one shallow drawer across the middle and a top inlaid with leather. Hawkes opened the middle drawer and pulled it entirely out, away from the desk, being careful not to spill its few contents. "Ah, it extends only one-third or so the depth of the desk." He did the same with the top right-hand drawer. It too extended only partially into the desk. Leaning down, Hawkes peered inside the vacant space, gazed for a moment and then replaced the drawer. He then pulled opened what appeared to be the large lower drawer on the right but was actually a door on hinges. The concealed safe came into view.

"It's not locked," spoke up Cullen.

Hawkes grunted and pulled open the safe door. "Yes, I see. There is no back or sides to the safe. There is a space here that, combined with that of the rear two-thirds of what should be the middle and right-hand drawers, permits a man of small stature to conceal himself. Tight squeeze, still it's adequate. It's the false appearance of separate drawers, separate small spaces that gives the illusion of there not being enough room to hide a man. Clever. What's this?"

"You see something?"

"A fountain pen," replied Hawkes, holding it up. "Here way in the back. One of those relatively new Waterman pens. Why didn't your men find it, Cullen? Didn't you shine a light in here?"

"Well, we didn't really do much more than look inside there," responded Cullen. "It looked empty."

"Yes, of course," said Hawkes as he put the pen away into a pocket. "Hum, what's this?"

"You see something else?"

Hawkes responded by again extending his thumb and forefinger toward Cullen as he had done when they were behind the drapes. "A twin to our other find," he said.

"Another piece of feather?" stated Cullen.

"Yes, another," responded Hawkes, pulling out another envelope and dropping it inside. He then produced his lens and carefully went over each part of the desk, starting with the outside surface and continuing to the inside, requesting a lantern for light when he put his gaze to the interior spaces. "A few scuffs. Nothing more," he announced at last. "Made by a man's shoes. That would be consistent with Greenleaf's story of hiding inside"

"You see nothing else?" said Cullen, clearly disappointed. "Nothing to put the lie to his tale?"

"I see what I've told you I see," replied Hawkes, his brow clouded. Then, after a moment of thought, he said, "Well, Cullen, I think I will look at the crime scene now. Is it available for examination?"

Cullen replied that it was.

"Let's be off then."

The bedroom was a large one and replete with lace and floral patterns on the bedspread and curtains, indicating the feminine touch of the deceased. A large armoire with delicate carvings in the wood stood against one wall. A bureau with five drawers stood near the wall on which, very near the floor, was a dirty smear, incongruous with the cleanliness of the rest of the room.

"This room's been cleaned," stated Hawkes with some pique.

"Yes, Greenleaf had it done. I stopped him from having his people completely erase the note Mrs. Greenleaf left behind when I found out what he was having done. There was a rug there with her blood on it there by the wall but that's been thrown away."

Hawkes grunted. Then, lens in hand, he stepped to the smear that constituted the remnant of Mrs. Greenleaf's last words, assuming the message was legitimate. There, he went down on his haunches and peered through the glass. "You did well to stop him, I can still make out some of the letters beneath the swipe of blood over them caused by the cleaners starting their work. Are there samples of her handwriting, Cullen? Her printing?"

Cullen produced a small address book. "She printed the names in here," he said, extending it to Hawkes.

"Very good, Cullen," responded Hawkes, accepting the small book and opening it. "Yes, a similarity in style, no doubt. But given the damage to the writing on the wall it's impossible to be conclusive."

"Detective Cullen?"

Both Cullen and Hawkes turned toward the voice. It was Clifford Greenleaf who'd spoken up, having just entered the room. A dark-haired man shorter in height than average but with a bearing, a haughtiness that seemed to add height to his physicality. Napoleon might have had much the same bearing. The goatee worn previously was now gone, his face clean-shaven.

"I know you asked me to wait, detective, but I am now running out of time. Are you about through?"

Hawkes stepped forward to respond. "Yes, we're about done here. I apologize if we are keeping you from other things but may I request a few more moments of your time? To ask a few questions?"

"And you are?"

"This is Simon Hawkes," spoke up Cullen. "He's assisting me with this investigation."

"I see." Then, talking again to Simon, "And do you share Detective Cullen's...ah, *opinion*...regarding this tragedy?"

Hawkes smiled at the man. "I share no opinions. I seek only to attempt to determine what has actually occurred here. Perhaps if you will answer a few questions that will help make things clear?"

"It's clear enough—to all but this...*gentleman*." The last word was thrown out, dripping with scorn. "Go ahead, ask your questions. Let's be done with this."

"Very good. You are an amateur magician. You were performing an...illusion, on Halloween night. May I ask why you placed the three lights in the room, and had Chief Inspector Devery flash them once your, ah, audience was in the room?"

Greenleaf blinked. "L-Lights? What do they have to do with anything?"

"I think that's why I'm asking. Why add them to your illusion?"

"Just an effect. I wanted the trick to be surprising, frightening even. What better way than to start it off by startling the audience? I wanted to do more than just perform a trick by rote. I wanted to set a mood. To enhance the whole experience. I do much the same with my parties."

"I see. The graphophone served the same purpose? To enhance the trick with a bit of eerie music?"

"That's right."

"You invited twenty to see the illusion, giving out the first invitations yourself and then letting your servant hand out the rest. Why didn't you distribute them all yourself?"

"What? Why didn't I hand off the remaining invitations? It occurred to me that it would add to the effect if people were selected arbitrarily. If I'd invited everyone, people might think they were acquaintances of mine. In on it with me, so to speak. Then the legitimacy of the search for me inside the room would be questioned."

"Questioned? Questioned by whom?"

Greenleaf blinked again. "By whom? Oh, by others who would later talk of the event, of course. I didn't want anyone to say that it was not a true illusion. I thought it might be said that the entire audience was part of the trick, that they told people they couldn't find me in the room simply because I asked them to say it."

"Hum, I see. It's the same as when a magician in a theater asks for a volunteer from an audience? Someone unknown to the magician?"

"Yes, that's right."

"So you didn't distribute all the invitations but you did give out some. May I ask how many?"

"W-What? Oh, only two as I recall. That's all."

"Who did you give them to?" asked Hawkes.

"Who? I don't recall now."

"You didn't know the people you gave them to?"

"No, not really. I just picked them arbitrarily as I told my servant to do."

"Did you give them out in numerical order? Did you give invitation number one to the first person you saw?"

"Yes, I gave number one to the first person. No particular reason except it seemed orderly."

"I see. Excuse me for this next question, but it must be asked. For the police record, you see. Primarily to dismiss the thought. How were things between you and your wife? Were relations strained at all?"

Greenleaf's spine straightened a bit. "My wife and I were very happy, Mr. Hawkes. There were no problems at all. Anything else?"

Hawkes produced the fountain pen he'd found in the compartment of the trick desk. "Is this yours?"

"Why yes, I'd lost it. Where did you find it?" said Greenleaf, accepting the pen from Hawkes.

"It was in your desk."

"Ah, I must have dropped it there, when I was doing my trick. Thank you for finding it. Is that all?"

"Your servant distributed the bulk of the invitations to your illusion. But when these people came to with their invitations surely you recognized who was there?"

"I recognized Mrs. Cleary, Mrs. Victor Cleary, and Joe, that's Joseph Taylor, the Wall Street banker. Other than that, I wasn't familiar with anyone. My guests often in turn bring other guests of their own. They're free to do that. Within reason, of course. I limit each invited guest to two additional people they can bring. So it's often the case that there are people attending who are unknown to me."

"I see. Would it be possible to obtain a complete list of the persons who were invited to your affair, those who attended at least as far as you know?"

"I-I suppose so. My servants would still have that list."

"There will be others who attended who will not be on the list, but we must begin somewhere. You've done away with your beard. It's my understanding you had one."

"Ah, yes, I've decided to do without it, for now anyway. But I'll grow it back, I think. What does my beard have to do with anything?"

"Just an observation. Well, then, I'd like a few words with your butler. With—Blake is his name? Is that possible?"

"I don't see why not. I'll ask him to come here to see you. Will that then be the end of this farce?"

"It will, I think, conclude our business here today," replied Hawkes. "Yes."

Greenleaf accepted Hawkes' affirmative with a curt nod of his head and walked out of the room without another word.

"He's not happy with us," said Cullen, stating the obvious.

"No blame for that," said Hawkes. "The man did just lose his wife and we are nothing more than an unwelcome nuisance."

"Mr. Hawkes, do you think I'm barking up the wrong tree too? Am I all wet with this?"

"I think…there are still questions to be answered," replied Hawkes. "Ah, here is Mr. Blake unless I miss my guess."

The butler was a man of medium height, with a softly wrinkled face topped with shortly cut salt and pepper hair. His eyes, sitting under a high forehead, contained more than a bit of sadness. It was evident the man had been crying recently. He was meticulously dressed.

Hawkes extended his hand. "Mr. Blake, I presume?" The butler confirmed this with a silent nod of his head and Hawkes added, "Thank you for coming. Just a few questions and we'll be on our way. Would you like to sit?"

"I'm fine, sir."

"You have been employed by the Pontseele family prior to Virginia's wedding?" asked Hawkes.

"Why yes, sir. I've been here for decades. Over thirty years. How did—?"

"It's clear you're in a state of sorrow. Unless you've suffered a loss of your own, which would be an amazing coincidence, it is reasonable to assume you were close to Virginia Pontseele."

"She…was…a wonderful person…." Blake responded, his voice cracking with sorrow. "I've known her for many years."

"Yet she had her disagreements, now and then, with her husband?"

"W-Why, sir? What ever would give you that idea?"

"We've just spoken with Mr. Greenleaf. He was quite forthcoming," replied Hawkes, putting a false implication toward the man.

"Oh, well then, it's true they had their arguments, sir. But doesn't everyone…now and then?"

"Yes, it's so. You are the gentleman who distributed the bulk of the invitations to Mr. Greenleaf's illusion on Halloween night, is that so?"

"Yes, sir. He gave me the cards and asked me to give them out, to no one in particular he said. So I walked about and gave them to people on the spur of the moment as he asked."

"There was no ah, criteria, as to how you should select those to whom you offered the cards?"

"No, not really. Oh, he did say to give half to men and half to women. But other than that there was nothing."

"Did he insist they be strangers?"

"Well, no," replied Blake. "Not strangers. Although he did say to make certain they were not close acquaintances of his."

"Why would he want people not close to him at his illusion? Wouldn't it be more natural for the man to want to show his skills to those he knows best?"

"I-I'm sure I don't know, sir."

"He explained that, Mr. Hawkes," broke in Cullen. "He said he wanted strangers so as to ensure no one thought the audience was in on it with him. That's what he said."

"Yes, that is what he said, Cullen. Thank you for reminding me." Then, turning his attention back to Blake. "Do you know how many cards he gave you, out of the twenty?"

"Yes, as a matter of fact I counted them. He gave me eighteen."

"Ah, do you know to whom he offered the first two cards?"

"No, I'm sorry, I don't."

"Did you know the names of anyone you gave your invitations to?"

"Actually, I can't recall, sir. I'm sorry, but my wits aren't about me quite yet, sir. Everything, up to Mrs. Greenleaf's death, sir, has become quite a blur."

"It would be good if you could remember. You heard the shout of robbery, the night Mrs. Greenleaf was killed?"

"Yes, sir. Terrible scream it was, sir. Full of fear. Hardly sounded like her so full of fright it was. I came running and—"

"Hardly sounded like her?"

"No, at first I thought it was someone else screaming. A guest. I was…quite shocked, when I saw it was her…."

"Yes, it is a terrible thing to find someone killed in such a violent way. You saw her by the wall there when you entered the room?" Hawkes pointed to where the smear of semi-washed blood was still on the wall.

"Yes. She was on the floor, her arm, her hand extended, looking like she was pointing to the words on the wall."

"And those words said?"

"Ah, well, sir, it was written there, ah, 'Cliff killed me.' But the police said that was a ruse, by the thief, sir. Mr. Greenleaf is quite upset by the…ah, implication."

"Yes, as anyone would be. We will need a list of all those invited to the affair. Mr. Greenleaf has said that you could get that for us. Is it available?"

"Yes, sir, I can do that."

"We'll appreciate it. We'll pick it up on our way out. Well then, thank you for your time, Mr. Blake." The words were a dismissal and the elderly man nodded acceptance of it, turned and left the room.

"I'm going to go about this room, Cullen," said Hawkes. "And then we'd best be on our way."

It took no more than a few minutes for Hawkes to complete the examination. "One thing of some interest," he declared as he put away his lens. "While it's been cleaned, there's still evidence of an accumulation of blood there a few feet distance from the writing on the wall. It's likely that it was there Mrs. Greenleaf was wounded and not by the writing where she ultimately died. Nothing else of interest," he announced as he put his lens away. "As expected since the room has been cleaned."

"What say you, Mr. Hawkes?" asked Cullen. "Are we still lost at sea? Do you see anything to help me in this? You heard that fellow Blake say Greenleaf did argue with his wife. Greenleaf lied about that."

"I heard him say that they argued now and then as do most married couples. If you believe arguing with your wife is a motive for murder then we mere mortals have many potential killers on our hands. Isn't that so? I remind you Cullen, that I'm not here necessarily to help you further a theory of yours but rather to find the actual truth if that is at all possible. Let's be off now. We'll get that list of guests and talk further during the carriage ride back to my room." With that Hawkes strode out of the room. After a moment, a rather dejected looking Detective Cullen followed behind him.

Chapter Seven

Hawkes and Cullen sat on opposite sides of the carriage, facing each other.

"There are a few points of interest, Cullen," Hawkes told the detective, as the carriage moved into traffic. "His response regarding his pen was one, was it not?"

"He simply thanked you for finding it," responded Cullen.

"Not quite," returned Hawkes. "I told him I found it in his desk. That could have meant in one of the desk drawers, a more likely place to find it. He immediately said he must have lost it there while hiding. He knew I'd found it inside his hiding place in the desk. It's a bit of a stretch, of course, a bit of speculation, but I think by his response and his manner, that it is very likely he placed the pen there and wanted it to be found. He might even have been a bit peeved that the police didn't find it earlier."

"I don't understand at all. Why would he plant his pen there? We're supposed to know he was in there, so what's the point?"

"Precisely, Cullen. If for the moment we assume our speculation to be correct, that he did indeed place the pen there to be found, then we must ask why. What other reason can there be then to have it represent some kind of physical evidence that he actually hid in the desk, but why would it be necessary to do that, if the man was in fact hidden there? It is something a person would do to convince others of a lie."

Cullen's face lit up with glee and he slapped one of his large hands upon his knee as though he'd just heard a rousing good joke. "You do think he did it! Good! I knew it! I knew it!"

"I have my suspicions, Cullen. For now that's all I have."

"The man is guilty as sin. You said there were a couple of points of interest, Mr. Hawkes?"

"The other is Mrs. Greenleaf's death declaration. The writing on the wall. Think what we must believe Cullen, for that message to be false. We must envision a thief entering the house, during the time in which the house is already filled with guests—"

"I've been told by Devery that the thief was most likely one of the attending guests," broke in Cullen.

"Yes," said Holmes without interest, then, continuing his initial thought, "we must envision a thief entering the *bedroom* then, while Mrs. Greenleaf is there, that the thief is then met by Mrs. Greenleaf and that he then kills her even as she calls for help. Finally, having been forced to kill her, he stops in his flight to write a false note in the victim's blood to incriminate Clifford Greenleaf. This despite the woman screaming for all to hear that a thief was present. That progression of events is in itself highly unlikely, is it not? In addition we now have evidence that the woman was actually wounded a distance from the wall on which the message was written, indicating either she had to crawl to the wall to write it or that her killer went to the trouble of dragging her dead body over there rather than simply writing the note on the wall closer to where she originally rested. It's more likely that, in the aftermath of the attack, she crawled the distance. That is, for me, conclusive evidence that the message was indeed written by Mrs. Greenleaf. It then follows as night the day that her husband is her murderer. But what I think is one thing. What I can prove is another, Cullen. We are a long way from bringing Mr. Greenleaf to justice."

"But we will do it, Mr. Hawkes?"

"That remains to be seen. Cullen, I want you to dedicate a man to the task of following Greenleaf during the course of his days. Even more, his nights. What we want to learn, besides his daily habits, is whether or not he is seeing anyone. Another woman."

"I'll work that out, Mr. Hawkes. Devery will resist authorizing it but now that you've put your own suspicions next to mine, he won't put up too much of a fight, I wager. Anything else?"

"We have our mysterious ostrich feathers, Cullen. And you heard what Blake said about the cries of Mrs. Greenleaf?"

"What he said…? What was that, Mr. Hawkes?"

"He said the screams he heard were so filled with distress that the cries *barely sounded like her*," stated Hawkes, putting emphasis upon the last four words. "This is a man who was well acquainted with Virginia Greenleaf, if we are to believe his own words. You must confirm that, by the way, Cullen. Check into the history of all the servants. That might prove helpful, or reveal nothing of interest but it should be done."

"Barely sounded like her? But that can't mean anything," returned Cullen.

"It may mean that Greenleaf himself did the screaming," stated Hawkes.

"What? Certainly that can't be. Why would he scream and so notify the household? It's precisely what he wouldn't do."

"No, Cullen, it's precisely what he *would* do," came back Hawkes. "Think. If Clifford Greenleaf killed his wife, then why should she scream that a thief was attacking her? The only possible explanation for that scenario to be true is that Greenleaf was disguised as a thief and she didn't recognize him right off but then realized it was him after shouting and perhaps receiving her mortal wounds. Why would the disguise be less effective then? Did he wear a mask and she then, in struggling, tear it off as the official police report declares? Two objections, why would Greenleaf bother with a mask when he went to the room with the intent of killing the only person there? You might say he did so as an added precaution should he be inadvertently seen by someone else. Unlikely given his small stature. Even with the mask he might be recognized due to that stature. The second objection is the stronger. Mrs. Greenleaf was stabbed in the *back*. Three times. It is therefore highly improbably that she was struggling with her attacker but was rather trying to *flee from him*. How could she tear the mask from his face if she had her back to him? Given that, we can say it is more probable, if the message written in blood is valid, that it was someone else who screamed out."

"I-I see. But...Greenleaf? I-I don't get it. Why would Clifford Greenleaf call out and alert the house after killing his wife?"

"Precisely because of his unbreakable alibi, Cullen. You see, it *must* be known to the world that Virginia Greenleaf was murdered while her husband was supposedly hiding in the desk in that room in order for his alibi to mean anything. If it could be said she was killed prior to his entering the room or that she was killed after he left it, then the alibi means nothing. It becomes worthless. He called out to make certain that the body of his wife was discovered while he still had his alibi."

Cullen's face illuminated with enlightenment. "Why, that's so, Mr. Hawkes. Of course. So then the screams had to be his!"

"It would seem so," responded Hawkes. "There however remains one problem with everything I just said."

"What's that?"

"It remains seemingly impossible for Greenleaf to have gotten out of that room. That is the heart of his alibi. That is why everyone is convinced the message in blood is false, and that a thief rather than her husband killed Virginia Greenleaf. Because it is apparently impossible that he did it."

"But he did! Mr. Hawkes, you just said—"

"Yes, Cullen, I'm more convinced than previously that he is our man. Still there is the very strong wall of that alibi that continues to protect him. It is his fortress. If that wall remains standing, I'm fearful that he may very well escape justice for what we believe he's done."

Cullen sat silent for a time, absorbing the truth of Hawkes' words, anger and befuddlement sitting on his features.

"We're not out of the game yet, Cullen," said Hawkes after a while. "You will do as I asked? Get a man or two to keep an eye on our Mr. Greenleaf? And try to get the names of as many who watched his little trick as possible? Unfortunately that will be a time-consuming task. We have the names of all those who were invited to his party, Blake has given us that list. Each name on it must be interviewed to learn if they attended Greenleaf's illusion, if they were one of the twenty. Also, ask each who else they brought with them. Perhaps a guest not on Blake's list was one of the twenty in that room. The more of these people we can talk to the more we increase our odds of learning something we don't already know. It is, as I said, a time-consuming task and it might ultimately avail us nothing of worth but it must be done. Also, find out the names of Mrs. Greenleaf's close friends. They might shed light on any difficulties at home with her husband. It's possible the woman confided in one or more of them."

Cullen replied that he would do as requested and Hawkes called up to the driver to pull to the curb. "I'll get out here, Cullen. I want to stop at the tobacconist and pick up some shag. It may be that in the smoke of my pipe the solution can be found. Good day, Cullen."

With that Hawkes stepped quickly out of the carriage and, without another word to the police detective, was gone from the rectangular opening of the carriage door window, leaving Cullen staring at the long morose face of an old wagon horse standing by the curb while its master, unseen as he was beyond the limited view offered by the window, called out to pedestrians to stop and look at his wares.

Chapter Eight

"Blake, make certain that the bedroom is cleaned," ordered Greenleaf the very moment Hawkes and Cullen walked out of his house. "I'll be going out now. I expect it to be clean by the time I return."

"Yes, sir," responded Blake. "I'll see to it, sir. Will you be wanting the carriage, sir?"

"No, I'll be walking." With that Greenleaf picked up his walking stick, which contained within it a hidden blade, necessary for protection, and walked out of the room.

As he strolled the streets, heading toward Black Pete's Saloon (modeled after the formerly infamous Kit Burns' Sportsman's Hall) his thoughts were on the two detectives that had just left his house. To call them *detectives* was of course to offer them too much credit. *Fools* is what they are, he concluded.

Although that fellow Hawkes seemed a little sharper than most. Greenleaf didn't like at all the way the man looked at him as he answered his questions. *And why was he asking me about the lights?* No one else had given the lights a thought. Certainly not that fool, Cullen.

Still, it would take more intelligence than that held by the entire New York City Police Department to fathom the truth of what he'd done. Take all the intelligence of those fools, collect it together and it still wouldn't fill a shot glass. That was his firm opinion. Damn his wife for living long enough to scrawl her message! If not for that, there'd be no suspicion directed at him at all. The fools would have been totally flummoxed. Still, it was one unseen flaw in an otherwise perfect plan, a plan so well thought out that even that one flaw couldn't wreck it. The two detectives had come, and they'd gone empty handed. Now it was time to get on with life. Black Pete's was a good place to start.

Black Pete's was a fairly new saloon determined to perpetuate the sport of rat baiting, which was then under attack as inhumane by the do-gooders in the ASPCA. Still, despite efforts to eradicate it, the sport survived in the city, albeit somewhat surreptitiously, in saloons like Black Pete's. The dogs were always fox terriers and well trained to fight any number of rats from a few up to dozens, with the admission cost of viewing the 'battle' rising in proportion to the number of rats provided. The minimum ticket cost of five dollars at Black Pete's was sufficient to keep out most of the riff-raff.

How much Virginia despised the sport! He chuckled to himself as he thought: *No more complaints from good old Virginia.*

A walk of a few city blocks brought him to the saloon. It was early afternoon but there was still a major show planned and, after paying the entry fee and stepping inside, it might have been night in any case. The interior was as black as Pete himself, with the windows covered and painted over to make certain no sunlight, nor the sight of the eyes of police or passing pedestrians, could enter inside.

The interior was lit by a few torches, giving the place a medieval feel. Almost the entire first floor was devoted to the amphitheater and the pit in its center. The 'pit' was in fact an unscreened box approximately four feet high, its sides made of thick wood lined with zinc. Matches, at this time, were private affairs catering to a dozen or more of the more wealthy of the city. Betting was in the hundreds of dollars.

As Greenleaf paid his entry fee and went in through the front entrance, a group of young boys, all poor and living in the lower East Side tenements, were bringing their "catches" to the back door, the rats they'd captured. They were paid up to twenty cents a rat by the saloon, a phenomenal amount of money to children living in poverty, money that very often put an evening meal on the family table.

Greenleaf nodded a perfunctory greeting to the others attending and then scrutinized the fox terrier that would be the first in the pit. Good looking dog, two years old with plenty of experience behind it. A killer if ever he saw one.

Bet against the rats, he decided. *This dog could kill a hundred of them.* He checked the time. He still had hours to fill before going to Jane's.

Chapter Nine

The "Jane" whom Clifford Greenleaf would, in only short hours, be visiting, had a history of her own, much of which was unknown to Greenleaf who believed her to be a child produced by an important "blueblood" family living in the south of France. A noble woman fallen on hard times. Jane Montane was in fact Jane Orleneff, born beneath a leaky sink in a tenement in the "Fourth Ward" in lower Manhattan.

She grew up for the first few years of her life surrounded by the theaters and saloons of the Bowery and so was fully aware of the fulfillment offered by the practice of *pretence*. When just sixteen years old she was selected to be a member of the *corps de ballet* in a revival of *The Black Crook*, one of the most popular plays ever to be presented in New York. There, clad in tights and ballet skirt, she began to be called "Frenchy" and, going along with the joke, learned how to affect a false French accent. The "variety show" was created on the Bowery, and it existed there not only in the theater but also on the Bowery streets where many played parts as ostentatiously as actors on a stage. Little Jane Orleneff was playing a part now both when working and when supposedly being *herself*. She very casually changed her name while appearing in *The Black Crook*. In 1892, Jane was further inspired by Little Egypt, the exotic belly-dancer who created such a fuss, a scandal actually, when she appeared in the Chicago Columbia Exposition. In fact, the "exotic" Little Egypt was born in non-exotic St. Louis right in the United States and not in the Orient as she claimed. And if a false history could advance a floozy from St. Louis then it couldn't help but advance Jane as well, or so Jane reasoned. She promptly tossed away her own family history, throwing it into the same trashcan in which her family name had gone, and created a new one that included the south of France, an impoverished winery that at one time produced some of the most renowned vintages in Europe, and the inherited blood of French royalty that continued to flow through her veins. Much of her family's property and riches were now lost in the uprising of the commoners during the French Revolution, thus her current "state" and lack of funds.

Her false history was readily believed by Mr. Greenleaf, who considered himself quite the ladies man to have attracted a woman of such breeding. And such a beauty besides.

While Clifford Greenleaf was enjoying the spectacle of the fox terrier battling the flood of rats coming at it, Jane Montane was making her way to the Tenderloin district, to her favorite opium den, there to purchase her "*li yuen*", the high quality opium, with money given her by Greenleaf.

No "pin-head pills" for her today. Let the people with little money go for the cheap stuff. *I'm riding high, ain't I?* she mentally told herself, forgoing her French accent to process the happy thought. *Got it made, now, Janie girl. Soon I'll be Mrs. Clifford Greenleaf, a member of the hoity-toity crowd. Not bad for a girl from near Beggar's Alley. Not bad at all.* The happy thought placed a soft smile on her full red-painted lips.

Night came to the city and the streetlights came on to replace the sunlight, transforming the gray litter-strewn streets into something more mysterious and, for some, a place more romantic, a brick and mortar star system of sorts, in the midst of which people walked and strolled; some seeking out those activities best savored at night, pleasures best enjoyed away from prying eyes.

Greenleaf, leaving the joyful amusement of rat-baiting and pocketing with pleasure his more than three hundred dollars worth of winnings (more than a year's pay for most), stood on the sidewalk outside Black Pete's for a moment contemplating a decision: Whether to return home for a change of clothes or head straight out to Jane's place. He then made a choice that, unknown to him, protected him that night from the forces that were beginning to swirl about him; specifically from the lone detective who now stood in the shadows across the street from his own home, awaiting his arrival so as to "pick him up" and begin the surveillance authorized by Chief Inspector Devery that afternoon, after much pleading by Detective Cullen.

Jane, having left her favorite opium den two hours earlier, was already at home, waiting for him to arrive.

She greeted him with a warm hug and a kiss. "Hello, baby," she told him (pronouncing baby as 'bebe' in her French accent). "It's so good to see you." She did not have to stand on her toes to kiss him, as she was just an inch shorter than him. "Hmm, I like you without the beard."

"I missed you too," he returned, kissing her once more. "But it was best we waited a couple of days."

"*Oui*, it was. But waiting is now a thing of the past. *N'est-ce pas?* Come, let's celebrate. I have a good wine, grown from near my old home. We can toast *us*." With a giggle, she turned away to retrieve the bottle of wine and two glasses. Greenleaf watched as she went away from him, admiring the lissome form so clearly evident beneath the velvet of her black dress, a dress that hugged her tightly, as though the cloth itself could not stand to be away from her. He then took off his jacket, threw it over a chair and went to the table where, he knew, the wine and glasses would be brought.

She returned with the bottle and two glasses, which she then half filled with the red wine. The darkly scarlet liquid was soft and gleaming in the gaslight that lit the room. Handing him a glass, she said: "Here's to our success." Then, with a smile, she added, "And to *our* future."

How much expectation was contained in that word: *our*? How much was taken for granted? The word irritated Greenleaf, but it was irritation insufficient for him to give voice to it. This was not a night for argument.

Returning her smile, he raised the glass to his lips and sipped the wine. It was exemplary and he told her so.

"The police no longer trouble you?" she asked. He sat down and swallowed the rest of the wine in his glass. She immediately filled it again and then took a seat as well.

"They finished up today," he said, at last answering her question. "They found nothing worth a mention."

"*Bon*, then we can get on with our future."

There again was the word. It proved more irritating the second time. "You seem to be intimating something, Jane. What is it?"

"Intimating…? I do not *intimate*."

"You've said '*our* future' more than once."

Jane smiled. "We are, how shall I say?, *bound* together now? *N'est-ce pas?* We, together, have changed the future. It is therefore *our* future, no?"

"You helped me, and you've been well-rewarded for it."

She leaned forward, putting her pretty face near his and pouting seductively. "And there have been no rewards for you?" she asked him.

He swallowed all the wine in his glass once again and the smile returned to his face as he placed the glass on the table. "Yes, there have been rewards for me," he said to her as he leaned forward toward the pouting lips in front of him.

Chapter Ten

The next day, when the time was nearing the hour of eight in the morning, Cullen, grim-faced, made his way past the clerk tending the desk at the Dead Rabbits, glanced up at the row of pegs on the board to see if Hawkes was in or out and, seeing the peg indicating Hawkes was in his room, went straight up the stairs, going to Hawkes' room. In his hand he clutched a few sheets of white paper.

Hawkes answered his knock, still clad in a dressing gown. "Cullen, come in," he bid the detective.

"Have I wakened you?" asked Cullen as he stepped inside. His eyebrows rose up on his forehead as he spotted a pile of pillows and cushions seemingly tossed against a wall. All of the bed pillows and the cushions from the chairs were there. Consequently there was no place in the room for Cullen to sit. The room was filled with the haze of tobacco smoke.

It was not the first time Holmes had fashioned a place of comfort for a lengthy contemplation. As described in Dr. Watson's reminiscence, "The Man With The Twisted Lip" it was Holmes' habit to go for days without rest as he thought over a particularly perplexing problem, looking at it from every angle, from every conceivable point of view. As in the resolution of that case, Hawkes had last night constructed his makeshift "Eastern divan" and, for the bulk of the night, pipe clenched in his teeth, eyes fixed vacantly upon a spot of no interest on the opposite wall, contemplated the circumstances surrounding the murder of Virginia Greenleaf.

"No, I've had a relatively sleepless night," replied Hawkes. "I have spent much of the night considering our little problem."

"Greenleaf…? Come up with anything?"

"I have at least a working theory which will serve until I find a better," said Hawkes.

"Oh, what is it?"

"Best I keep it to myself for the time being," responded Hawkes. "It is my habit not to speak of theories until I have some certainty of their validity. Have you put a man on our Mr. Greenleaf?"

"Yes, I've been given two men. For now at least. They'll work twelve hour shifts keeping an eye on him."

"Is that what brings you here to my room?" Hawkes jabbed his pipe stem toward the papers in Cullen's hand.

"What?" Cullen looked down at his hand as though surprised it held something. "Oh, yes, it's the list of names we got from Blake, plus some names we added due to the interviews we've made. Those additional guests brought by those actually invited to Greenleaf's Halloween affair. It's only a partial list of course, we've a long way to go, but I thought I'd bring it over in case you want to look it over. I don't see anything of interest but you do seem to see things that many others miss."

"You seem to be particularly grim for someone bearing only a list of names. Is something wrong?"

"Wrong? No, not really. Just a…." Cullen shrugged his shoulders. "I don't have to tell you of the wide use of opium and morphine, Mr. Hawkes. That German drug, Heroin it's called, is becoming a problem too. Too many people taking them all too freely, by my judgement. Once in a while we find a body, someone who is careless with the amounts they ingest or inject. I just came from a young woman's apartment. A hypodermic needle did her in. Pretty young thing. An actress though, but still too young to be dead like that. A tragedy really."

Drug use, and addiction, was, at this time in the United States, rising in more than direct proportion to the population and was beginning to be viewed by some as a societal problem. Laudanum (opium mixed in alcohol) was freely given to adults and children alike. "Drug kits" could be purchased over the counter by almost anyone. These kits contained a glass barreled hypodermic needle and vials of morphine, heroin and/or cocaine, all packed in a neat and attractive tin case. All as common as tobacco. Some women of the higher levels of society spent part of their days injecting themselves with these drugs, usually using more expensive, decorated syringes. A few years earlier, the U.S. Congress imposed a tax on opium and morphine in a supposed attempt to lower use and addition. It failed. The newspapers of Hearst were publishing stories of white women being seduced by Chinese men, the stories more prejudice against the

"Yellow Peril" than a true effort to slow the use of opiates that remained so much in vogue. The news stories were generally careful to avoid mention of the history of the prominent Astor family of New York, specifically John Jacob Astor who had joined the opium smuggling trade decades earlier, having his American Fur Company purchase tons of Turkish opium for later sale. The "tongs", Chinese criminal organizations, were now scapegoated for the widespread use of opiates in New York (and elsewhere) but in fact dens were everywhere, not only in "Chinatown" as publicized but in the Tenderloin district and along the Bowery and the drug trade was largely in the hands of people other than the Chinese. The rich who indulged often had their own drug paraphernalia, fashioned of gold and silver.

Hawkes, whose own "seven-per-cent solution" was not far away from where he stood, only nodded his head in response to Cullen's words, his eyes indicated little interest in Cullen's "tragedy" as he took the papers from the detective's hand. "Anyone of interest on the list?"

"I'm not sure what I should be looking for," replied Cullen, somewhat uneasily.

Hawkes' eyes fell upon a name with a line drawn through it. "What's this?" he asked. "Why have you crossed this name off?"

"Her? She's gone," stated Cullen. "Jane Montane. She's that woman I was just talking about, the one found dead this morning. I drew a line through her name since we won't be talking to her."

Hawkes gazed at the man in wonder, not only amazed by his words but equally astounded by the detective's opacity of mental vision. "Are you telling me, Cullen, that one of the guests at Greenleaf's affair on the night of his wife's murder is now herself dead?"

"Died of ingesting too much opium," replied Cullen, with another shrug. "It happens. 'Specially to these showgirl types."

Hawkes' face was suddenly energetic with fresh excitement. "Have you disturbed the scene of this accidental death?" he asked sharply. "I'd like a look."

"I only just left. I wager it will be a while before the body's picked up and taken away. Why—?"

"Give me the woman's address, Cullen," demanded Hawkes in a sharp tone. Write it down there on that paper and then go back to her apartment. Make certain nothing further in the apartment is touched. I must get washed and into fresh clothes. I'll be ready in a few minutes and will follow you."

"What? Go back? Why? What do you think—?"

"Go! I'll be right behind you!" barked Hawkes, and Cullen, with a double-blink of his eyes serving as his farewell, carrying a befuddled vacancy in those very same eyes, obediently turned and went out of the room.

It required scant minutes for Hawkes to perform his morning ablutions and don his clothes. In little more than a quarter-hour he was riding in a landau toward the brownstone apartment in which the late Jane Montane had resided and in which, with a little luck, her body still rested in her final sleep. The carriage passed a stable, and Hawkes viewed momentarily the sight of a few horses being curried by young boys, the horses' breath, puffed from their nostrils, white in the chill of the air. A brief image through the window, then the stables and horses were gone from sight, replaced by the more common storefronts of the avenue. It was a cold November day, the sky blotted out by heavy gray clouds that threatened either rain or snow, depending upon how low the temperature fell. Hawkes nestled deeper into his heavy coat as the cold permeated the interior of the carriage, listening to the sounds of the city as they entered inside and came to his ears, a diffuse static heard above the hiss of the carriage wheels.

He considered again the fact of this young woman, now found dead in her home. It was speculation on his part, he knew, that drove him now to view the body, to contemplate that she was connected with Clifford Greenleaf and the murder of his wife, Virginia, but it was a supposition that had a very good chance of probability, given his determinations following his night of contemplation on his self-constructed "Eastern divan".

Still, Cullen was not wrong in stressing the popularity of opiates among the show-business types so prevalent now in this city. It seemed there was a nightspot, theater or museum on every corner. It was entirely possible, at least at this moment, that this young woman died as Cullen had concluded and had no connection to the Greenleaf affair.

A drive of a few minutes brought Hawkes to the front of the three-story building in which the late Jane Montane had lived. A few steps up brought him to the entrance of the boardinghouse. Opening the door he stepped through to the inside. A quick glance down the hall offered him the sight of a uniformed police officer standing before a door; the presence of the man told him immediately which room held the body of the deceased.

The officer, recognizing Hawkes, simply nodded his head, a silent greeting, and stepped aside to allow him to enter the room. Cullen was inside, seated in a chair, smoking a cigar. Seeing Hawkes, he stood, maintaining possession of the cigar. The room was dimly lit, illuminated by only the half-light coming in through the windows. Outside the gray day peered inside like a flat piece of roof slate pressed against the pane of glass.

The room was, despite a few garish touches, tastefully put together. On the mantle by the unlit hearth, Hawkes viewed the display of a few of the woman's possessions, an alabaster Russian viewing egg; a wood carving of a Western "cowboy", evidence she was taken up by the "Western craze" then popular in the East; a colorful vase devoid of flowers, displayed for its own design; a charming ceramic statuette of a small child. Above these knick-knacks was a framed print of a poster advertising "The Black Crook". In one corner of this print was a photograph of a grinning Jane Montane, one dancer in the midst of a chorus line of four.

The furniture was of good quality, but only a bit above common and no more; consisting of a table and chairs; a nice but not overly expensive sofa, and a few other little more than ordinary pieces. The only extravagance was displayed by the presence of an elegant, highly polished Weber Square Grand Piano that stood by one window. Thirty or forty years old but still in extremely good shape. It stood on hand-carved legs that terminated in ram's head feet. On a sunny day, the light from the window would fall upon the sheet music that was now opened, as though waiting expectantly to be read, to hear its written notes and chords played for enjoyment.

One wine glass sat on the table near Cullen, a splash of wine at its bottom. "Her glass?" asked Hawkes. "I see the lipstick on the rim."

"What? Yes. Apparently our young lady had a glass of wine last night before retiring to her bed and her opium."

Hawkes leaned over and studied the glass. Then he went around the room. Finished with his quick, efficient examination, he looked again at Cullen. "Where is she?" he asked, as Cullen, now standing, gazed at him.

"Oh, in the bedroom. Through there." He pointed the cigar at the open door to Hawkes' left.

Jane Orleneff rested on her back on her bed, her eyes closed, clad only in a night gown that was in a slight disarray upon her body. Her chestnut brown hair was dark against the white of the pillow. Her shoulders and arms were bare, the arms resting akimbo at her sides; her legs were splayed, her feet pointing toward each wall beside the bed. The position of her limbs, arms and legs, made her appear almost comical in death. It was not the way in which an actress, careful of image and appearance, would have played her own death scene if given the part to act on a stage. Before an audience, on a stage, her death would have been made glamorous, a scene worthy of applause if played correctly. This display here and now had the appearance of farce.

To the side of the bed was a bureau, the top of which was covered with various cosmetics and other objects. A large mirror reflected the image of the deceased back into the room. An armoire stood on the other side of the bed very near the window. A door by the bureau led to the relatively newly installed bathroom. A washstand with ewer and basin stood near the bathroom. The washstand was now made irrelevant by the existence of the bathroom by which it stood but was retained anyway by its owner either for its quality of design or as a precaution in the event she would one day be forced out of this apartment into a lesser one in which a bathroom was not yet installed. If the latter reason, it indicated a sense of pragmatism in the now deceased young lady.

"Where's the hypodermic?" asked Hawkes, after briefly scanning the scene in front of him.

"I put it over there on the bureau," stated Cullen.

"Yes, I see it. Tell me, Cullen, be as precise as possible, where did you find it before moving it?"

"It was on the floor," replied Cullen. He pointed to the floor by the foot of the bed. "She must have injected herself, started to feel the effect of the drug, dropped the needle and then lay down on the bed where she died."

Hawkes grunted, and began a closer examination of the body. It required only moments. "There is a puncture wound in her left forearm," he announced. "Hello, what's this?"

"You see something?" asked Cullen.

"Look here, Cullen, her left shoulder, on the side of the deltoid muscle, another puncture wound."

Cullen stepped over. "Why, it's so, isn't it?" he murmured. His hand went up to scratch the top of his head, as though the words that explained this second wound was tangled in his hair and could be shaken loose with a scrape of his fingers. "She must have taken a second dose," he concluded. "That must be what ultimately killed her."

Hawkes was already at the bureau, on the top of which sat a curling iron, some whitewashes for creating the pale-looking skin still popular, a status symbol as it indicated the woman did not have to work outdoors, and some jars of powder and rouge. Also on the bureau top sat an open box of drug paraphernalia which grabbed Hawkes' attention. Beside the open box was the opium pipe or "joint", so called because such pipes were often made of jointed pieces of bamboo, and the *yen shee hop*, the box used to hold the ashes of smoked opium.

"You saw this of course, Cullen, this *yen hop* as the Chinese call it." Hawkes looked into the box and there inside were all the other tools needed for the smoking of opium; the dipping needle; the opium lamp and various other items. Hawkes then turned his attention to the opium pipe and the *yen shee hop*. "This pipe was recently used," he stated. "Most of the ashes are in the *yen shee hop* but some have fallen to the floor. The pipe was smoked in this room. Hum, this is three-quarters filled, containing many more ashes than she would have smoked at one sitting. She was saving the ashes. As you may be aware, Cullen, opium ashes are often saved and later used to generate a "high" by poorer addicts, those who do not always have the money to purchase a fresh supply. Any port in a storm. But she wasn't needy. Perhaps she sold the ashes to others, or gave them away to friends less well off."

Cullen, unseen by Hawkes, nodded his head.

"The pipe is well used," added Hawkes, still without looking at Cullen.

"I saw that," said the police detective. "She was a doper, no doubt about that. And that second puncture absolutely explains her death. Accidental death due to the injection of too much of the drug."

Hawkes grunted once more. He had opened a drawer and was looking at a letter, partially completed by Jane, that he'd found inside, resting there waiting to be completed.

"She was writing a letter to her parents," he said at last. "Her real name is Orleneff. Her parents live in lower Manhattan. Hum, look at this." Hawkes picked up the incomplete piece of correspondence and handed it to Cullen.

"What? What am I supposed to be looking at?"

"The slope of the letters, Cullen."

"Slope…?" His hand returned to top of his head, to there scratch once again.

"So what?"

"She's left-handed," responded Hawkes. "Hello, what's this?" He withdrew a pair of eyeglasses. "She had problems with her sight?" In the next moment he added, "No, the two lens are clear glass. What do you make of that, Cullen? Why would someone order spectacles of clear glass? Rather thick too. Unbecoming to say the least."

"I'm sure I have no idea," responded Cullen.

Hawkes was now at the washstand and noted that the basin and ewer were both half filled with water.

"She continued to use this at times apparently, despite the presence of the bathroom," said Hawkes. "Or perhaps she kept it handy for visitors to use. It might be she didn't want all her visitors to use the bathroom."

"Visitors…?" murmured Cullen with derision. "A nice way of putting it. A showgirl and a doper, I'd say she no doubt had her *visitors*."

"Hello, what's this?" spoke up Hawkes, staring at the water in the basin. "See this, Cullen? A very small piece of cork and the residue of some wine, I'd say, settled at the bottom of the basin."

"Cork...?"

Hawkes was now at the woman's armoire, looking through the garments that hung inside. After a few moments of rummaging he emitted a sigh of satisfaction. "Look what we have here, Cullen," he said, turning around and displaying for Cullen's eyes a long black velvet dress. It contained a jabot bordered with an edging of the tips of ostrich feathers.

"A dress...?"

"Note the feathers, Cullen. Note the feathers."

"They're fairly common now, Mr. Hawkes. Currently the rage, as they say in the magazines. A lot of the better dresses have them."

"Very true, Cullen, and in itself it is not proof of anything. Still it is another link in the chain, is it not?"

Cullen scratched his head once again. "Mr. Hawkes, I'm not really certain at all where you're going—?" There was some exasperation in his voice.

"Unless I'm off the mark, this dress was worn by this young woman to Greenleaf's party on the night of his wife's murder. We will have to try to confirm that. Perhaps someone will recall her wearing it."

"What will that give us, Mr. Hawkes?" The exasperation in his voice was now overlaid with perplexity.

"My dear fellow," said Hawkes, "can it be you don't see how strongly this dress bears upon our investigation?"

Cullen shook his head. "I'm sure I seem a fool to you, Mr. Hawkes, but I don't see the point of anything about any of this. She's a showgirl and a prostitute as well, most likely anyway, who happened to kill herself with her opiate habit. She happened to be at Greenleaf's affair, but so what? Probably was there to keep one of those rich cats happy that night. I don't have to tell you what these cheap Bowery actresses are like, do I, Mr. Hawkes? They're free and easy with themselves."

"Quite a plethora of surmise and conclusions in your words, Cullen," stated Hawkes with a frown. "If only there was some reasoning contained in your processing of data, your conclusions might then be impressive. Come, we'll go back outside and sit at the table where you can dispose of the increasingly large amount of ash forming at the end of your cigar. There I'll explain what I believe occurred here. If I am right, and I have no doubt I am, then this was not an accidental death at all, Cullen, but rather a cold-blooded murder designed to appear as one."

Cullen gazed at Hawkes without speaking, his eyes two question marks.

"And we have some reason," continued Hawkes as he started out of the room, "to believe also that her killer may very likely be none other than our own Mr. Clifford Greenleaf. Our man may very well have killed again."

Cullen's jaw dropped open, and then closed again. "The devil you say!" he exclaimed after recovering from his initial disbelief and finding his voice. He followed Hawkes out of the room as the ashes of his neglected cigar fell onto the bedroom floor just prior to his stepping outside. His free hand was once again scratching the top of his head in perplexity as he entered the parlor.

Chapter Eleven

Hawkes did not immediately sit next to Cullen at the table but instead went to the cupboard near the kitchen sink. After a moment he uttered a sound of satisfaction as he withdrew a wine glass, a twin of the one already on the table.

He carried this second glass with him into the parlor and, as he sat down at the table across from Cullen, placed it beside the first, the glass with the lipstick on the rim. The dress he'd taken from the armoire he lay across his lap.

"See that, Cullen?" he asked, pointing to the second glass.

"See what…?" Cullen's hand continued to scratch his head, harder this time. He was increasingly in danger of wearing away a patch of hair.

"Those drops of water at the bottom," replied Hawkes. "The glass was recently cleaned."

"Oh?" It was clear from his expression that he had no idea as to the significance of Hawkes' find.

"Recall, Cullen, what we discovered in the water basin in the bedroom. The small piece of cork and the subtle residue of wine, very easy to miss as diluted at it was, but it was there. We didn't miss it. Now we have this glass. Surely it's clear that there was someone else here last night, Cullen. Someone else who shared a glass of wine with our departed Miss Orleneff. It was therefore someone she was reasonably acquainted with or at least expected to entertain. The second wine glass was taken into the bedroom and later rinsed in the basin, then replaced in the cupboard. Clearly an attempt to make it appear that no one was here with her last night, to make it appear she died alone."

Cullen's hand at last came away from his head. "I see," he said, "but that still doesn't mean she *didn't* kill herself, does it? Perhaps a friend, or a *client*, was here last night, and then, seeing she accidentally killed herself, decided he didn't want that fact known. Maybe he has a wife and family, or is in a high position. He would do that, wouldn't he? That's understandable, isn't it?"

"That could be granted as a possibility if it wasn't clear that she *didn't* kill herself. It's elementary. You saw the pipe? It was recently used. No doubt last night. It's unlikely that this young woman would smoke her opium, as was clearly her normal habit, and then would also choose to inject herself. If she wanted more of the drug, she'd more likely use the pipe again. Addicts normally choose to use one method or the other at one sitting, seldom do they use both at the same time."

"Seldom, but it's still possible that's what she did."

"No, recall the letter I showed you," responded Hawkes.

"The letter? Oh, the one she was writing to her parents. What does that have to do with her drug habit?"

Hawkes recalled his old friend, Dr. Watson. He realized once again that he'd done his old comrade an injustice when criticizing him for failing to comprehend what, to Holmes, was easily and clearly comprehensible. There were others even more incapable of observation than his old friend and one of those others sat now across from him at this table.

"The letter writing, the slope of the letters, shows she was left-handed, Cullen. Left-handed. Now recall that the puncture wounds from the two injections were on her left arm and her left shoulder. It is much more likely, with her being left-handed, that the puncture wounds would be on her *right* arm and shoulder if she'd injected herself, for she'd naturally be using her left hand to do the injection, isn't it so?"

Cullen mulled it over for a few seconds. "Yes, it is," he answered at last. "Just as I, being right-handed, would as a matter of course put the needle into my left arm."

"Yes, except for long-time addicts who need fresh areas of their body to inject the drug, that would be the normal and expected thing. And there were no other puncture wounds," continued Hawkes. "This was clearly the first time she'd injected the drug. Or at least she hasn't done so recently until last night." He leaned forward in his chair. "Think what we must believe to conclude she killed herself, Cullen, first she smoked her pipe, achieving what must be her normal opiate high. Now, already enjoying the drug, she suddenly decides she will also inject herself for the first time and then, having done it once, decides to inject herself again. What is the probability of that, Cullen?"

"Unlikely…." said the detective, frowning with thought.

"Now we add to that unlikely scenario the fact that the injections were made on her *left* side," went on Hawkes. "This combined with the fact that she was left-handed is very near absolutely conclusive, Cullen. But, even on top of this, we also have one of the injections being made on her shoulder, not in the front of the shoulder but rather toward the side. To reach that part of her with a hypodermic needle, she would have had to twist herself dramatically. Would someone already under the heavy influence of the drug do that, Cullen? No, of course not. Not even if we first grant that she used the wrong hand to inject herself which is itself highly unlikely. No, we must conclude she did not inject herself but rather was injected by another, most probably while under the influence of her smoked opium. Someone else put the excess drug into her, someone who was a guest and who was in the room with her at the time. There is no other reasonable conclusion."

Cullen nodded his head. "Yes, it must be so," he agreed.

"What else do we know, Cullen?" asked Hawkes.

"What…else…?" responded the befuddled detective.

"Is it not likely that Miss Orleneff's visitor is *not* himself an addict? Note that the second glass of wine was brought with him into the bedroom where the opium was smoked. An addict looking forward to the drug would more likely abandon the wine as Miss Orleneff did and leave the glass outside. A bit of a stretch but not an unreasonable one."

"How do you know he brought the glass into the bedroom?" asked Cullen.

"Because that is where the glass was cleaned," replied Hawkes. "If it had been left on the table here and then cleaned, he no doubt would have rinsed it in the kitchen sink which is much closer than the basin in the bedroom. So we can surmise the two retired to the bedroom, she to smoke her opium and he to continue to drink his wine. Perhaps he refilled his glass before going there. They may have been intimate, most likely were, but it is irrelevant to us. She, no doubt in the stupor commonly caused by the drug, was resting on the bed when she was injected. Then, to be certain of death, a second injection was made."

Cullen simply nodded his head again.

"Let's continue with our speculation. Since we have surmised that her killer was not an addict, it must follow that either she purchased the hypodermic kit herself, perhaps considering the possibility of injecting the drug in the future, or perhaps meaning to give it to another addict—recall the saving of the opium ashes, Cullen—or that her killer brought the hypodermic with him. Since he was not an addict that would mean he likely came with the intention of killing her. If not, and she purchased the kit herself, then we must consider the possibility that the killing was not premeditated but rather was a murder of opportunity. Perhaps at some time during the night, they had a falling out of some kind, and he, seeing a chance to rid himself of her, took it. I would put a man on it, Cullen. Try to find out if she was supporting another's drug habit. A brother or old lover, perhaps? An actor with whom she is friendly? If she was *not* supporting another's habit then it would mean it is very likely that Greenleaf himself purchased the hypodermic kit and, with a little investigation, we might be able to discover when and where he made that purchase. That would go a long way in making a case against the man. You should also have your men question her neighbors. Perhaps someone saw Greenleaf arrive and leave. What time did your man spot him going into his home last night?"

"Ah, a little short of ten."

"Well, then he might have left her close to half-past nine, assuming he went straight home. Ask if he was seen at that time. And anytime earlier of course."

"Yes, I will do that, Mr. Hawkes, but I still don't understand why Greenleaf would want to kill this woman. Even if they had a falling out, so what? Whores are common and not too hard to find, certainly not for men with money. He'd just walk away from her if she and he had a falling out, wouldn't he? Why bother to kill her?"

Hawkes lifted the dress which he, up to now, had held on his lap. "This is why, Cullen," he stated, displaying the dress. "This is why. That list of persons invited to Greenleaf's Halloween affair proved important as it contained Miss Orleneff's name. Have one of your men question the Greenleaf servants as well. Find out who among the female visitors that night also wore a dress with ostrich feathers on it. I know ostrich feathers are fairly universal in fashion at this time but that is true more of feather boas, which have longer feathers, than the smaller tips we see here. If we continue to be lucky the list will not be long. If other names appear, we will no doubt shortly eliminate the others from it once we question them. We will, I'm certain, end with just one name, that of the deceased. Then we will have confirmed, at least to my satisfaction, why she was killed."

"And why is that?" inquired Cullen. "Nothing you've said is telling me the why of it."

The muscles of Hawkes' jaw rippled before, looking keenly at the police detective, he replied. "Recall the feather tips I found when examining Greenleaf's room, the one in which he did his illusion. They came, I am almost certain, from this dress. Our Miss Orleneff is, most probably, a coconspirator in the murder of Virginia Greenleaf, Cullen. She was, I believe, a willing participant in the plot to kill that woman, an integral part in the plan to grant Mr. Greenleaf his so-called *perfect* alibi."

Cullen's jaw dropped once again. "You astound me, Mr. Hawkes. She helped him kill his wife?"

"I believe it to be so. And that fact, if fact it is, may also tell us why Jane Orleneff is suddenly no longer among the living. Dead men tell no tales, it is often said, but I think the truth of that old adage would apply to the opposite sex as well."

Chapter Twelve

The Bowery, once the premier area for entertainment in a city that hungered for it, had lost ground over the past decade to competition from new theaters springing up along Broadway. By 1893, the "Gay White Way" was in bloom, a stretch from the mid-twenties to the mid-forties, ending at Forty-forth street. Democracy was in full force along this stretch, especially in the night's shadows (as it was in the Bowery). Thieves and thugs mingled with the newly rich and aristocrats, self-proclaimed and otherwise. Prostitutes and opium dealers, playboys and gamblers, politicians and pimps could all walk and mingle here and all could purchase tickets to any of the shows along the way. The Bowery paled in comparison to the events now appearing on Broadway; it simply could not offer grand spectacles such as that offered by Cody's "Wild West Show" in which many entertainers and literally hundreds of "injuns" and horses were featured, all in one place at one time. Nor could the Bowery offer entertainment the size and scope of the great circuses appearing on Broadway.

Still the Bowery went on, presenting shows (melodramas much of the time) for the less affluent. Theaters and museums, though less prestigious now, continued to survive and present their unique types of entertainment. But it was neither on Broadway nor on the Bowery where the searched-for friend of the deceased Jane Orleneff was at last located by the police. Rather he was found in a theater that existed on neither of these famous lanes, a place of entertainment located on Water Street called The Grand Duke's Theater.

The Grand Duke's was unique in that it was run by and for a youth gang composed for the most part of young teenaged boys. The boys produced, wrote and performed in their plays. Like most "gangs" the boys who ran the Grand Duke's had a name: "The Baxter Street Dudes". Their leader was a tough known as Baby-Face Willie. A night-out to The Grand Duke's could prove to be more than a theatrical experience as the theater was often attacked by rival gangs, even while the shows were under way.

One of the actors appearing in the show now being offered was a teenager by the name of Peter "Re-Pete" Orleneff, Jane's young brother of seventeen years of age and an opium addict for at least four of those seven plus ten years of life.

Holmes and Cullen arrived at The Grand Duke's at a few minutes before nine. They arrived alone, just the two of them, unaccompanied by uniformed police as the presence of a uniform would do little else except cause a disturbance in the theater. Even their own presence would be noted as a curiosity here for the Grand Duke's theater crowd was for the most part composed of young boys and "newsies", teenagers, as was the cast and crew who ran the theater. This audience held little affinity for police authority.

Hawkes paid the necessary two dimes (ten cents each for Cullen and himself) and he and Cullen entered, being given the "fish eye" by the seller of the tickets from the moment they purchased their tickets to the time they made their way inside. The play was already well under way.

The theater was dark, lit by stolen tallow lamps here and there, lamps spaced well apart so that there were puddles of dark shadow throughout between them. The stage was better lit, dim by Bowery theatrical standards but bright enough, illuminated by a row of kerosene lamps that were also stolen. (Almost everything needed to produce the night's entertainment here was either filched or salvaged from somewhere.) The benches up front were all crammed with young bodies and Hawkes and Cullen made their way toward the back of the theater, going to a literally tossed-together balcony composed of piled-up boxes. They accessed this gallery by walking up a stepladder, one of a pair. Youthful eyes, filled with distrust, followed them along their route and up the ladder but once Hawkes and Cullen were seated in the dark they were quickly forgotten, swallowed up from thought as thoroughly as two tugboats that had floated into a heavy fog and were gone from sight. All eyes returned to the stage.

The show being presented was one of some slight social commentary. In the less than overly bright light of the kerosene lamps the facade of a tall building was on "fire". Only the first three stories could be seen before the height of the building brought it above the curtain top and out of sight. The fire was cleverly represented by a red cloth cut jagged on top to represent flames. This was pulled up ever higher, consuming more and more of the building, by wires overhead. This building and cloth-fire stood on the stage to the right while in mid-stage two separate fire companies were busy brawling over the right for their fire company to extinguish the flames. As they fought and cursed each other, the conflagration (the cloth) grew ever higher and screams and calls for help, the voices increasingly hysterical, came from within the building. Now and then a dummy made of sandbags and clad with a dress and a mop for hair would land on the stage, a simulation of "jumpers" fleeing death by fire by choosing instead to leap from unseen windows high above.

Cullen chuckled at the scene. "You may not know this, Mr. Hawkes," he whispered, "but there's truth in what you see. Up until twenty-five, thirty years ago, this city had competing fire companies, volunteers, and they very often fought with each other while the fire raged. At times they kept right on fighting even after the building burned down to the ground."

The police detective's smile faded in the next instant when there appeared on stage a uniformed police office carrying a baseball bat for a nightstick. "Where's the fire," screamed the officer on stage. "Where's the fire?" This while the flames over his shoulder grew higher and another sandbag "jumper" landed at his feet. "Where's the fire?"

The youthful audience roared at the policeman's stupidity while Cullen chafed under its presentation. Apparently any thought of "truth" in this particular performance was dismissed.

A young man, dressed as a woman, appeared on stage and went running up to the uniformed policeman. "My baby's inside the building!" shouted the actor in a falsetto voice. "Sir, save my baby!"

"That's him," whispered Cullen to Hawkes. "That's Jane Orleneff's younger brother, Peter." Hawkes grunted an acknowledgement.

On stage, the police officer began drubbing the distraught "mother" with his overly large nightstick and the audience roared with laughter at the sight of the beating.

"A police officer would never do that," complained Cullen, bristling at the representation of the police, his fingers rubbing his mustache. "This is disrespectful to the force."

"Yet quite amusing," stated Hawkes, smiling at the detective's umbrage.

All around them the audience was laughing uproariously as the beating on stage went on, and would continue until every laugh was drained from the scene.

Behind the beating, the competing fire companies, the members of which had apparently gone off to the conflagration armed to the teeth, began producing pistols and shooting at each other, some of the shots hitting passing pedestrians.

"We'll go backstage when this farce is over," said Cullen, "and talk to Peter Orleneff there." He had to speak up to be heard over the laughter of the audience around him.

Peter Orleneff was a slight, even overly thin, young man with a pale long face topped with greasy black hair that apparently hadn't seen soap for weeks. The hair was tied into a short ponytail in the back. The wig he'd worn on stage was gone now but the dress he'd not yet discarded. He was still wearing it as he gazed with suspicious eyes at the two gentlemen now in front of him. It was short-sleeved and Hawkes noted immediately the needle wounds on the boy's thin arms.

Even in the dim light of the nearby tallow lamp Peter Orleneff immediately concluded that both men were members of the police department and so was instantly wary of their presence. He looked at Hawkes and Cullen as though fully expecting one or both to produce a nightstick similar to the baseball bat used on stage and start beating him with it right then and there. A beating similar to the one he'd received on stage but given with more reality of purpose. "Yeah, I'm Pete Orleneff," he said in response to Cullen's calling his name. "Wha's it to you?"

"Charming lad," responded Cullen. "Let's keep a civil tongue, boy. I'm here about your sister."

"My sister? What about her?"

"You haven't heard? I'm sorry boy, but it's my unfortunate duty to tell you that she's…passed on. Her body was found in her home, just two days ago."

The young man's tough façade disintegrated with the news of the death of his sister and sorrow flooded into his features replacing the thuggish attitude that formerly resided there. His eyes were immediately filling with tears. "Janie…?" he murmured, staring at the two men with a now stricken gaze. "No…not Janie…."

Other boys, actors in the play, walked by and glanced at the detectives and Peter, wondering what trouble the authorities were dragging into their theater. One boy, noticing the stricken expression on Peter Orleneff's face, stopped and asked him if he was all right. To this the boy didn't respond, instead he sought out a nearby chair and placed himself down into it. "Janie…" he murmured again. The tears were now streaming down his face.

"How about getting him a drink of water?" suggested Hawkes, speaking to the other boy who'd stopped to inquire if Peter was all right. The boy nodded his head and went off to do as requested.

Hawkes placed a gentle hand on the boy's shoulder. "My sympathies," he said with real feeling. "Can you compose yourself?, he added after a few moments. "It's important that we ask you a few questions."

"Q-Questions…?" came up the feeble voice of the boy.

"Your sister didn't just die," stated Cullen. "She was murdered. And we're hoping you can tell us something that might help us catch her killer."

The other boy returned with a tumbler of water and presented it to Peter who took a swallow and then simply held onto the glass with both hands, glass and hands in his lap.

"Let's talk in this room," said Hawkes, pointing to a small and vacant dressing room. "It'll be good to have some privacy. Cullen, take that lantern there and bring it inside for light."

Cullen nodded his head and took possession of the lantern as Hawkes helped the boy to his feet. All three went into the room with Hawkes closing the door behind them. Peter's friend, the boy who had brought the glass of water, stood outside silently, staring at Hawkes with questioning eyes until the door was shut.

Chapter Thirteen

Hawkes produced a handkerchief and offered it to the crying youth who, once inside the room, immediately dropped himself into the nearest chair, falling into it heavily. "Here, dry your eyes," said Hawkes, "and compose yourself." The words were more a quiet demand now than previously. "You will be of greater use in assisting us in trying to attain justice for your sister, if you are able to answer our questions."

The words provoked the young man into an attempt at self-restraint and, after a few more passing moments, he told Hawkes and Cullen he would help them in any way he was able.

"Good man," responded Hawkes. "You have the marks of a hypodermic user on your arm. Many such marks. Is opium your drug of choice?"

"Y-Yes, but what does my usin' the opium have to do with anythin'?"

"Please just answer the questions. It was your sister who obtained your drugs for you, was it not? At least periodically?"

"Sure," replied the boy with a shrug, "she could afford it better than me. I was goin' over to see her tonight, right after, but what does that—?"

"Your sister smoked opium," interrupted Hawkes. "We know that from the pipe we found in her room. Did she, to your knowledge, inject the drug as you do?"

"Janie? No, never. She was 'fraid of needles," answered Peter. "But what—?"

"Your sister died of an overdose of opium. An overdose that was given to her by injection," stated Hawkes.

Enlightenment dawned on the young man. "No, no! That can't be! She didn't do that to herself. Like I said, she hated needles." His voice was rising now with heat. "It was someone else! Someone else stuck the needle in her!"

"Calm down, we suspected as much," said Hawkes. "Otherwise we would not have told you her death was a homicide. You just mentioned that you were planning to see her tonight. When was the last time you saw her?"

The young man took a deep breath and settled down. "What? Oh, just three—no, four days ago."

"At which time you took what supply of opium she had purchased for you? Yes, then these items used to kill her were most likely purchased by her for your use, and, if so, within the last four days. You were close with your sister? She spoke of her private affairs with you? To some degree at least? We need to know the names of her friends and acquaintances, of any enemies she might have had. Can you give us that information?"

"Enemies...? What enemies? She didn't have no enemies," declared the young man. There was no power to his declaration for it was clear, even as he spoke, that his older sister did have at least one enemy. "Friends? Y-Yeah...that I know. Well some anyways. She didn't tell me too much about what she did other than the shows she was in, her work. I know the names of some of her actor friends."

"She didn't mention any...male friends? Lovers?"

The young man shook his head. "No, we didn't talk about thin's like that," he said glumly. "You think it was a boyfrien' did her in...? No, she didn't tell me...."

"She went to a Halloween party recently. Did she talk about that at all? Was she accompanied by anyone to that party?"

Peter considered the question for a few moments before answering. "Why yeah, now you ask, she did talk about that a little bit. She thought it was a big deal, to be invited to mix with the swells at a fancy shindig like that. She said this fat cat named... what? Green somethin' invited her. So I guess she went with him."

"Greenleaf?"

Peter's eyes widened with the memory. "Yeah, that's it. Greenleaf it was. That's right. Greenleaf. You thinkin' it was him did Janie in?"

"We're trying to determine just who it was. That Halloween affair was held at Greenleaf's home. That's how his name probably came up. She mentioned she was going to the Greenleaf house, but she didn't go there with him. That's certain. In fact, it's doubtful they knew each other personally. Are you sure she didn't say with whom she was going there with?"

"W-What? You saying he just gave the party? No, she talked like she was goin' there *with* him, with this Greenleaf fellow. Now I think on it, she talked like she was kinda, well, a little gaga over him, you know." He shrugged his shoulders again. "But if you're sayin' they didn't really know each other, maybe I got it wrong. That's just the feelin' I got when she talked about it."

"Did she have any particular friend or friends she would confide in? You said you knew the names of some of her actor friends, was she more close with some than others?"

"There was one girl, an actress too, that she hung with a lot. They're friends for a time, since Janie left home to be on her own. What's her name? Alice somethin'. She's part of a group of girls callin' themselves "Floradora-Mora". They do comedy bits and dances and such. She maybe does a "Little Egypt" type dance too. One of Janie's friends did that anyways, and I think Janie said it was this Alice friend of hers. Anyways, she's workin' up in the Tenderloin, at a place called Cushman's Palace of Delights.

"Do you know of any reason your sister would wear a pair of eyeglasses, spectacles with clear glass for lenses? A set was found in her room."

"Uh, no, not unless she was in a play, I guess, and they were needed for a role she had. But she wasn't. In a play. She was a dancer."

Hawkes was satisfied that he'd learned all he would learn from the young man. "Thank you," he told him, his voice turning gentle once again. "You've been helpful. Again, I express my sympathies for the death of your sister. I assure you that we will do all we can to bring her killer to justice."

The young man gazed up at him, his eyes beginning to fill with tears once more. "T-Thank you, sir…" he murmured. "She was a good girl. I know there's people think otherwise 'cause of how she had to earn a livin', but she was good…she was more mother to me than my own mom…took care of me…" The interview over, he had no further need to keep his sorrow in check and so it was released, let free to reign over him once again. His face twisted with grief as he gazed up at Hawkes and sobs broke suddenly from his throat and mouth. The glass of water he held dropped from his hand and shattered on the wooden floor at his feet. Its destruction was ignored as, at the same time, his eyes squeezed shut, his head dropped into his hands, and, sobbing, he began to rock to and fro on the chair.

A good girl, he'd said. The fact that Jane Orleneff was suspected of assisting Greenleaf in murdering his wife was left unspoken by either Hawkes or Cullen. Why snatch away the boy's illusion? The two took their leave of him, leaving the young man alone with his grief, and made their way back out through the darkened theater by way of the now deserted stage and up the aisles to the front entrance. Not until they were standing in the night on Water Street did Hawkes speak.

"As much a miss as a hit," he announced. "The boy could only say that he suspected his sister was friendly with Greenleaf but couldn't confirm it. Perhaps this 'Alice something' he told us about will be more able to do that for us. If so, then the boy's offering us the name will prove valuable."

"I know of Cushman's. Pretty risqué place but no worse than many others and better than some. It'll be going full steam about this hour. By carriage, we can be there in a few minutes."

"This young man was adamant about his sister's dislike of needles. With that we have confirmed absolutely that she was murdered. Not that that is truly helpful since we didn't need more evidence of that. At least we are certain now why the hypodermic kits were in Jane Orleneff's room. She purchased them for her brother to use. That closes one door of opportunity for us as that would mean Greenleaf didn't make the purchase. The method of murder was merely available to him that night and he decided to take advantage of it."

"We were coming up empty on that road anyway," said Cullen. "My men talked to every store in the vicinity of Greenleaf's home and in the vicinity of the victim's home. No one could recall Greenleaf buying the kits."

Hawkes grunted. "That coincides with what we've learned here tonight. Well, let's hope that 'Alice something' can tell us more about Miss Orleneff's private life than her brother. I'd like to achieve viable proof of her relationship with Greenleaf and, right now, we still have little more than our own suspicions."

"We have a little more than that regarding the troubles in his marriage," came back Cullen. "One of my men spoke to a Mrs. Morgan, a close friend of Virginia Greenleaf's, and it turns out that Mrs. Greenleaf was thinking seriously of ridding herself of him. She'd begun to think her marriage was a mistake that had to be fixed."

Hawkes nodded his head. "Good work, Cullen. In that we have our man's motive, no doubt. Well done. You still have a man trailing him, of course?"

"Yes, he's kept to himself a lot. Goes almost daily to a place called Black Pete's for the rat fights. Eats out now and then. Other than that he's been a stay-at-home."

Cullen waved a carriage over to the curb, a hansom cab, and both he and Hawkes climbed inside. It was Cullen who shouted their destination to the driver who immediately put on his face a very knowing expression, thinking that here were two gentlemen away from their wives for a night, seeking the entertainment such freedom allows.

Chapter Fourteen

Places of prostitution existed in the Tenderloin. Other establishments took advantage of the reputation of the area to offer not the real thing but rather a tease of prostitution. The latter was a specialty of Cushman's or, as the sign said above the entrance, "Cushman's Palace of Delights". The sign was illuminated at night with gas lights, electricity not having conquered this area of New York yet. Below the sign, to the left and right of the entrance, behind glass, were a series of transparencies of beautiful woman, none of whom were actually inside or employed by Cushman's as implied by the presence of the transparencies. One of the pictures was of Lilly Langtry, the famous actress who, despite her own scandals, would no doubt be appalled to see her likeness exhibited outside the place.

Patterned after similar establishments that dotted both sides of the Bowery, Cushman's employed women as either waiter-girls or as supposed customers sitting alone at tables, a lure for the men to purchase drinks in the hope of female companionship of a more intimate nature than mere sitting at a table. The woman's drinks would be, for the most part, nothing more than colored water and the gentleman would be charged twice as much for the woman's drinks as for his own. All the women worked on a percentage basis and so ordered drinks as fast as they were able. Seldom was sex truly offered or given and customers who grew angry at being "strung along" were generally given a last drink "on the house" which contained knockout drops and then deposited in the gutter outside.

Entertainment was offered, most normally in the form of a small musical trio, but now and then specialty acts would appear. One of these was the "Floradora-Mora" comedy and song-and-dance group. All of the women of this group were expected to act as lures to entice male customers to buy them glasses of colored water when they were not performing on stage.

Alice 'something' turned out to be Alice Lake, whose real name was Alice Steffens from New Jersey. She was there at Cushman's, sitting at a table with a gentleman happily plying her with expensive colored water, when Hawkes and Cullen arrived. She was pointed out to them by the bartender who nodded a friendly greeting to Cullen. Cushman's had nothing to fear from the police as the management dutifully made their monthly protection payments in order to be left alone.

Cullen flashed his badge at the gentleman and shooed him away. Then both Hawkes and he sat at the table across from a peeved Alice, who, for the moment, thought only of the loss of income stemming from the loss of her gentleman.

On the stage a trio played music, a piano, violin and cornet, all the musicians including the piano player, wearing boxing gloves while they performed to the delight of those few patrons who paid attention to them. Most ignored them and the music had to fight mightily against the sounds of eating and raucous conversation in order to gain any dominance in the large room.

Alice Lake was a very pretty young woman whose facial features surprised Hawkes immediately in their similarity to those of Jane Orleneff. Except for the difference in hair coloring (Alice Lake's was blonde rather than dark brown), a slight elongation of the nose of Miss Lake and the curvature of the bones of the cheeks, all of which Hawkes noticed immediately, they were close in appearance. They might have been sisters or, at least, first cousins.

Despite being "inconvenienced", Alice offered both men a charming smile as she studied the police shield displayed by Cullen. "Have I done something wrong, gentlemen?" she asked, a wry smile on her lips, her fingers touching the glass of colored water sitting before her on the table.

"We're here about your friend, Jane Montane," stated Hawkes. "This is Detective Cullen. I'm Simon Hawkes. With your permission, we'd like to ask a few questions."

Hawkes polite manner pleased Alice and her smile widened in response to it. "Well then," she responded, "what has my friend done wrong to bring the police after her?"

"It's not her we seek," replied Hawkes. "You haven't heard. Unfortunately then it falls upon me to tell you…that Miss Montane's body was found…in her apartment. Two days ago now. We're investigating her murder."

The young woman gasped her shock, her small hand going up to her mouth, her eyes widening in surprise. "Jane…?" Her face was suddenly pale, so that the rouge on her cheeks and the red on her lips stood out more dramatically than before. "Murdered…?"

"Injected with an overdose of opium," responded Hawkes. "We believe the killer to be someone she knew." His eyes were keen as he gazed at her. "Someone she was close to."

"You don't think that I—"

"No, Miss Lake," responded Hawkes in a soothing tone. "We're here because her brother Peter has told us that you and Jane were good friends. That is so, is it not?"

"Yes, Jane and I are…were…friends."

"May I say it is remarkable how much you resemble her. You're not related, are you?"

"What? No. Not at all, but yes, we did look alike." She turned her head to the side so as to present her profile to him. "She was prettier than me though. I have this bump on the bridge of my nose, see? Her nose was straight. She had prettier eyes too."

"Then they were beautiful indeed," responded Hawkes with a smile. "We were hoping you could tell us of anyone she was seeing, any male callers, that is. Did she mention anyone, any name or names, to you? It may prove important."

"Names…? Oh, my…my mind seems to have gone quite blank…" Her hand went up to her forehead where a line of perspiration formed and, for a moment, Hawkes was fearful the young woman might actually faint dead away at the table. He asked Cullen to go to the bar and get a glass of brandy and this Cullen did, jumping the bar and pouring it himself. In almost no time he was back at the table with the brandy. He hurried not out of any sympathy for the young girl for, as he sat and listened to Hawkes' sensitive way of questioning her, he thought it misplaced. This woman was after all, to his mind, nothing more than a lowly showgirl and a whiskey tout in a saloon. Probably worse than that as well. Still, she might have information they needed and so he hurriedly brought her the drink requested by Hawkes. The London man knew very well how to extract information from people and Cullen was content to sit and listen and learn. If kindness got them what they wanted then kindness was a tool to be used. Without a word, he placed the glass of brandy on the table in front of Alice Lake.

It was Hawkes who spoke to Alice. "The brandy may prove more beneficial than the colored water you have in front of you," he said to her, the words accompanied by a gentle smile.

"Thank you, kind sir. You may be right," said Alice, gazing with appreciation at Hawkes as she picked up the glass of brandy. She took a deep swallow and returned the glass to the table. "God Almighty…Jane…."

Hawkes waited a few moments. "Can you answer our questions now?" he asked, seeing the color return strong to her face.

"I'll help in any way I can," replied Alice.

"Excellent. Did Jane at any time mention the names of any gentlemen she might have been seeing currently?"

"She was seeing Johnny Dobbs a while ago, a bartender at the Burnt Rag. He was sweet on her but she was looking for something better. She hasn't seen him for a while, I don't think. She liked Harry Talmage, a play writer and poet. They were going out to Buchignani's down on Third Avenue a lot. Sometimes they'd go to the East Side and eat with the anarchists in Schwab's on First Street. He had an explosive temper at times, she told me. One time she had this black-and-blue on her face where he hit her. You don't think he—"

"We'll have to see. Anyone else?" While Hawkes talked Cullen dutifully wrote down the two names offered by Alice, the expression on his face clearly revealing his disappointment that the identification of Clifford Greenleaf was not forthcoming.

Alice lowered her voice. "Well, I don't like to speak ill of the dead, but she did tell me she was seeing this married gentleman. She liked him 'cause he could spend money on her. Had it to burn, you see, at least to hear her talk. She told me she thought he would leave his wife for her but I told her she was daft. That kind of thing only happens in books and in fools' dreams, I told her. She wasn't wearing any glass slippers and there's no prince out there waiting to find either one of us. She laughed and told me I was wrong. She told me that she was pretending to be a French aristocrat with him and so didn't need any glass slippers. He didn't know who she was really and thought she was his princess. That's what she told me."

Both Hawkes and Cullen registered an immediate expansion of interest in the young woman's words. "What was this man's name?" asked Hawkes, leaning forward in his chair.

"Oh, it was…Greenleaf. Yes, that's what it was. Cliff, she said. She told me his name when she showed me these great looking diamond earrings he'd just given her. If he didn't steal them, then he was a big spender from the sight of them, at least if they were real."

Cullen wrote down the name, smiling this time as he scratched the words into his notebook.

"Did she say anything else about this man?"

"She was excited about going to a party she said he was giving, I remember. A big shindig it was supposed to be. Given on Halloween. She needed a good dress to wear and I think it was he who took her to some fancy place or another to buy her one. She pretended to be a French aristocrat but one that had fallen on hard times. So it was up to him to get him the clothes she needed to be dressed properly at the party. That was a pretty dress. She showed it off to me one time."

"What did it look like?"

"What? Oh, it was long, elegant, mostly black velvet. There was a jabot in front bordered with an edging of ostrich feathers which was really nice. It was really pretty. She looked grand in it."

"Do you know where it was purchased?"

"Why, yes, she did say," replied the young woman. "It was a place she couldn't afford on her own and she was pleased as punch to be able to go in and play the lady in a shop like that for a day. Brookstone's Shop, 96 Green Street is the place. And she bought shoes and a purse, and a jacket to wear over the dress but not at the same shop. She bought those things at Bloomingdale's. That store way up north by the stop on the Third Avenue El. The one with the famous "inclined elevator" all the squares used to go to gawk at. He took her there by carriage rather than the train. She was really happy the day she showed me all those things they bought. Giggling like a little girl." Alice's hand reached out and grabbed the glass of brandy. She lifted it to her mouth and took another swallow, a smaller one this time.

"That is all extremely helpful. Can you think of anyone else she was seeing?"

"There was only Charlie, Charles Jerome. He's a faro dealer, works for some gaming house off the Bowery. I don't know which one. She was sweet on him for a while. I don't know if she stopped seeing him or not. But I think she did. Stop that is. She hasn't spoken about him for a while. That's it. No one else that I know of."

"Thank you, Miss Lake," said Hawkes, getting to his feet. "You've been quite helpful." Cullen, following Hawkes' lead, also pushed himself out of his chair.

Hawkes reached into his pocket and produced a five dollar gold piece which he placed on the table next to the half-filled glass of brandy. "For your time," he told her. "Be assured, we will do our best to bring your friend's killer to justice."

"Thank you, Mr. Hawkes," replied Alice. "You're very kind." She picked up the coin and tucked it away immediately, considering its sparkling presence on the table to be too great a temptation if seen by the eyes of the many thieves and pickpockets in the place. As Hawkes and Cullen took their leave, the gentleman they'd shooed away from the table walked back and took his place once again at the table with Alice, who greeted his return with a perfunctory and well-practiced smile.

"Well, you certainly treated her like the princess of the ball," declared Cullen with a smile as they stepped outside back onto the street.

"There are some who create their own circumstances," replied Hawkes, "through their own weaknesses and decisions and there are others who are tossed into circumstances that are very much beyond their own total control. Miss Alice Lake strikes me as a strong intelligent woman who is doing her best to survive in the circumstances she finds herself."

"Circumstances beyond her control?" returned Cullen, frowning now. "It seems to me she's chosen to work in that den. Doing God knows what for her money."

"She entertains on stage according to Peter Orleneff, an endeavor that, as far as I am aware, is not condemned by any code of morality, and, when not performing, she induces men to spend money while offering them a smile," said Hawkes. "As long as that's as far as it goes, there is little to denounce in my opinion. I am reminded of a conversation I had recently with Mrs. Agatha Willis—I spoke to her in connection with our previous, ah, collaboration, the Hammond affair—and she spoke passionately of her desire to help woman gain their rights regarding labor laws. There are many women working in this city's factories, and in other factories in other cities, for less than a half-dollar a day, and that for a twelve-hour day. It seems to me that society cannot limit women to such unendurable conditions in regards to earning a living and then, at the same time, condemn those same woman for seeking opportunities outside those very conditions. With such miserable wages being offered elsewhere, she all but has no choice but to work in places such as this. Here she'll make more in one night here than in weeks of working in the factories. I see little additional virtue in slaving for penurious wages."

Cullen offered Hawkes a grunt, being neither convinced of the point nor able to argue it. "Well, at least we have confirmed that Greenleaf was having an affair with Jane Orleneff. But we're still a long way from proving he killed her, aren't we?"

"Miss Lake has presented to us additional important information, Cullen. More than simply the confirmation of a connection between Jane Orleneff and Greenleaf, as important as that is. She's given us the name of the shop in which the dress Jane wore on Halloween night to his party was purchased. What's more, it was he, Greenleaf, who purchased it. Brookstone's Shop, 96 Green Street. That information may prove to be very valuable. Tomorrow, we will make a visit to that shop and confirm that the dress was purchased there. And, unless I am completely off the mark, confirm also that it was not one dress that was purchased there by Greenleaf, but rather two."

Befuddlement returned to Cullen's face. "Two? Two dresses? What do two dresses have to do with anything?"

Hawkes smiled. "I must continue to ask for your indulgence, Cullen. Come, we have done all we can this night." He stepped to the curb and hailed a passing cab over to him. "I'll return to the my room at the Dead Rabbits and obtain some sleep and I suggest you go to your apartment and do the same. Tomorrow morning I'll go to Brookstone's on Green Street. There's no reason for both of us to go."

He stopped talking to Cullen for a moment to give his destination to the cab driver and then turned back to the detective. “After going to Green Street I’ll ride the elevated train to the Bloomingdale’s shop she mentioned. If that store keeps any records at all, I’ll determine what was purchased there as well. It may be helpful. Good night, Cullen.” With that, he opened the door to the cab. “Be assured,” he added as he climbed inside, “that we are drawing our net close ‘round Clifford Greenleaf. We may very well have our man shortly.” With that optimistic declaration Hawkes slammed shut the carriage door and, with the crack of the driver’s whip, was gone from view as the cab swiftly pulled away from the curb.

Cullen’s hand went up to scratch the top of his head once more as he gazed at the rear of the departing carriage. “Two dresses?” he murmured. “What the deuce do two dresses have to do with anything? Who cares how many dresses he bought?”

Chapter Fifteen

The New York Elevated Railway Company was organized in 1872, more than two decades earlier. Prior to that organization, an experimental railroad a half-mile long was built on Greenwich Street. Its success prompted the expansion of the elevated railway and, by 1876, it extended from the Battery to 61st Street. This elevated railroad was built upon a system of single posts to support the tracks above.

In 1878 another system, the Metropolitan Road, was completed, a double-track railroad system that filled nearly to capacity the narrower downtown streets of Manhattan it occupied and rumbled through the middle of the wider Sixth Avenue up to 59th Street.

In 1879, the two systems were leased to the Manhattan Company, thus effectively forming one management and the railroad system expanded periodically until its branches stretched up to 158th Street and the Harlem River and into the relatively rural area of the Bronx. On the East Side of Manhattan a Third Avenue Railroad was created and it was this branch of the system to which Hawkes made his way the following day.

The fare, during the early workingmen's hours was a mere nickel and the trains, consisting of a steam locomotive and four cars, normally ran less than four minutes apart with the trip to 59th Street consuming no more than twenty minutes. With any luck Hawkes would be back downtown by ten, in less than two hours' time.

He'd decided to reverse his original intent to visit Brookstone's prior to going to Bloomingdale's once he learned that the former shop would not open until ten in the morning. Rather than waste the time simply waiting for Brookstone's to open its doors, he would ride the rails uptown.

It was the first time Hawkes had taken the elevated train and he had to admit it was an unusual sensation at least initially to be riding along atop posts nearly sixty feet high while looking down upon the rooftops of passing buildings and into the windows of the top floors of others. It was almost like flying. Although it was clear the sensation of wonder passed eventually as most of the other passengers, workers on their way to their jobs, barely bothered to glance out the windows at all. Many seemed bored by the ride.

Hawkes was fortunate. The clerks at Bloomingdales kept good records of their sales and he was able to determine quickly exactly what articles of clothing and accessories Greenleaf and Jane Orleneff had purchased. He made identical purchases and returned to downtown Manhattan ladened with a bag holding his procurements. It was after ten now and he went straight to Brookstone's where, as expected, the purchases of Greenleaf and Miss Orleneff were also quickly verified. After returning to the Dead Rabbits to drop off his packages, he went straight to the police precinct to meet with Cullen. The time was nearing half-past eleven. He was immediately told that Cullen was not present in the precinct but was on his way to the Burnt Rag to arrest the bartender Johnny Dobbs for the murder of Jane Orleneff a.k.a. Jane Montane, a statement which startled Hawkes into speechlessness for a moment after he heard it spoken. Then he turned around and went back outside where he immediately hailed a cab to take him to the saloon called the Burnt Rag.

It more than lived up to its name, the walls of the Burnt Rag (inside and out) being so shabby and dirty they might have been composed of stiffened rags rather than wood and brick. They were walls filthy to the point of appearing they'd been blackened by flames. A uniformed police officer was outside the entrance and, nodding his head to Hawkes' inquiry as to whether or not Cullen was inside, stepped aside to let Hawkes enter.

It was a low place, a "two-cent" restaurant and saloon to which only the poorest of citizens would go to drink and eat. The bar was nothing more than a couple of barrels set a few feet apart from each other with two planks running over them in between. Grime covered everything including the bartender Johnny Dobbs who was now seated in a chair in front of Detective Cullen, the seedy-appearing man bawling his eyes out. He'd just been dragged from his cot in the back room where he slept each night and had been placed in the chair in which he now sat. If Hawkes' judgement was right, Mr. Dobbs had gone to sleep the previous night after polishing off at least one bottle of some alcoholic drink or another. He was unkempt and unshaven, with two days' growth of stubble on his face. His blood-shot eyes gazed out of the grime coating his face like two small desert rats staring out of two holes in the ground. Drool fell from his slackened jaw down his unshaven chin, gaining good purchase on the stubble of his beard and remaining there, refusing to drop to the floor.

"I did it," he moaned as Hawkes approached. "I did it. It's my fault Jane's dead. Mine. All mine. I did it...I did it..." Tears poured past the grime that surrounded his eyes. He was a man legitimately distraught.

Cullen glanced over to Hawkes. "This puts a hole in *your* theory," he said. "Dobbs here is confessing to killing Jane Montane. That means it's not Greenleaf as we thought."

"What made you hunt him out today?" asked Hawkes, frowning. This had to be wrong.

"A neighbor of Jane's came into the precinct early today. An elderly lady, lives across the street. She said she'd seen this Dobbs hovering around the place and thought she'd let us know. He frightened her more than once you see. And she knew that he was friendly with Jane at one time."

"And when you arrived here?"

"He was dead to the world in his cot back in that stable he calls a room. It took me near a quarter-hour to get him conscious, he'd so much liquor in him. No sooner do I tell him Jane Montane is dead then he confesses, blubbering like a baby. Just like you see him now."

Hawkes pointed to Dobbs' right arm. "You are a needle man, I see," he said. "When you're not drinking."

The glazed eyes stared at him. "I killed her..." he moaned. "I killed her..."

Hawkes looked at Cullen. "What did you tell him when you sobered him up? As much as it is possible to sober him up in any case. Did you tell him that Jane Montane had died of an injection of too much opium?"

"Yes, sure, why not?"

Hawks turned his attention back to the slobbering Dobbs. "What do you mean by saying you killed Jane?" he asked. "Speak up man!"

"I-I killed her…" moaned Dobbs, focusing on Hawkes due to the sharp tone of Hawkes' voice. "My fault she's dead…my fault…."

"Your fault. How is it your fault?"

Dobbs' head fell onto his chest. "I-I killed her, you see. It was me…"

Hawkes reached down, grabbed the man by the shoulders and shook him violently. "What do you mean, your fault! Tell me!" he shouted.

"I-I acquainted her to the drugs," said Dobbs, finally attempting to fully explain his meaning. "She-She never took them before she met me. It's my fault you see. My fault…isn't it so?" He gazed at Hawkes, his eyes transformed to question marks.

"Do you think her accidentally taking too much of the drug is your fault, man?" asked Hawkes. "It was an accident, that's all."

"No, my fault. She wouldn't have taken the drug at all if not for me. She killed herself 'cause of me. My fault. I killed her…I did…I killed her…."

Hawkes released the man and he fell back into the chair, very nearly slipping to the floor. "There's the reason for his *confession*, Cullen. He introduced her to the opium and now feels responsibility for her death, because her death was caused by the same drug he'd first drawn her toward using. He's not our killer, not at all."

Cullen gazed at Hawkes. "You certain? He seems a right good candidate to me."

"We're wasting our time here," responded Hawkes. "Come. Let's go." Without another word he turned and walked away from the sorrowful Dobbs and the detective. Cullen, after a moment's hesitation, too abandoned Dobbs and followed Hawkes out onto the street.

Outside, Cullen dismissed the uniformed officer and he and Hawkes walked away from the Burnt Rag.

"He's a man who's fallen far quickly," stated Hawkes. "Did you see the quality of his clothes? First-rate, yet filthy now and left to go to ruin. He had money once, and has since lost it, or lost his ability to get more. That explains how he could once attract a woman such as our deceased Jane Montane yet look as miserable as he does now. Do you think a man in that condition, with so little funds available to him, could be the same person who shared a glass of wine with Jane on the last night of her life, Cullen?"

"I-I suppose not," grumbled the detective. 'It's just that when a man confesses I have to take him seriously."

"That wasn't a confession. Rather a blurting out of the sting of his own conscience. It's startling, is it not, how one person can retain such a surfeit of conscience that he will feel guilt over a crime that is barely related to any actions he took, while another can kill outright, then go home and sleep like a babe resting in its mother's arms. Why the unequal distribution of this ability to feel guilt, Cullen? Of conscience? Is it something men are born with or something learned? Or perhaps both?"

"I-I'm sure I don't know," replied Cullen, scratching his head.

"Hawkes nodded his head. "Nor do I. Back to the business at hand. We have drawn our net fairly tightly around our Mr. Greenleaf. I'm certain he's our man yet, at the same time, I must state that our evidence is purely circumstantial. And he strikes me as being a man, intelligent as well as absolutely selfish and arrogant, who will not easily cave in under the normal pressure of an interrogation. With that in mind, I'd like to suggest to you that we rattle the man's cage, so to speak. I have a plan in mind that may succeed in shaking up our Clifford Greenleaf. It will require some dramatics but it just might triumph where other methods will not. Are you game, Cullen?"

"Mr. Hawkes, without your help, I'd still be cursing the fact that I couldn't touch the man, and quite likely would have arrested Mr. Dobbs just now. There's much pressure from the higher-ups to put someone away for Virginia Greenleaf's murder. At this point they don't much care who it is, but I'd very much like it to be the right man even if it doesn't matter to them."

"Well said," replied Hawkes. "I too like to see true justice done and not simply a facsimile of it which is polished up and presented for public consumption. I have seen such occurrences take place much too often. All right Cullen, let me tell you what I have in mind, and let me warn you in advance what will be the toughest task to perform."

"Task? And what might that be?"

"We must convince Clifford Greenleaf to grant us permission allowing us back into his house, there to perform what we shall present as a necessary reenactment of the crime. Necessary in order to finalize the *elimination* of him as a suspect; that is the best way to put it, I imagine. He will surely not be able to resist watching the police declaring his own innocence of a crime he knows he is guilty of. In fact…" Hawkes here stopped dead in his tracks as a new thought came to him.

"What is it, Mr. Hawkes?" asked Cullen, halting in his step beside him.

"I think it might be wise, after all, to have Mr. Dobbs put into the custody of the police. Yes, he might serve our purposes well. Come, let's return to the Burnt Rag, Cullen. You can then place Johnny Dobbs under arrest. He will, I'm certain, prove of use to us."

Chapter Sixteen

Clifford Greenleaf's expression contained an odd mixture of exasperation and self-satisfaction as he watched Hawkes and Cullen prepare for the reenactment of events leading up to the murder of his wife. He clearly wanted this spectacle, somewhat ridiculous to his mind, to end as quickly as possible. On his face was the recent growth of beard, the man wanting back the goatee he'd so recently discarded. Standing beside Greenleaf was his servant, Blake, who looked uncomfortable over the presence of so many police arriving in the house.

They were gathering in the hall outside the small room in which Greenleaf had performed his Halloween night's illusion. The room, seen through the door, was as dimly lit as it was on Halloween night, with only one gaslight to push away the shadows within. With Hawkes and Cullen were a group of uniformed police, a dozen in all, and, standing now in their midst, was Johnny Dobbs, hands bound by a pair of Bean Patrolman handcuffs, more sober now than previously. Occasionally he meekly protested his arrest. When not speaking against the injustice being offered him, he stood silently, glumly, his head drooping, his eyes on the floor, looking much like a beaten dog living with no hope of anything coming along in its future except further beatings.

"We thank you, Mr. Greenleaf," said Hawkes, "for permitting us into your home. This enactment may very well answer a few as yet unresolved issues regarding our case against this man here. As I said previously, he has already confessed to killing another woman, Jane Montane, and we believe it's likely he's also responsible for your wife's murder as well. Still, it's not entirely clear how he gained entry to your home, nor made his way to your bedroom. Certainly he was not an invited guest, nor did he accompany any other guest inside as far as we're able to determine."

"He must have come in through a window," stated Greenleaf. "As I imagine most thieves gain entry to homes." Inwardly he was pleasantly surprised at Hawkes' repeat of his statement that this handcuffed man was the killer of Jane Montane as well as the murderer of his wife. It appeared to Greenleaf then as though good fortune had indeed chosen to smile upon him for some inexplicable reason. He may not have earned that smile but there'd be no objection from him for having gained it. "Looking like that," continued Greenleaf, "he certainly wouldn't have been permitted in by my servants, so he must've crept in through a window. Perhaps the French Doors. But I still don't understand fully why this full reenactment is necessary. What does it matter what I was doing while he was breaking into my house?"

"Well, sir, as I said before, there are some—" Here Hawkes glanced at Cullen for effect, "—who are not totally convinced that, ah, how to put it, that you are not still involved in some way with your wife's death. This will hopefully erase all doubts of your innocence."

"I don't understand. Involved…? In what way?"

"I'll explain further. The theory, weak as it is, is that you abetted this man's entry into the house and that, while he actually did the terrible murder, you were present in the bedroom at the time and are therefore equally culpable in that crime." Hawkes was here presenting to Greenleaf a tale, an imaginary tale, created for no other reason than to justify the reenactment of the crime before Greenleaf's eyes. They presented to Greenleaf a pretence that they, Hawkes and the police, were there to prove Greenleaf's total innocence, a deception that Greenleaf accepted as truth. "I see," he replied slowly, mulling over Hawkes' words. "So some still think I could have been involved in the murder of my dear wife." He shot Cullen a look of anger. "Shameful," he declared, fairly flinging the word at Cullen, if it'd been a rock it would have dented Cullen's skull. "Well, go on then. Let's have this done and over."

"Excellent," responded Hawkes, smiling pleasantly. "Bring in the crate then," he said, turning to Cullen. The detective in turn made a motion to his uniformed men, four of whom turned and left the hall. In a few moments they returned carrying a six-foot long wooden crate, each man supporting one corner of it.

"Put it inside the room there," said Hawkes, pointing to the door leading into the room. The men obediently went through the doorway and deposited the crate inside.

"What—What in the world is that?" asked Greenleaf. "What is that crate for?"

"For convenience sake," declared Hawkes. "It will serve the same purpose for me as your desk did you. I'll go inside the room as you did, and will conceal myself inside the crate just as you concealed yourself inside your desk. As you can see, my height makes it impossible for me to enter the hiding space in the desk itself. Ten of these officers (we couldn't obtain the full twenty) will be given numbered tickets as your own guests were offered numbered invitations on the night of the murder. Cullen here will serve the function Devery did on that fateful night. That is, he will be the so-called gate-keeper. He will accept the tickets from each man in numerical order. Once they are all inside, the door will be locked, as it was then. Now I believe the time permitted for the guests to search the room was ten minutes, is that correct?"

"Ah, no, fifteen…" replied Greenleaf, a frown on his face. "But I still don't see why all this is necessary."

"For the sake of brevity we'll set the time today to simply one minute—then, after the fifteen minutes passed, the door was opened and all the guests exited the room while you remained behind, still hidden in the desk. Is that correct?"

"Certainly"

"The door was then locked by Inspector Devery and he and a guest remained standing outside until the cries of murder were heard. Within that space of time, time in which you *must* have been inside the room, Dobbs here had to have entered the house (unless already within, that is still possible) and made his way to the bedroom where, once there, he murdered your wife. Is that also correct?"

"Yes, absolutely correct," stated Greenleaf. "So there's certainly no way I could have been in the bedroom with this man at the same time."

"Yes, that is one of the issues we will resolve today," said Hawkes. "We will then proceed with our analysis of how we believe the murder occurred, how Dobbs here wrote the bloody message on the wall and fled the house. Again, all within the time frame in which you were inside the room. Do you see any objection to any of this?"

Greenleaf replied that he did not.

"Good, then we will proceed. I will take the place of Mr. Greenleaf here and enter the room. The crate is a little short for my height but I will bow my head for the few minutes I must be inside. Cullen here will act as both time-keeper and gate-keeper. Ten of these officers have their numbered tickets and will, after a minute has passed be allowed to go inside after me. After another minute Cullen will open the door and allow them to leave, again in numerical order, giving back their numbered tickets as they exit. Then the door will be locked as it was that night. At that point Dobbs here will be taken to the bedroom, there, as I said, to be presented with the facts of how we believe he killed Mrs. Greenleaf and then made his way out of the house. Clear? Good, then let's get started."

Hawkes stepped forward and went to enter the room. "Oh, with your permission, Mr. Greenleaf," he said, halting and turning around, "I'd like to play the same music as was played that night as well. Is the music still the same on the graphophone?"

"Yes, it hasn't been changed," replied Greenleaf. "But I really don't think—"

"Thank you," interrupted Hawkes, not offering the man an opportunity to voice an objection. "I'll go inside now, Cullen. Close the door after me and then, after the minute passes, let the others in."

Cullen grunted an acknowledgement of the instructions and, the moment Hawkes had passed through the door, quickly pulled it shut. He immediately produced his watch and began watching the second hand.

The hall grew silent as the men waited. There was no sound except the ticking of a nearby grandfather clock and that of Dobbs' murmurings. "I didn't do it," he said, speaking barely louder than a whisper. "Not me…Jane…sorry she's dead…my fault…all my fault…Jane…poor Jane…"

Then the music came through the door and into the hall, Hawkes having turned on the graphophone inside the room, drowning out the sonorous tick of the grandfather clock and Dobbs' barely audible words. His lips continued to move but no one could any longer hear what he was saying.

"Is that really necessary?" protested Greenleaf. "To play music…?"

Cullen lifted his eyes from the watch for a moment, offered Greenleaf a noncommittal shrug of his shoulders, and then returned his gaze to the second hand. All stood waiting as the music, as eerie as it was on Halloween night, played within the room.

"All right, time's up," declared Cullen all of a sudden. He opened the door and peered inside. The crate stood directly ahead, Hawkes was nowhere in sight. "Come on, men, hand me your tickets. Number one first. Come on."

In moments Cullen held ten tickets and the door was again locked. Cullen's gaze went once more to his watch. In the hall near Cullen stood the two excess officers, one on either side of Dobbs, watching the prisoner. A short distance from them, a few feet, stood Greenleaf and Blake. No one spoke, not even Dobbs, and the only sound in the hall that was audible was that of the music playing on the graphophone, floating out from behind the closed door of the room.

"Time," spoke up Cullen at last after the second minute had passed. He opened the door and the patrolmen filed out, one at a time, he handing them their numbered tickets as they stepped out into the hall. As number ten left the room, Cullen pulled the door shut and locked it again. "Come on," he said loudly, "we're to go to the bedroom now. All of us. Bring Dobbs along as well."

"Shouldn't someone stay in front of the door?" asked Greenleaf. "Just as Devery and a guest did that night? To make certain Hawkes doesn't leave while we're away?"

"The door is locked," said Cullen.

"Couldn't he pick the lock?" said Greenleaf. "I think, for the sake of accuracy, someone should remain here."

"I don't believe that will be necessary," spoke up a voice from within the group of the dozen uniformed police standing in the hall. Greenleaf and Cullen both looked at the speaker who, to Greenleaf's amazement, straightened up before his eyes, adding two or three inches to his height, and then removed his hat. With that removal, Greenleaf's face blanched white, his eyes opened wide and his mouth dropped open, for there standing before him, *outside* the room, clad in the uniform of the police, was none other than Simon Hawkes. So profound was Greenleaf's shock that, for many seconds, all he could do was stare in utter amazement at the tall man in front of him.

"You-You got out..." he declared at last, his astonishment as present in his voice as it was in his face.

"Yes," responded Hawkes, staring keenly at the shaken man. "In the same way you did, by pretending to be someone else, by substituting myself for another. Cullen, open the door."

Cullen put key to keyhole and then pushed the door open. Out stepped another police officer, a few inches shorter in height than Holmes.

"You thought we were incapable of being able to reason the means by which you managed to leave the room while all the time seeming to remain inside, but we've here proven you wrong," declared Hawkes. "You've stated repeatedly that it was impossible for you to have exited the room but, as has been demonstrated here today, it is entirely possible. For here I stand, having left the room under your own eyes, while you watched the door to it yourself. In exactly the same way you were able to exit the room, walk down the hall, enter your bedroom and brutally murder your wife."

Greenleaf's eyes remained fixed on Hawkes but now pure loathing began to mix with the astonishment that resided there. "Damn you, you are clever. Damn you." Removing his gaze from Hawkes, he looked about him at the police surrounding him. "All right, so you've proven I could have left the room, so what? That still doesn't mean I actually *did* leave, does it? I still maintain I was inside that room when my wife was killed. Who are you to say otherwise? Who is anyone to say otherwise? Arrest me if that's your intent. I'll still foil you in court."

"Cliff..." A voice, a youthful female voice, came then from within the shadows of the small room. The voice, mild yet strong, was heard clearly above the music that continued to pour forth from the graphophone.

Greenleaf turned toward the sound of his spoken name and for the second time in mere moments his face drained white, this time his features also going entirely slack with incredulity and pure disbelief. The sight that greeted his astounded eyes was the figure of none other than Jane Montane, standing within the shadows of the room and clad in the same black velvet dress, adorned with the same accessories, as she'd worn the night of the murder. She repeated his name and stepped forward nearer the entrance of the room, stopping just prior to stepping into the hall.

"Jane!" he shouted. "But-But you're dead. You're dead!"

"Did you think your attempt to kill her succeeded, Mr. Greenleaf?" said Hawkes in a severe tone of voice. "No, while in a grim state for a time, she was able to survive the double injection of opium you gave her that night. She survived and is here to speak against you. To condemn you. You called me clever but I cannot take credit for cleverness. It's *she* who has revealed to us how she assisted you that night, how she aided you in your desire to rid yourself of your wife. Indeed, without her to tell us, how else would we have known?"

"It's the electric chair for you for certain," declared Cullen. "Yes, you'll be riding a Black Maria straight to your executioner. Right now there's a wagon waiting outside to take you to the stationhouse. From there you'll go to the Tombs."

Greenleaf's eyes narrowed into slits. "No! No!" he shrieked suddenly, a wild hoarse scream that was nothing less then the howl of a frightened animal; with that shout, he was off. A powerful shove pushed aside the police officer nearest him and that officer tumbled into others in the group throwing the men off balance. On the instant Greenleaf was off and running down the hall, racing toward the room at the very end of the hall. It was a few seconds before the police officers started after him.

Blake then spoke up. "Careful," he shouted, directing his words primarily to Hawkes and Cullen, the others already a distance away, "he keeps a pistol in that room."

Cullen shouted caution to his men even as Greenleaf entered the room he'd run to and slammed the door shut. "Careful, men!" he called to them. "He's got a pistol in there!"

The warning was heeded, and the men closest to the room pulled up short of bursting inside, taking the time to draw their own pistols. Another few ticks of the grandfather clock went by and then, to the surprise of all in the hall, a gunshot was heard from within the room into which Greenleaf had fled.

Hawkes and Cullen exchanged glances. "Careful, men," cried Cullen, going up to the front of the pack of police while drawing his own revolver. “We don’t really know what’s in there. Get back, I’ll open the door.”

With extreme caution, he pushed the door open and there to greet his eyes, as expected, was the body of Clifford Greenleaf, sprawled across the bed in the room, a great stain of blood by his temple, a shout of scarlet against the cream-colored coverlet on the bed. The pistol he’d used to end his life remained clasped in the unmoving claw of his hand.

“Well, he won’t be going to the Tombs,” spoke up Cullen as he put his pistol away. “The body wagon will do for this one.”

“Justice, self-inflicted,” stated Hawkes, as he turned away from the sight of Greenleaf’s body and found himself face-to-face with Alice Lake, her eyes vast, her hand to her mouth. She had pushed herself through the crowd of police to glimpse the bloody destruction of Clifford Greenleaf. “G-Goodness, Mr. Hawkes,” she said, “I didn’t think…I didn’t think something like this would happen. All that blood….” Standing behind her, his eyes nearly as wide, stood Blake, Greenleaf’s servant no longer, his services terminating with the piercing of Greenleaf’s skull by the bullet fired from the man’s pistol.

“Nor I,” replied Hawkes, stepping up to the trembling young woman and putting an arm around her shoulders. “Who would have thought he’d take the quick way out? Come, sit over here. Can I get you something? A glass of brandy perhaps?”

He led her to a deacon’s bench that stood in the hall by the banister and there she sat down on its cushion. Here she removed the brown wig she wore for the impersonation.

“Blake, some brandy,” requested Hawkes.

“No,” said Alice, “I’m fine…now. Was he the one, Mr. Hawkes? The one who killed Jane?”

“Yes, yes, he was,” replied Hawkes. “Without a doubt.”

After a few seconds in which she considered Hawkes’ words, a smile slowly made its appearance on her lips, arriving as gradually and softly as a sunrise. “Then I’m glad, Mr. Hawkes,” she said at last. “Then I’m glad you asked me to help you.”

Chapter Seventeen

"I've no doubt I seem thick to you, Mr. Hawkes," said Cullen, "but I swear, even after all that's happened, even after you telling me how he did what he did, I still don't have it quite clear in my head."

The two men, Hawkes and Cullen, were seated by the fire in the main room of the Dead Rabbits, Hawkes sitting in the chair nearest the blazing hearth, the light from the fire burnishing the side of his lean, angular face. He offered Cullen a smile in response to the detective's words. "I explained it rather quickly," he replied, "and perhaps not in the detail required for a full understanding. I remind you of the night I purchased a large pouch of shag and gave myself over to consideration of this very unique puzzle. It required hours of thought before I grasped it, the means by which he made his way out of that room when it appeared impossible that he could do so. I'm not surprised that my very quick and admittedly hasty clarification offered to you should not be entirely sufficient. Let me give you a more complete explanation of events." Here Hawkes stopped to light up his cherrywood pipe. After a few seconds, with a shake of his head and a soft chuckle, he broke the silence. "You must admire his cleverness," he declared. "His plan was most imaginative if also most *outré* as the French say."

"Sorry, Mr. Hawkes, but I fail to see anything admirable in it," replied Cullen.

"It is the cleverness that is worthy of some appreciation," responded Hawkes. "Certainly not the purpose to which that cleverness was directed. There is no delight to be found in the crime of murder."

"I agree wholeheartedly."

"Now to explain. Upon first sight there seemed to be no way Greenleaf could have done this deed, to have murdered his wife under the circumstances as presented to us. Indeed this appears so obvious that his alibi no doubt would have been accepted as absolute truth if not for his misfortune in failing to immediately end the life of his wife. That is, she survived his attack long enough to write that accusation of his guilt on her bedroom wall in her own blood. If not for that, he may very well have succeeded in escaping punishment. As it was, even with that dying declaration, he still very nearly escaped."

"True enough."

"His innocence appeared to be a given. But what if, I thought, instead we simply flip that around and take it as true that he did do it? That he is *not* innocent. What then?

"It was determined, first by our friend Conroy, then by the police and finally myself, that there was no hidden way in or out of the room. Unless this hidden means was so well concealed that all of us missed it. That was unlikely. So the question became one of discovering how it was possible for the man, in some other way other than a secret door of sorts, to leave that locked room under the strict conditions he himself offered. How could he possibly get out, under the eyes of twenty people and Chief Inspector Devery? That is the question I took to my room that night with my supply of shag. Happily my time was not wasted. The answer did indeed reside in the smoke of my pipe and by two in the morning I had the answer, or at least *an* answer, a possible means by which the man might have left the room while appearing to remain inside.

"I reasoned he had an confederate. Most likely a woman," continued Hawkes, "one among those selected to serve as witnesses to his magic trick. Having come that far, I also determined it was very likely it was a woman who had a close relationship with Greenleaf. A mistress most likely. An assumption but a probable one. Thus, when you appeared that very morning with that list of attendees to Greenleaf's affair, a list with a line drawn through the name of a woman who was now suddenly deceased, I immediately considered the possibility that here was the very woman who assisted the man in his crime. In that consideration I was subsequently proven correct. Jane Montane was indeed the same woman who helped Greenleaf execute the murder of his wife. Without her participation it could not have been done."

"Yes, and my hat's off to you for figuring that out, but *how* did you know that, Mr. Hawkes? What made you determine a woman helped him? I have to say I've strained my brain trying to understand all this and it still beats me."

Hawkes smiled. "It was indeed, as Greenleaf himself told everyone, a magic trick. But it was one which had a different purpose than making people think he was *out* of the room. Gone over to the other side, as he said. It's true purpose from the beginning was to make people believe he was *inside* the room. If they were convinced of that, then he had his alibi."

"So how did he do it?"

"One circumstance as I contemplated the facts of the murder began to stand out in my mind. That was, the *time of the occurrence of the murder*. It did not take place during the fifteen minutes when the twenty so-called witnesses were searching for Greenleaf inside the room, but rather during the ten minutes *after they'd completed their search and left*. As I thought about it, that fact gained dominance in my mind. It seemed increasingly to me that the key to solving the mystery resided in that fact."

"The key??" asked Cullen, feeling about as intelligent as one of the nightsticks he used to swing as a patrolman prior to becoming a detective.

"If Greenleaf had a secret way out of the room, then wouldn't it be more likely the murder would take place during the first fifteen minutes when he would use the hidden means to get out of the room? More, how secure would the man be, if his plot for murder depended upon a secret door of some kind? Wouldn't he worry that the police might discover it? And he'd be right, the police most likely would discover it. Once they did his alibi would be gone. No, it wasn't good enough. A secret way in and out of the room was too obvious. So I concluded that all our searches within the room did not miss anything. There was no secret way in or out of the room.

"Concluding that, it must stand to reason he got out another way. A much less obvious way. And here was where the time of the murder gained importance. Virginia Greenleaf was murdered during the minutes coming *after the room was vacated by the guests invited to witness Greenleaf's disappearance.* I began to think that, there being no secret way in or out, there existed only one opportunity for the man to leave the room. That is, he had to walk out of the room when the others did, exiting with the twenty guests invited to witness the illusion."

"But he couldn't have. They'd have seen him leaving. The inspector would have seen him."

"That is the precise objection to the theory, Cullen, I myself voiced. I congratulate you. But if we grant that the theory is correct anyway, as I did, the question then becomes: How could Greenleaf have managed it? How could he walk out of the room right under the eyes of all the others and not be noticed?"

"And don't forget that business with the cards," broke in Cullen. "Each person who went into the room after him, gave a numbered card to Devery. They got back the same card as they left. Only twenty in and twenty out. He couldn't have just mixed in with the crowd and walked out with the others."

"It seemed so. That is precisely why the ingenious Mr. Greenleaf instituted the necessity of the numbered cards," responded Hawkes. "Nevertheless, I was becoming certain that somehow he *did* walk out of that room. There was no other way. So how did he manage it? That was when something Conroy had told me came to mind. The blinding flash of light that occurred in the room just after the door was locked. Do you remember him speaking of that? What if that light had a purpose?"

"What could that be?" asked Cullen, as perplexed as ever.

"Greenleaf was an amateur magician. I had the good fortune to pass by a theater, one which featured a magician and I thought I'd pass my little puzzle by him. He told me that, in his opinion, the flashing light might very well have been used to serve as misdirection. A magician's best friend, he told me. To misdirect the eyes of the audience *away* from what is important toward what is irrelevant. He suggested to me that the blinding lights were a crude way of doing exactly that, a means of getting people *not* to see something that was taking place. He could offer me no further insight but still it was an important point."

"So the lights blinded people? To get them *not* to see something? What could that be?" repeated Cullen.

"Precisely the question to be asked. Recall the tips of ostrich feathers we found behind the curtains covering the window. True, they might have fallen there off a dress of one of the so-called guests searching the room, a female guest looking behind the curtain as

Conroy said he did, but that possibility was effectively eliminated when we discovered similar feathers inside the desk where Greenleaf was supposedly secreted. What if these feather tips had fallen off the dress of someone who was hiding behind those curtains? What if that someone was Greenleaf himself, who was not hiding in the desk as he told everyone afterwards, but was instead *simply concealed behind the drapes as the twenty entered the room?* What if, during the minutes he had before the others entered, he didn't use the time to conceal himself within the trick desk but rather changed his appearance? *What if he disguised himself during that time? Putting on a woman's dress and assorted accoutrements?* Then the flash of light would allow him, at the moment the door to the room was closed, to slip from behind the drapes and simply join the others, wouldn't it? He would then be part of the crowd in the room. He would then be hiding *in plain sight*."

"Impossible. They'd spot him right away. His beard would give him away."

"Remember how dark the room was kept. That was done purposely. He could easily escape notice if he changed his appearance sufficiently. What if his distinctive beard, his goatee, was now false? The original beard shaved off and replaced with an artificial one? What if he removed this artificial beard once inside? Then also took off his tux to put on a dress he had concealed in his secret compartment in the trick desk? A dress that was the same or very much like that worn by one of the twenty witnesses? What if, during the time he had, he quickly put on some rouge and eyeliner? What if, in short, he disguised himself *as a woman*? Again I ask you to recall how dimly lit the room was and that it was filled with people who were all either complete or relative strangers to each other. Recall too Greenleaf's small size and his youthful features. Could such a transformation work?"

"It did work." replied Cullen. "Since you've been long proven right. His beard. That's why he was clean shaven afterward for a time. He didn't want to wear his false goatee after it'd served its purpose for fear it'd be noticed as a fake."

"Yes, so I thought, but still my thoughts were more supposition than anything else. I reasoned that the tux that Greenleaf wore into the room was thrown into the desk, along with his imitation goatee, thrown behind the door of that false safe within the desk. From the same space he removed the dress and woman's paraphernalia he'd previously placed there and put them on. All of this, the tux and false goatee, he would retrieve later, after his wife was dead. His transformation complete, he waited behind the curtains while the others were allowed in and until the flash of bright light permitted him to come out and mingle with the others. No one noticed that there was an additional women in the room. But it was of course possible he would be noticed. The plan had the distinctive advantage to him that, should someone at some time become aware of his disguise, he could simply shrug it off, congratulate the man or woman who recognized him for discovering the secret of his trick and then *not* go through with the murder. Thus it contained its own safety mechanism. But once he was actually out of the room and still undetected, he knew his plan was a success. Only then did he proceed with the murder of his wife. Only then did he believe there was no way anyone could prove he was the killer."

"But it's still not clear, exactly how did he get out of the room? If you're right, then there were twenty-one people walking about in the room. But Devery only let twenty out. That left one who couldn't leave as there was no twenty-first ticket. And it was him who had no ticket."

"Having figured out the machination of the ruse up to this point, the rest was simplicity itself. His accomplice, a woman who was the same approximate height and weight as himself and who entered the room, as I said, wearing a like or very similar dress as he now wore, secretly approached him as the crowd wandered about, and, I later surmised, based upon the spectacles we found in Jane Montane's room, passed to him a set of false spectacles which she wore when she entered. That was most likely their purpose, to partially conceal her features when she went into the room and do the same for Greenleaf when the time came for him to leave. The spectacles were a clever touch for they made it more likely that each, Montane and Greenleaf, would be taken for the same person. The woman remained behind in the room while Greenleaf walked out past the chief inspector."

"Those eyeglasses we saw in her room," murmured Cullen.

"Precisely. We could talk to Devery to see if he recalls a young woman with thick spectacles being one of the twenty witnesses to Greenleaf's illusion, but at this point I don't think that confirmation is necessary. Spectacles or not, Greenleaf and Jane Montane changed places with Jane remaining inside the room while her lover, Greenleaf, went out, walking past Devery."

"Greenleaf must have given her ticket bearing the number one," said Cullen, suddenly inspired. "The servant who went through the party handing out the tickets was only given eighteen to distribute, so everyone else, having a higher number, had to *follow* Greenleaf out of the room. That way, they had only his back to look at and not his face. He only had to get past Devery. Devery was the only one who really had a chance to study his face closely."

"Excellent, Cullen. There is hope for you. Yes, that is correct. And Devery's eyes obviously couldn't get past the woman's spectacles, assuming we are correct about that."

"If I know Devery, he had enough drinks to make the face of everyone there blurry," stated Cullen. "I wonder if Greenleaf picked him because he was a drinker."

"That is possible. Again I congratulate you for good thinking. In any case, while the others lined up to follow Greenleaf out of the room, Jane fell behind, went to the back of the room and then, unseen, slipped behind the drapes. Greenleaf now went off and brutally murdered his wife. Then he, raising the pitch of his voice so as to sound feminine, made the cry of thief and murder. As I said previously, the cry was necessary at that moment as it was imperative to his plan that everyone know without a doubt the killing occurred while he was supposedly locked in the room. She *must* be discovered dead at precisely that time if his alibi is to be effective. So he drops the knife to the floor and, pretending to be the victim, screams to bring witnesses to Virginia's death. He then leaves the bedroom the back way, while the servants and guests are running to the entrance in the hall."

"Damn, the man had nerve," murmured Cullen. "To cry out like that just after stabbing your wife to death…to bring people running right to you…"

"The screams served another purpose as well. They pulled Devery and Conroy away from the door of the locked room. While all attention was turned upon the murder, his accomplice, holding a second key to the lock, opened the door and, careful to avoid being seen, left the room. Greenleaf, still disguised as a woman, then himself went back to the room and changed back into his tux and reapplied his false goatee to his face. It was done. All that was left was for Greenleaf himself to show up in the bedroom and play the part of the grieving husband."

"He gave away two tickets," said Cullen. "I wonder who he gave the second to?"

"No doubt a stranger. He gave away two tickets as his conferral of just one might make it more apparent that he had a confederate. Two made that fact less obvious."

"I wonder why he ended up killing her, Jane Montane I mean."

"A falling out of sorts, I suppose. Perhaps she, thinking she now held power of him through possession of her knowledge of the murder, made excessive demands upon him. I've seen it happen many times before. Or perhaps he decided he didn't want anyone living with the knowledge of what he'd done. Both Greenleaf and Montane being no longer able to tell us, we'll never know for certain."

"Their plan would have succeeded, as you said, if not for the message in blood accusing him of killing her."

"Absolutely," replied Hawkes. "After receiving her mortal wounds, the poor woman lived for a minute or two after her husband left the room, and so she was able to tell us who her killer was. That message did what it was intended to do; it brought her murderer to justice."

"But without you, he still would have gotten away," responded the detective. "I tell you, if that happened, if he did get away, it would have been something that chewed on the inside of my belly for as long as I lived. Thank you again, Mr. Hawkes. I owe you big. If I can ever be of assistance to you, in any way, just give me a holler."

"No, Cullen, you give me too much credit. For it is without *you* that the man would have certainly gotten away with his vicious crime. I remind you that it was your own insistence that the man was guilty, insistence in the face of what appeared to be overwhelming evidence of his innocence, which convinced me to consider the possibility of his guilt. It's therefore to you that the soul of Mrs. Greenleaf must now offer thanks for the attainment of the justice that permits its peaceful rest."

Cullen smiled, taking some pleasure at Hawkes' words. "Well then, both of us, Mr. Hawkes," he said, the smile broadening. "It was both of us."

The Adventure of the Captive Forger

Chapter One

"After all, who can explain what *Art* even is?"

Bespectacled William Marsden Lancaster tossed out the question and then leaned back in his chair as though abandoning the words he'd just spoken.

The son of James Ossian Lancaster, he bore a noticeable resemblance to his father, both men being athletically lean and each possessing a countenance that clearly spoke of their relationship, of common ancestry. James Lancaster was a Wall Street financier who'd recently become known to Simon Hawkes through his request to Hawkes for help in a criminal matter, a matter resolved to satisfaction. Lancaster was referred to Hawkes by the police commissioner (who had himself been assisted by Simon in a matter requesting some extreme delicacy).

Having thrown out the question (for which he did not expect an answer) William Lancaster pulled a handkerchief from his pocket, removed his gold-framed, wire-rimmed glasses and began to casually wipe the rather thick lenses.

Sherlock Holmes was a man of whom it was said (by Doctor John H. Watson) possessed an absolutely "nil" interest in literature. If one can be said to possess what one lacks it was certainly an accurate assessment. Holmes "held" an equal level of interest in the talents of drawing, painting and/or sculpture. The skills of the portraitist, landscape artist, the gifts of a master carver or sculptor, held little appeal to Holmes, unless of course such skills (or their results) applied in some manner to a crime in which he had an interest. Holmes in travelling to America, specifically to New York City (and there assuming the name of Simon Hawkes for the sake of concealment from the danger directed toward him by Moriarty's men) did not in his travels suddenly acquire a deeper interest in the arts. So it was that he offered the young Lancaster nothing more than a curt nod of the head in response to the man's words. The nod was followed by a puff on his cherrywood pipe and additional silence as he returned his gaze to the open newspaper before him.

Both men were seated in the main room of The Dead Rabbits Society, Hawkes seeking time with his newspaper, Lancaster seeking company. Although Hawkes was tempted to be rude to the man, he resisted that temptation, instead simply offering Lancaster a lack of enthusiasm for the conversation. Surely the man would take the hint and either sit in silence or be off and away, either choice being acceptable to Hawkes.

Lancaster's question was rhetorical and he spoke again, the words coming from the other side of the Times held in front of Hawkes' face. "I think *I* can explain it," said Lancaster. "Or at least I can offer *an* explanation."

William Lancaster was a man with one overriding intellectual passion, his love of the Fine Arts. As a young man, he'd immersed himself in the study of drawing and painting, believing himself to be the next Raphael or Ingres. However, after years of study and struggle, he ended by coming in second best to the demands of that which he wanted to do. While possessing some skill, he discovered soon enough that what talent he held was not enough to allow him to achieve what he wanted. After years of struggling against his own limits, he was forced to accept the fact that he would never be anything more than a mediocrity doing what he loved to do. Recognizing that truth about himself, he walked away from that which, up to that point in his life, he had dedicated himself.

But he did not walk away entirely. His love for Art remaining inside him, he shifted course a bit and became an art dealer (as well as an active supporter for those struggling artists in which he saw evidence of the talent absent in his own hands). In regards to his new career, he, over the years, emerged with a reputation for being able to discern forgeries patterned after the styles of the great artists of history. This latter ability was much appreciated by many private collectors who at times summoned William Lancaster to pass judgement upon a painting or sketch being offered for sale, to vouch for its authenticity if its lineage was in any doubt whatsoever. More than once, he'd saved the wealthy from purchasing a work of art offered as legitimate but pronounced a fake by William Lancaster.

He also kept with him a small drawing pad, little bigger than a good-sized notebook on which he sketched now and then when he saw a scene of interest. It was this drawing pad that he now produced as he continued to interrupt Hawkes' reading.

"As a philosophical exercise, I've given the matter some thought and I think it *is* possible to define what Art is. At least in general terms. I'm considering publishing my thoughts. Let me show you this and you can tell me what you think." Hawkes was at last forced to lower the newspaper.

He watched with less than true interest as Lancaster pulled out his pen and, pen-point to paper, began drawing circles and writing. In less than a minute, he displayed what he'd produced to Hawkes. The drawing looked like this:

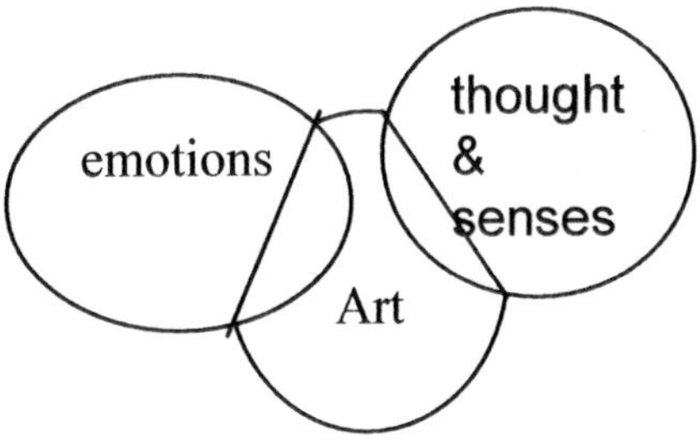

Hawkes grunted.

Lancaster smiled, tenderly it seemed, at his illustration. This was obviously a theory very close to his heart. "The small parts—where Art overlaps the circles—that is where genuine Art is created. And those are also the common points where humankind communicates, as we can only communicate through our arts, of which even our common language is a part. They are the means by which we talk to each other. All the rest, where there is no overlap, is unexplored territory. My point is—what?—that genuine Art, and not the work of imitators and artisans, whether it be painting, music, poetry or something else, depends, in my opinion, upon *both* the ability of the artist to push further into the unexplored circles of human emotions and/or human senses and then, completing that exploration, to find a way to communicate what is newly discovered to others. Art is thus twofold, first an exploration into the soul so-to-speak, and then a kind of conquering, that is, conquering a means of communication, whether it be paint, words or music, so as to be able to place the results of that exploration in front of others. Art, true Art is a very rare thing. Much of what we call 'Art' is really nothing more than simply a pretence to it."

Hawkes couldn't help but smile at the man's enthusiasm for his subject. "That does sound quite reasonable," he responded, chuckling.

"I think many people have had the experience of reading something, or of listening to a song, and suddenly experiencing the sense that the words written on the page or the song being sung is expressing exactly what they were feeling inside. Many of us feel things inside but have no means of *putting what we feel into words for others to understand.* The Artist however finds a way and so does a service to all of us who feel the same thing but cannot explain that feeling to others. There are truths we sense inside us which we have no way of grasping because we do not have the means to grasp them. The Artist finds a way to grab hold of those truths and display them to others. The imitator, the forger, sometimes quite technically skilled in their own right, simply walk the path the artist has opened."

Hawkes warmed a little to the subject. "I think I agree with you. I am fond of music, the violin in particular, I think your idea would be the same for that as well. Yes, I do. It's the difference between the originator and the skilled mimic, isn't it? You speak of art and forgery. And, as you say, often the forger's technical abilities match or even surpass that of the artist he's imitating. What the forger ultimately lacks is the creative power, the genius, to invent great works of his own."

"Yes, or to put it my way, he lacks the ability to explore the human soul. To push the boundaries of Art further into these two other circles."

"Quite an interesting thought. Yes, it might very well be so. It certainly does offer a generalization of that very hard to define subject we call 'Art'. Well done. It recalls to my mind a case I was involved with a while ago. Back in London. An art dealer was found in his salon, dead with the sharp point of the handle of an artist's paint brush pushed into his eye. Quite unusual circumstances surrounding that incident, I must say."

Lancaster blinked, and then blinked again. "Good Lord," he responded at last. "In the eye?"

Hawkes nodded his head. "Yes, a case with some interesting points to it. No pun intended." With that, he picked up the newspaper, snapped it into attention and let his eyes return to reading. The rising of the newspaper once again did not dissuade William Lancaster from further talk.

"Speaking of forgeries, I got a call yesterday from someone named Charles Buonocore. He lives in the Bronx. Wants me to come up and take a look at some drawings being offered to him for sale. My meager reputation seems to have extended itself beyond Fifty-ninth Street."

"Hardly a meager reputation, I understand," replied Hawkes, lowering the newspaper once more.

"Thank you," said Lancaster, truly appreciative of the compliment. "I didn't want to go at first but he's offered to pay me a bonus on top of my normal fee to compensate for the travel time. So I'm going. Money talks. I'm to take the city rails up to the last stop and there he'll have a cab waiting to take me the rest of the way. Says his house is a short distance from the train, so I expect another few minutes of travel time at least. I'm going up there late tomorrow. He said he'd be away until the evening, so I'll take the late afternoon train up. I've never been up in the Bronx that far. It should be a nice little trip, being in what is essentially the country for a time."

Hawkes surrendered, realizing there would be no peace in the Dead Rabbits for him that evening, not by the hearth in the main room. "I trust the trip will prove not to be too inconvenient," he said, folding the newspaper and tucking it under his arm. "Please excuse me, I find time has run up on me and I must be, ah, *somewhere*. Good day to you, and please relay my good wishes to your father."

"You're going…?"

"Yes, I must be off," replied Hawkes, having risen and already presenting his back to the talkative young man. He strode purposely out of the room, leaving Lancaster alone to contemplate his business trip to the Bronx.

A nice little trip, he'd told Hawkes. Words that would very shortly prove to be mockingly ironic, for William Lancaster's "nice little trip" would prove to be nothing less than a dangerous threat against his very life, a perilous journey bringing him very near to death.

Chapter Two

It was nearing six in the evening of the following day when Hawkes, sitting once again in front of the hearth in the Dead Rabbits main room, enjoying a before-dinner pipe and reading the daily newspaper while waiting for the dining room to begin serving supper, was suddenly confronted by none other than the financier, James Lancaster. The man's face expressed some concern as he hastily placed himself in the chair near Hawkes.

"Good evening, sir. I'm glad to find you here. I've come at the insistence of my boy. He's back in the house. He's asked I request you come to him. He wanted to come himself but he's not quite up to travel in my opinion and so I told him I would do it for him. And so here I am."

"Not up to travel? What's happened to him?" asked Hawkes. "Is he all right?"

"He's fine. Bruised but all right, thank the Lord. Please, will you come? He's quite anxious that you do. I fear he will not be satisfied until he talks to you."

"Is it that urgent?"

"For him, yes."

"Then of course."

A smile of appreciation appeared on the elder Lancaster's lips. "Excellent. I will make it worth your while. I'll tell you what little I know in the carriage ride over to my house. Then you'll hear his story from his own lips. Oh yes, one more thing."

"Yes?"

"Be prepared to refuse him his request for travel. Foolish boy wants to go back up to the Bronx tonight, to the farmhouse in which this damned fellow Buonocore is staying. Tell him you won't do it."

In minutes, Hawkes, snatched away from the comfort of the hearth, was with Lancaster in his carriage, the men making their way through the dreary, cold and gray November evening, going uptown to Twenty-ninth Street where stood the stately Lancaster home. The glow of the lamps of the streetlights of New York City were gauzed in a strong evening mist, looking like bits of abandoned cobwebs, the spiders fleeing for warmer places to be. As the cab trotted at as good a pace as was possible through the crowded streets Lancaster informed Hawkes of the basic facts of his son's experience in the Bronx the night before. He spoke quickly of it, stating only the broad particulars, and ended his brief statement with the remark that it was too bad one could not depend upon the police to handle the matter. It was their inability to do anything that was causing his son to want to return. "Boy doesn't realize how lucky he is to have not have been hurt worse than he is. There're no police up there, not really. All farms and dirt roads. He could have been killed." Then, suddenly recalling another purpose of his travels, he called up to the driver, telling him to stop on Fifteenth Street where his son maintained his own small apartment.

"He's lucky. Nothing broken except his eyeglasses," commented Lancaster, explaining the additional stop. "I'm going to William's apartment to pick up his spare pair of corrective lenses. Won't hurt to get him some fresh clothes either. His are a bit of a mess."

"You don't know why he was attacked?" asked Hawkes.

"He was clubbed—right in Buonocore's home. I know little else," responded Lancaster, gritting his teeth with anger. "He'll explain more fully when we arrive, although in truth, after listening to him myself, I find he knows little else as well."

Hawkes and Lancaster were at the Lancaster home on Twenty-ninth Street in less than twenty minutes, including the time needed to stop at William Lancaster's apartment. The two men went immediately inside the house, a large townhouse of brown stone patterned after the style of the home of J. Piermont Morgan, the Wall Street banker who so strongly impacted the U.S. economy in the 1880s. That was a period of time in which European confidence in U.S. securities waned, shaken by the fragmented and highly competitive railroad industry in the United States. Morgan convinced rail executives to ease competition, settle several disputes and merge their traffic. He later reorganized several major railroads, issuing stocks and bonds to refinance them. As he did, he gained control of their boards and so now ruled fully one-sixth of all of America's railway system.

His wealth and success made him worthy of imitation in style and manner. Other bankers and financial men moved uptown to live nearby the great man with the Midas touch and James Lancaster was one of these men.

William Lancaster sat on a sofa by a large window in a small room adjacent to the drawing-room. A part of his cheek was purple with a bruise and the top and one side of his head was covered with a large bandage. The man had indeed suffered a hard beating. He was hunched on the sofa as he sat waiting but pulled himself upright the moment his father and Hawkes entered. Looking at them, his head poking out of the top of a robe like a turtle's head coming halfway out of its shell, his eyes squinting so as to see as clearly as possible with his bad sight, he appeared, for a brief moment, as sad and forlorn as a lost child.

"Father! Hawkes! Thank goodness you're here!" he called out, relief coming into his battered face. He didn't rise but remained seated as the two men went to him.

"How are you?" asked Hawkes as the elder Lancaster handed his son the spare pair of glasses. The father then went and placed the change of clothes over the back of a nearby chair.

"I've been better," replied Lancaster, putting on the glasses. "Although I'm told by the doctor I'm not as bad as I might appear. Ah, I can see again. Thanks Papa, for bringing these, and the fresh clothes too." Here he stood up, a bit wobbly on his feet.

"You're sure you're all right?"

"Still a little dizzy. Some bruises. That's it. No other harm done. I guess my sleeping away most of the day has fixed me up."

"Good. Your father mentioned that you spoke to the police? Wanting them to go up to the Bronx?"

"They came and took my statement. Left over an hour ago. They won't go there. Even if they would, what good would come of it? I can't tell them exactly where I was in any case. I'm not sure where the damned house is. But it's the woman I'm worried about, Mr.

Hawkes. I think she might be in trouble. In very serious trouble. Surely there's some means by which we can help her."

"Woman?"

"The woman," he replied. "There's a young woman—she's being held against her will—at least I think so—in Buonocore's house. There's something wrong going on there! I don't—" Here he began to turn white, for a moment it appeared as though he was about to pass out.

"Are you sure you're all right," asked Hawkes, grabbing him by the arm.

"I-I think she might be in danger," said William, ignoring Hawkes' inquiry of concern, "but…but I don't know what to do about it."

"Steady. Here, sit back down. Perhaps a drink?" Hawkes threw the question at the father rather than the son, and the man responded by going to a nearby liquor cabinet and pouring a double-shot of whiskey. "Good Irish whiskey," he said, extending the glass toward his son. "Take some, Bill," he said. "It'll do you good. Help steady you."

William accepted the drink, took a deep breath and then swallowed down the entire contents in one gulp. "Thanks," he said as he returned the empty glass to his father.

"Now," said Hawkes, "if you're up to it, tell me what happened to you and explain just who this woman is you're evidently so concerned about. Just state the facts as clearly and precisely as you can."

"She's in trouble, Mr. Hawkes, bad trouble—" groaned Lancaster, touching a particularly nasty-looking bruise on his cheek with his fingertips. "Bad trouble, I fear."

"It will be best if you start from the beginning, otherwise we might never know what truly happened to you."

"She's in the house—Buonocore's house. But I don't know how to get back there. It was too long a ride, and too confusing—too twisty—but we've got to try."

"Start from the beginning." Hawkes' voice now had the sound of a reprimand rather than a request.

"All right, yes, of course, from the beginning," said Lancaster, responding to the tone of Hawkes' voice, and, after taking and releasing a deep breath, he commenced to relate to Hawkes the unusual events that had led him from his Manhattan apartment to the sofa in his father's home:

"I left Manhattan yesterday evening," he began, "as I told you I was going to do. At the Rabbits, remember? Of course you do. Yes. Anyway, I took the train as instructed. Took a little time, about half an hour. Still, it was dark by the time I reached the last stop. I knew I'd have more distance to go for Buonocore had told me so. I stood alone. There was no one else there at the station. Buonocore was reasonably prompt and I had only a few minutes wait when the carriage pulls up and he comes up to me and shakes my hand. The first thing he does is apologize for the long trip in front of us. Long trip! He tells me his home is another damned hour and a half or even two hours or so away! I expected another quarter-hour at the most, so I was not happy with this news. I didn't say so but I felt I was conned into this trip for now it was clear to me that the man no doubt thought if he'd told me right off how far his house was from the station, almost twenty miles he now told me, I might not have taken the job. In that he was correct, I wouldn't have accepted it.

"He said he anticipated my dissatisfaction and so brought the sketches with him. Perhaps, he said, I could give them a look right here by the sidelights of the carriage? The carriage was a good one, and all polished up and gleaming as though made ready for a president's inaugural day. At least he showed me that respect and I have to say the sight of the shining carriage did mollify me a bit. If that was indeed the intent of his polishing it up, it worked. Still I was not looking forward to two hours in a cab and so I was very tempted to do an analysis right there by the brass lights as he requested. Believe me, I was. But I do have my reputation to uphold, small as it is, and my integrity took hold of me. I told him no, the carriage lights were inadequate to study them properly. I swear he looked as disappointed as I was. At that point, with no other choice, we decided to go to the house.

"His driver was there of course, a great large brute who looked like he belonged in a circus. What was his name? George, I think it was. Yes, that's what Buonocore called him. I greeted him and George said something back and to my surprise Buonocore then told him to button his lip and just get moving. Very rough with the man. George nodded his head, and flinched, as if he was afraid of being physically beaten by Buonocore. He didn't say another word on the trip."

"There was one horse pulling the carriage?" asked Hawkes.

"Yes, that's right."

"Did you see what type of horse it was? Any distinguishing marks?"

"I did glance at it as the carriage pulled up. An appaloosa, I think. White mostly, with some spots"

"It was tired, or fresh?"

"Didn't notice."

"Still, an appaloosa, almost pure white, might be noticed. Pray, continue."

"At first, as we traveled, Buonocore began interrogating me, subtly of course, about my credentials and my experience. Then we rode in silence for a time, over some rather dusty roads. It's been a dry October and November as you know. I had to lower the window shade on my side to keep from inhaling all the dust. It didn't seem to bother Buonocore though as he keep his shade up. We rocked along then for a time in silence until he began to discuss the drawings he was planning to purchase, pending my approval of course. He grew excited as he described them. He did so in great detail. He was ecstatic about buying them. Very much so, and so his disappointment was consequently great when I later examined them and declared them to be forgeries."

"They turned out to be fakes?" asked Hawkes.

"Yes, good ones, but fakes. I did need the proper light to judge them correctly."

"How long did it take you to get to his home?"

"Just over an hour and a half. I checked my pocket watch when we reached the house. I wanted to know how long it'd take me to get back to the train station."

"Do you know what direction you went in?"

"I don't have a clue. Or rather every direction. It was a lot of driving on twisting country roads in the dark. We passed a farmhouse now and then, homes I could make out in the black only because a lamplight was burning in a window. Other than that, it was like riding in a darkened tunnel. Really just a lot of woods and empty country."

"You said it was a twisty ride. Hum, I'm reminded of a case I came across once, years ago. Did you see anything? A landmark? Cross a bridge?"

Lancaster groaned. "Nothing. It was all just darkness. Wait, there was something. I just remembered. When the ride was almost over, right at the entrance to a road we turned into, was an old large white-painted wagon wheel leaning against a tree. Had a few broken spokes. I suppose it was put there as a marker, to indicate the presence of the road. It was very narrow and overgrown with shrubs. Without something to mark it, it would be easy to ride right past it otherwise in the dark. The road I mean. It was maybe a mile or two from the house we were going to. But that doesn't help us at all, does it? I still have no idea where that road is. It'd be as hard to find as the house."

"Well, it is something.... Go on with your story."

"I-I was surprised by the condition of the house. People who buy expensive art usually don't live in houses that are in disrepair. It was a good-sized old farmhouse. Wood frame, white with black shutters on the windows. A big porch in front that went half-way around the side. Fixed up it'd be a nice sight but this was in poor shape. Some of the wood was even rotted away in places, at least on the porch, the part which was lit up by the light over the door. It was dark and difficult to see clearly the rest of the house as it was standing in silhouette in darkness for the most part. Buonocore must have seen surprise on my face at the state of the house because he immediately explained it away by telling me he'd only just purchased the property. It was his plan to restore it to its former beauty, or so he said.

"We went inside. George the driver went off somewhere and Buonocore offered me a drink and a bite to eat before getting down to business. It was after eight when I finally viewed the drawings. It's serious work and I take it seriously. To declare an authentic work a forgery would be tragedy, not only financially to the owner but to the World of Art. There was a baker's dozen in all. Drawings with pencil or pen, and some watercolors too. The one pencil was by Ingres, a superb draftsman, placed lines on paper as though his hand was guided by the angels. The watercolors, three of them, rather quick sketches, were by the American, Winslow Homer. You know of him? No? He's popular now. And some drawings by the Frenchmen, Degas and Renoir, who are creating a stir here of late. They call themselves Impressionists. Some very wealthy people are starting to collect them. You know I'm especially careful with sketches. They're easier for good forgers to create and much more difficult than finished work to judge as real or fakes. These were good forgeries, but after a time I finally declared them all to be what they were and, as I always do, I suggested Buonocore obtain a second opinion to confirm my own, should he think it necessary.

"Buonocore looked as though I kicked him in the stomach. That's how disappointed he was. A natural enough reaction, I suppose. He grew angry as well. I saw the blackest rage pass over his face for a moment. He recovered quickly enough though and thanked me for saving him from what was obviously a bad investment. As mad as he looked for that moment you'd think he'd already paid for the sketches. I checked my watch—it was nearing ten—and I told him I'd have to find a place to stay the night. Could he recommend a place? He hesitated a bit but at last suggested I spend the night in the farmhouse. I think he'd have preferred if I left, but good manners at last prevailed. He then showed me up to my room, the stairs creaking with age and neglect with each step we took. He offered me a spare robe, and I then went straight to bed. I was so tired that I just removed my suit and then climbed into bed. I was asleep almost as soon as my head hit the pillow.

"A while later—I don't know how much time passed—I was awakened by a strange sound, a faint low squeal-whine of sorts that drifted into the dark of my room. A dog, or so I thought at first. Then I heard another low sound mixed with it, this more easily recognized, the growl of an angry man. What else but Buonocore scolding the whining dog? Nothing more, I decided and immediately I dropped back to sleep.

"But in minutes I was awakened again. A cry! Not from a dog. And the shuffling of feet. Now right outside my door! The sudden sound startled me, frightened me actually. I rose up and sitting in bed I saw, beneath the space between the closed door of my room and the floor, a shaft of yellow light, someone with a lantern in the hall, and the movement of shadows. Another sharp cry! I wasn't certain but I thought I recognized it as being the sound of a woman or the cry of a child, in either case struggling against someone. A cry of distress or hurt.

"I decided to investigate. I put on my glasses, jumped out of bed, found my robe and went to the door. I stuck my head out into the hall and what do I see but Buonocore struggling with a young woman, a beautiful woman, dressed in shirt and pants. Their struggles had taken them down the hall a bit, away from my door where I'd first heard them. He held her arms tight at the wrists and they faced each other, she viciously attempting to bite his hands, to claw at his face with her nails, to hurt him in any way she could, but failing for the most part to do damage. He was too strong for her. I shouted his name—Buonocore!—and he turned toward me, still retaining enough presence of mind to keep his grip on the struggling woman. I started to walk to them—wondering what in the world was going on, and not knowing at all what to do about it—when suddenly I felt a tremendous shock on the side of my head and the world went black. Literally, the next thing I knew I was lying on the steps of the rail station I'd left hours before. They'd apparently put me in the carriage and taken me back, leaving me there, dumped like refuse. When I came to, I was still clad in skivvies and robe! But beside me was my suit and coat. I looked inside my overcoat pocket and found my wallet still filled with what money I had. At least they hadn't robbed me. I then went off into the trees to put my clothes on, slipping and muddying my clothes in the process, and then went up the station stairs and there waited for the train to come and take me back to the city.

"I made it back by dawn and, came here, to my father's house instead of my apartment. I've been asleep for most of the day since then, as I said."

"That was humane of them at least," remarked Hawkes. "Very humane, I would say."

"Humane?" broke in the father. "They just left him on the ground like a dirty dog."

"They could obviously have done worse," responded Hawkes. "And they did take him back to the station before abandoning him."

He then turned back to William. “The bruise on your face, how did you get it?”

Lancaster’s hand went up to the bruise on his face.

“I don’t know. Maybe I hit my face on the floor after I was whacked. We must go back and rescue her. She’s being held there, a prisoner. We must free her.”

“You saw Buonocore fighting with a woman and you assume somehow she’s a prisoner? What makes you take that giant leap? How do you know it wasn’t just an angry confrontation with his wife, or daughter? People in families have been known to fight with each other.”

“Precisely what I told him,” said James Lancaster. “You should have seen some of the battles I had with my wife. Real screaming matches. She could—”

“Papa, please, reminisce some other time,” interrupted the son, his voice sharp with exasperation. “Mr. Hawkes, I-I don’t have an answer, not an explicate one. But if you could have *seen* her, you’d agree with me. It looked *wrong*. Not just a wrong in a family way, but wrong. Terribly wrong. And the look that sprang up in her eyes when she saw me—it was *hope* I saw in her eyes—the look of a prisoner at last getting a chance for freedom. ‘Help me’ she said to me, or started to say. Then the lights went out. I know she’s being held there against her will! Even if she’s married to him, I still say it. Wife or something else, she’s being held there as a prisoner. Against her will. I’m convinced of it.”

“What did the police say about your *theory*?”

“They weren’t convinced. Like my father, they’re of the opinion it was a domestic dispute of some kind. Even if they thought otherwise, they told me they’d have no idea where to start looking for this house, since there’s no way I can tell them precisely where it was. Somewhere well past the King’s Bridge. Many miles past it. But we must try to find it. We must!”

“Hmmm, I wonder,” Hawkes now turned to James Lancaster. “Mr. Lancaster, can your man drive us to a train station at this end of the—the Third Avenue line it was, wasn’t it?” He directed these last words to the son. “Isn’t that the train line that extends into the Bronx?”

"Yes," said William, smiling with enthusiasm. "You will go. Thank God. And help me find where the house is. How wonderful of you, Mr. Hawkes. Isn't it, Papa?"

The father was less than pleased. "*Wonderful* is not the word I'd use," he snarled, glaring at Hawkes who ignored both his words and his obvious ire. "Isn't this a waste of time, son? How will you find the house? You said yourself you don't have a clue as to where they actually took you."

"We'll start at the train station," declared Hawkes. "It is the place to begin. Then we'll have to see what we find."

"You're determined to go," said James Lancaster, speaking to his son. "Then I'll go as well. And I'll bring my revolver with me. We most likely won't need it, but it still won't hurt to have it."

The station at the termination of the elevated railroad sat in darkness except for a pair of white lights that were on either side of the entrance just below the shingled roof. Once the train pulled out, the place was as silent and deserted as a graveyard at midnight. "This is where you met Buonocore?" inquired Hawkes as he followed William Lancaster to a place in front of the train station. Lancaster replied that it was indeed the same place.

"Now all we need is a bloodhound," said William's father, not without sarcasm. "The dog can pick up the scent of the carriage and we can follow it to the house."

"Perhaps the station attendant has such a dog," responded Hawkes, and immediately he went off to find the attendant. "Wait here, I'll be right back."

"What?" called out James Lancaster. "It was only a joke, man—" He gazed at his son in the dim light, his eyes questioning Hawkes' sanity.

A brief search by Hawkes produced a youthful, stubble-chinned, rather discombobulated appearing station attendant who, although he was working when found, looked as if he'd just been roused from a deep sleep. His eyes widened and stared at Hawkes as though surprised to see the existence of another human being who actually wanted to talk to him.

After a few moments of conversation, Hawkes was back, a smile on his face. "He's been of great help to us," he told the Lancasters. "We hit a bit of luck there, for certain."

"Help? What did he tell you?" asked William.

"Where the farmhouse is, of course," replied Hawkes rather matter-of-factly. "We'll have to get a carriage to take us there. We have good fortune in regards to that need as well. He told me there's a stable just around back of the station and about a quarter-mile distance. We'll walk there and get a dog-cart to carry us. It will suffice. We don't have too far to travel."

Hawkes had to act as driver of the cart, no driver being available for hire. The horse, dissatisfied with being pulled from the comfort of its stable, was stubbornly morose as it moved along and it required a steady tap of the whip by Hawkes to propel the animal forward. The beam of a lantern held by William Lancaster stretched out in front of them like the light from a miner's helmet, momentarily bleaching white the tree branches it fell upon as they drove by. After a few minutes of dark, winding road, the wagon wheel spoken of by William Lancaster appeared out of the deep gloom of night. If not for the light of the lantern, they'd not have seen it at all.

"This is it!" cried an astonished William Lancaster. "Look, there's the wagon wheel, leaning against that tree! How—?"

Hawkes didn't respond but instead asked a question of his own as he directed the trap onto the dark and half-concealed path. "Do you recall how long you were on this road?"

"A few minutes. That's all. We're not far."

"Best to do away with lantern, then. We don't want anyone to see us approaching." Lancaster immediately did as requested and the three men were plunged into a deep blackness that pressed in against the cart on either side of them. Deep shadows, even blacker than the dark of the night, crowded them on both sides. They strained their eyes to see through it and the darkness on each side gazed back at them like sentries posted at a border line guarded by opposing armies. The dirt road here was very bumpy and so they had to move very slowly. It was like riding the trap into a cave.

A few cautious minutes and they were through the woods, breaking out into a large expanse of relatively clear ground that was more undulating meadow than woodland. Up ahead a sharp angled silhouette sat against the sky. "There it is," shouted the young Lancaster. "The house, right up ahead!"

There indeed, off in the distance before them, stood the silhouette of the peaked roof of a house, rising above the surrounding darkness to make its mark against the blue-black sky. Other than the roof, nothing else of the house was visible at first to the eye, the bulk of the structure remaining obscured by the black of the night.

"You brought your pistol with you? As you said you would?" asked Hawkes, directing the question to James Lancaster. He replied that he did.

"I too have one. We might have need of them if your son is right about what's going on in there."

As they continued on, rolling along the now softly curving road, they saw, in the distance, an eerie glowing light coming from behind the window of one of the rooms of the house, the light shining behind a curtain.

"What's that light?" asked William. "It's awfully bright."

"It's fire!" shouted Hawkes. "The place is in flames!" He cracked the whip hard and the horse, for the first time that night, was forced to gallop forward.

Even as the dog-cart bearing them pulled up in front of the farmhouse, the first floor window through which the fire was shining suddenly exploded outward, spewing shards of broken glass onto the porch and beyond. The sense of the countryside nighttime tranquility was instantly ripped apart at the seams by the explosion of glass. A bright tongue of yellow-orange flame leaped out through the destroyed window and took a gleeful swipe at the night air before proceeding to dig a claw into the wood on the side of the house above the window. There it quickly multiplied, sprouting Hydra-like heads, each licking and chewing at the wood as though each possessed the tongue and teeth of the ravenous legendary beast. "Lord!" cried Lancaster. "The whole place is going up in flames!" They could hear the explosions of other windows, coming from the side and the back of the house.

The fire, now offered the additional fuel of the oxygen of the night air, raced throughout the house rapidly, the old dry wood being gobbled up by the flames like free lunches served at a Manhattan saloon.

William Lancaster, running onto the porch, was halted from going through the door only by Hawkes' shout: "No! Don't go inside! The house may already be empty!"

There occurred then a horror that proved Hawkes' supposition false. Suddenly the very door in front of which the undecided Lancaster now stood was flung open and there emerged through it a large roiling flume of flame, a living flailing monolith of fire that charged outside like a crazed bull running at a matador's red cape. It was George, the giant driver described by Lancaster, the man now wrapped horribly within a cylinder of furiously dancing flames, his arms flapping and fluttering in silent agony, his lungs and voice already seared away by the intense heat. Like a strange manifestation of a flaming ghost, a lost soul set afire and pushed through the gates of hell to burn itself out, George whirled and shuffled before them.

Hawkes, removing his overcoat, ran over to the fiery specter to throw the cloth upon it, an attempt to extinguish the destroying flames. As he did so, as though the very weight of the fabric of the coat was too much for him now to bear, George sank to his knees and then fell to the ground, still burning, mercifully oblivious to his pain before he dropped to the earth.

Suddenly a scream of the utmost terror came to them over the night air. A woman's shriek. From inside! On the instant William Lancaster was through the front door of the house, racing into the fire. All sight of him was immediately obscured by the furious flames and smoke inside.

"Bill! Don't!" screamed his father, the shouts already too late for his son's ears to hear.

The flames seemed then to take on a kind of mocking disdain for the elder Lancaster's fear (and Hawkes' fear as well) for his son's safety as the fire rose even higher into the sky, raging over the entire roof of the house. All they could do then was stand back away from the inferno, stand and wait, and pray, for the reappearance of the brave young man.

Long seconds ticked by. Furious blazing eternities. The house sizzled and crackled in front of them. "God…please…" moaned James Lancaster, tears appearing in the corners of his fear-filled eyes. "God…please…"

Then there occurred what appeared to be nothing less than a miracle, perhaps a response by the Almighty to Lancaster's pleas. William Lancaster suddenly became visible in the frame of the very door through which he'd minutes ago entered into the fire, materializing out of the thick smoke billowing from within the conflagration like a fiery angel advancing out of a sky filled with thick black thunderclouds. Before the amazed and joyful eyes of both Hawkes and his father, he was suddenly there on the porch of the house, alive and well. And there, cradled in his arms, like a sleeping child, was the young woman he sought to save, resting unconscious against his chest, oblivious to the brave effort that was necessary to rescue her. William's face and that of the young woman in his arms were both covered with black ash, a touch of the foul breath of the raging fire.

The young man stagger-stepped down the porch as Hawkes and his father went forward to help him. Off the porch, his strength gone, he sank to his knees, his now exhausted arms falling, no longer containing any strength at all, and releasing the burden of the young woman onto the grass before him. He was suddenly coughing, convulsing like a consumptive patient attempting to expel the destroying disease from his lungs through nothing but the power of his cough. Was the woman alive? Or were Lancaster's efforts to save her in vain? That question was answered only when she too, in imitation of her savior, began to cough, almost as violently as Lancaster. Both man and woman were alive.

In relating the story to Doctor Watson years later, Holmes would tell him: "They were blessed wonderful sounds, those terrible hacking coughs, for they were life, struggling to push the powerful hand of death away. And succeeding in doing it. I don't know how the young man made it through those flames to get back outside. To this day, I consider the rescue to be nothing less than a miracle of God. Let the atheists scoff, but let them realize too that their own scorn requires much more a leap of faith than does my own simple belief. For they must then believe in nothing—in nothing—and how do you easily do that when surrounded by a world—a universe—so filled with miracles? Miracles both large and small."

The above quote was written in full in Doctor Watson's notebook.

Both Lancaster and the young woman survived their ordeal with no ill effects at all. The young woman rescued from the flames was, it was discovered, a trained and talented painter and draftsman. It was those skills that had very nearly led her to her death, as would become clear when she, the next day, recounted her recent history.

While she rested in a bed in the Lancaster house, having largely recovered from the effects of inhaling much smoke from the fire, she told the facts of her captivity by Buonocore, for captive is what she was. William Lancaster was absolutely right about that.

Annette Ballard was beautiful, but it was not solely physical beauty that made her so. Rather it was an *enhancement* of her physical countenance, her features embellished from within by the mysterious glow of her own internal nature. Pretty enough to begin with, she was transformed to beauty by the gentle radiance of her own soul. There was a kind of dancing light about her that made it a pleasure to be in her company. But it was beauty marred, her face damaged by a three-inch scar that ran across and down her right cheek.

Following in the steps of the great Mary Cassatt, an artist and woman she much admired, Annette Ballard studied art at the Pennsylvania Academy of Fine Arts in Philadelphia. Had she the money, she would have followed in Cassatt's footsteps and gone to Paris, just as Cassatt had done in 1874, but the funds to allow her such freedom were not available and so she traveled instead to New York City, there to be a struggling artist, to practice her skills and perhaps gain a reputation. Her small apartment was then paid for by monthly funds she received from her loving parents. For a full year, she worked slavishly and eventually succeeded in having a few of her works displayed (and one sold) in a small gallery located on Eighth Street.

Then misfortune struck her parents, and they regretfully told her they could no longer support her, although they wanted to. It appeared that her career as an artist was coming screeching to a halt. She would have to return to her home in Philadelphia.

It was in the gallery in which her work was displayed that she had the misfortune of meeting Mr. Charles Buonocore (although at the time it seemed to her to be a stroke of great luck). Spotting her work, he expressed great interest in it, presenting himself as an art dealer of the first rank. He told her he would assist her monetarily, paying her living expenses and the costs of a studio in return for a percentage (a large percentage) of the future profits he was certain would come their way once her work began to sell. He seemed sincerely interested in her art and she decided to trust him.

"It seems foolish now in light of all that's happened, but I believed him," explained Annette. "He told me it was possible, with my skill, to produce works that would sell well in the right galleries. The implication was that he was capable of getting me displayed in those galleries. He paid my expenses, set me up in a studio in that farmhouse—it was so roomy after being stuck in my little apartment—and let me paint. There I could develop my own painter's voice and not worry about money. I fairly leaped at the opportunity. It seemed perfect."

"Did you think it appropriate? A young woman, alone in that farmhouse?" asked James Lancaster. There was a touch of criticism in his voice.

Miss Ballard's eyes flashed with anger at the tone of Lancaster's voice.

"No more or less so than the work many other woman take. If I'd taken a position as a governess or a housemaid, my only other alternatives in this society, I'd also have to live in the home of strangers, essentially trusting in people I don't know. Women who need to earn a living do it all the time. I see you have a few working for you here."

Lancaster grunted and his son smiled slightly at the words. Then the young woman continued her narrative:

"After a few days he started suggesting I begin copying the works of a few of the known artists, old and new, especially of the new Impressionist Movement, 'to let me get a feel' for the methods and the styles is how he put it. He said I would gain much knowledge in imitation. I objected, I had my own 'voice' to find, I told him. He insisted and to placate him I made a few Degas and Cassatt-like drawings. A Winslow Homer and others. They weren't hard to do. He told me they were good and then demanded I make not copies but 'original interpretations' of their styles. Sketches and drawings that would be signed with the artists' names. Forgeries.

"I refused. It was suddenly clear what he wanted to do. Create forgeries that could be sold through galleries as the real thing. Art collectors are following on the heels of the Havemeyers who are now building their collection of Impressionists Art. There's a good market for that art right now. There's money to be made.

"As I said, I refused to be used in such a manner. As a result I was immediately taken prisoner and threatened, starved and beaten until I agreed to cooperate. With little real choice, I-I at last did so." Here, at this point in her account, her hand went up to the red scar that ran across her cheek. "This was done by Buonocore," she said in a soft, almost bemused voice. "He…cut me. With the blade of a long knife. Threatened to slash my face to ribbons unless I did as he asked. I-I had no choice."

"The lousy son-of-a—" grumbled Lancaster, rage at the woman's mistreatment coruscating in his eyes. "If I had him here…."

Annette smiled at him with obvious appreciation of his anger against the harm done to her. "I was forced to create some forgeries," she went on. "And Buonocore wanted to test them, to see if they would pass for the real thing. So he decided to contact you. He knew if they fooled you, he could easily market them as originals without fear of arrest. Unfortunately for him, you declared them to be fakes.

"That night, after you'd gone to your bed, he came up to the room they kept me locked in, an attic room. My roomy studio was now a thing of the past. He was outraged at me, accusing me of purposely producing substandard work to make sure he couldn't sell them. I-I wasn't. I'm…not brave enough. He frightened me. I was able to push past him, and I ran. I got downstairs to the second floor when he caught me, right in front of your room as it turned out. God, I fought him, but—"

"I remember," came in Lancaster. "I came out of my room and saw you struggling with him."

"Yes, and only then did I know you were still in the house. I'd thought you'd left. While you were looking at me and Buonocore, before you could do anything, George came up behind you and hit you over the head with the butt of a pistol he always carried with him.

"While you were unconscious, they argued over you—over what to do with you. George wanted to kill you and bury you out back. But Buonocore was against that. At least the man is not a cold-blooded murderer. He told George to put you into the carriage and they'd dump you back at the train station. They didn't think you'd be able to find the house, not after the precautions they'd taken. Nor would you be able to direct the police to it. Not soon enough to matter at least. They were planning to leave the farmhouse, and would stay there only a few additional days. Buonocore felt that was the safest thing to do. They didn't own the house. It was empty and they had just appropriated it for a time. George changed a few of the locks, the one on the front door and the one on the door of the attic room they kept me in. And they cleaned it up a little bit for your benefit."

"Lucky for me," said the young Lancaster, "that the man wasn't a killer, I mean."

"How did you find the house, Hawkes?" asked James Lancaster, giving voice to the question that had puzzled him the entire night. "That is, how did you know enough to ask the station attendant where it might be? To do that you had to already know the house was in the local vicinity, didn't you? That it was not miles away? The local station attendant would have no knowledge of a house miles away but might very well know the local area. How did you know to ask him?"

"Yes, I knew that the long ride in the carriage was simply a precaution taken by Buonocore," responded Hawkes. "Taken in the event that for some reason your son would want to return to the house, or to tell the police about it. As it turned out, it was a wise precaution for Buonocore to take, although it ultimately failed him. As your son related his tale to me I was reminded of an instance that occurred years ago—the similarities in some ways are striking—involving a young engineer by the name of, of Victor Hatherley if my memory serves me. He too was taken on a ride in a carriage, a ride meant to fool him into thinking the destination to which he was being taken was a distance off, when in fact it was quite close. In that case, it was clear that the long ride was a subterfuge as he'd told me that the horse that pulled the carriage into which he entered was fresh and not tired. If the carriage had just come a long distance—as it would have had to do since it had just come from the very place to which it was to return—then the horse should have shown signs of weariness. Quite elementary."

"Yes," said William Lancaster. "I remember you asking me if the horse pulling Buonocore's carriage was fresh. Now I understand why. But I also remember telling you that I didn't know, that I didn't get a clear enough look at the animal to tell. So how could you have known the long carriage ride was a ruse in *my* case?"

Hawkes smiled. "The truth can at times be attained through various paths. While you didn't get a good look at the animal pulling the carriage you did observe the carriage itself. Enough to declare that it was clean and shiny. 'Polished up and gleaming as though made ready for a president's inaugural day' is the way you put it. At the same time you told me that the ride back was so filled with dust that you had to lower the curtain of the carriage window to escape it. Now how could that carriage have traveled over that same road in coming to the station and yet remained so untouched by the dust as to be 'gleaming'? No, it was immediately obvious that the long ride was nothing more than a ruse to throw you off the track as to the actual location of the house in which they stayed. Elementary. Since station attendants are very often familiar with the area in which they work, I sought him out and asked if he knew of a road marked by a wagon wheel. He immediately replied that of course he did. If he had not known of it, I'd have been forced to ask the locals, a nearby pub being the first place of choice for information—I'm almost certain the station attendant would have known of one if I'd asked him *that* question—but it wasn't necessary as he did know of the road we were seeking."

"Yes, yes, I see," murmured James Lancaster. "Yes, the dust. That's…so obvious. I should have picked up on it myself."

"The truth is often obvious—once it's pointed out," responded Hawkes.

"Well, they fooled me," remarked William. "I thought the house was miles off in the country just as I was told. I didn't pick up on it at all. Thank God at least you had your wits about you, Mr. Hawkes, otherwise, we'd never have gotten to the house in time to save Annette from the fire."

"Yes, the fire," said Hawkes. "What happened there? What started the house burning?"

"That was my fault," said Annette, somewhat sheepishly. "I-I started it. I-I was so upset that I failed in getting away. And I was so desperate. I thought if I started a fire someone would notice, that the police and the local fire company would be summoned and I'd be freed. Or if not that, once my room was on fire, my captors would have to open the door to get me out and then maybe in the confusion I could get away. I didn't stop to think about how isolated the house was. I heard them talking about leaving the place the next morning, and I knew I didn't want to go with them. I'd rather die. I broke a leg off a chair in my room and used it to make a hole in the plaster of one of the walls of my room. Then I soaked a rag with turpentine, used my lantern to set it afire and dropped it inside the wall. Apparently, it fell down, inside the wall, all the way to the first floor. In fifteen minutes or so, I heard George and Buonocore shouting. Next thing I knew the whole place was burning, and no one came to get me. I started screaming myself."

"It was very daring," stated Hawkes, "as well as extremely foolish. If not for the courage of Bill here you would have perished in that fire."

"Yes...I would have..." she replied somberly. She turned and gazed gratefully at Lancaster, almost sadly. Then in the next instant she brightened, a great luminous smile spreading across her face. "But I didn't die! Did I?!" Her simple joyousness was so infectious that all three of the men, including James Lancaster, responded in kind, with smiles of their own. "I'm alive!" she added. "And I'm free!"

Six months later, William Lancaster and Annette Ballard announced their betrothal. In a few years, William was a renowned art appraiser and Annette Lancaster a respected artist. Both lived happily in their spacious home in Manhattan surrounded by drawings, paintings and small children. "They're my best works of art," Annette very often was heard to say, when referring to her children. "My very best works of art. My babies."

A thorough search of the ruins of the farmhouse in Haverstraw failed to turn up the remains of another body lying among the ashes. Charles Buonocore had escaped the flames, and, in so doing, had successfully evaded the justice of this world. Escaped for the time at least, as he must still eventually stand before the Higher Authority to which we must all answer some day.

The Adventure of the Glass Room

Chapter One

Sherlock Holmes, alias Simon Hawkes, sat in the main room of The Dead Rabbits Society reading a news story detailing the recent tragedy of the Sea Islands in the American state of South Carolina. It was in August of 1893 that a raging hurricane hit that area with the full wrath of Nature, devastating the area and leaving more than 30,000 people homeless and starving. The astounding Clara Barton, working with the American Red Cross, was leading efforts to assist the people harmed by the storm. Many of the volunteers were African Americans who had fought in the Civil War a few decades previously.

His attention was drawn away from the brave compassion of Clara Barton and the volunteers and directed toward the person of Alwyn Pritchett, who, having cleared his throat to announce his presence, smiled once Hawkes' newspaper was lowered. "Mr. Hawkes, a good morning to you. I see you are waiting for breakfast to be served as I am."

True enough. Hawkes had finished his before-breakfast pipe just minutes earlier. He responded to Pritchett's words with a wan smile and a nod of his head, once again recalling the pleasant atmosphere of the Diogenes Club back in London and regretting the absence of its rules here in the Rabbits Society.

Alwyn Pritchett was a former client of Hawkes, having sought his assistance in a small matter involving some thievery in his household, a matter that Hawkes agreed to look into only because the alternative would have been to seek out his morocco case containing his hypodermic syringe. The matter offered him little more than a couple of hours' diversion yet it had sufficed to greatly impress Pritchett with Hawkes' abilities.

Alwyn Pritchett was, as Hawkes was well aware, a believer in the existence of the spirit world and a devotee of the incredible concept that it was possible to achieve contact with the souls of the dead. The man, Pritchett, on most other subjects was a complete bore but regarding this topic he was able to generate great inner enthusiasm and thus create some interest in those who listened to him speak of it.

And it was of his latest plan to contact the dead that he spoke of now, a plan to assure there was no trickery when next he utilized a psychic medium with extrasensory abilities to achieve contact with the other world.

Hawkes had met such men before and was continually bemused by how otherwise intelligent men allowed themselves to be swept up by spurious claims, myth and, inevitably it seemed to Hawkes, outright fraud in the area of spirituality. Belief in the existence of an afterlife was one thing, belief in the contact of it totally another. That possibility was—as far as Hawkes was concerned—nothing but pure foolishness. Hawkes was a man of logic and plain-sightedness in all aspects of his life and could not accept as true the astonishing proposition that conversations with the dead were distinctly achievable. Certainly that claim could not be accepted blindly, without evidence and hard physical data to support it.

Still, he held some sympathy for Pritchett regarding this belief of his, for it was an outgrowth of his great love for his deceased wife. No one ever loved his spouse more thoroughly, and the man's heart, aching for her, simply refused to let go of that love.

He continued to search for her in the only manner left to him, hoping to find contact with her soul on the other side of this worldly physical existence.

Pritchett himself was no longer the completely gullible fool he once was in his enthusiasm, and having already been the victim of more than one fraud made against him, now also sought some tangible evidence to support the claims of the mediums who came to him. He spoke to Hawkes now of the latest procedure he was implementing to assure the true powers of any medium who might come his way, the building of a "glass room" in his own parlor.

"I'm in contact with a medium whom I believe has genuine extrasensory powers," he told Hawkes after bringing up the subject. "However, I am as concerned with fraud as you would be, and so I'm setting up a rather extraordinary means to assure the authenticity of any psychic phenomenon that might occur at the séance I am paying her to perform."

"Assure authenticity? And how are you going to do that?" asked Hawkes, genuinely interested.

"I've had erected," explained Pritchett, "right in my own parlor, a wooden frame, a cube, eight feet by eight feet. On this wood frame I've had attached sheets of glass to serve as the walls to the cube. Entry into and out of this glass room can only be achieved through a door cut into one wall. The door is also glass. This way I can be certain there are no hidden wires and such in the walls. The paraphernalia of the false psychic cannot be hidden behind glass. The séance will take place entirely within this room. During the séance the single entryway will also be bolted shut. From the inside. It is by this means, by completely isolating the medium from external influences, that I will assure myself that any paranormal activity which does occur is truly paranormal and not simply a clever trick. The only furniture I am permitting inside the room will be a small table and two chairs, one chair for me and one for the psychic. Nothing else. This furniture has been examined but will be thoroughly examined again before being placed inside. Also, to eliminate the possibility of any confederate assisting the medium, only two people will be present during the actual seance. That is myself and the medium. No one else will be present in my parlor when the séance takes place. In fact I'll even have the parlor doors locked."

Hawkes leaned back and chuckled in appreciation. "Extraordinary, to say the least" he declared. "That certainly *is* taking precaution. In fact I cannot imagine being any more cautious. So, if I understand it, you and the psychic will seat yourselves within this glass room, as you call it, the door will be bolted, and then anyone else present in the parlor will leave and your parlor doors locked behind them. You and your medium will then be left alone behind your glass walls, and alone in the locked parlor as well. Is that right? Yes. Well, that certainly is strong precaution against any trickery I must say."

"As drastic as the whole setup appears, it will serve the purpose I intend. That is, it will eliminate the possibility of any fraud by the medium. In fact, my glass room is so effective a deterrent against trickery that I've had a very hard time even getting a psychic to agree to work under the conditions I've devised. This is so although I'm offering quite a substantial amount of money to any medium who achieves success. There can be no other conclusion but that my precautions are already serving a good purpose, isn't it so? That is, my glass room is eliminating the imposters right from the start."

"I would agree. So you've gotten somebody to actually perform a séance under your strict conditions? Who might that be?"

"A Charlotte Davreux, who is from New Orleans. She has quite a substantial reputation there locally, or so I'm told. Looks like the real deal, at least in the photographs of her I received. I'll be very curious as to how the grand experiment turns out. I'm looking forward to the results. The séance is scheduled to take place tomorrow."

"Good luck to you," responded Hawkes. "I congratulate you on your precautions against fraud and I wish you nothing but success. I am a man of logic but I do believe that logic can be applied to the spiritual realm as well as to the events and consequences of this world. I have often looked at the beauty that occurs in our world, that of a rose for instance, and concluded that it is an extra of life. It seems to me that it is only the goodness of Providence that grants us such an extra. It may very well be possible that a kind Providence will grant you success. I do wish you well."

Hawkes' wish of success offered to Pritchett was destined to end in disappointment, for Pritchett, having once having entered his precautionary "glass room", would not emerge from it alive. He and Charlotte Davreux would both be found dead behind its glass walls, their skulls penetrated by bullets, their bodies sealed within the transparent chamber behind the glass door bolted from within.

Chapter Two

The next day, in mid-afternoon as the clock neared four, a Detective Blaine appeared in the Society and approached Hawkes, requesting a moment to speak to him. In the next moments Hawkes' face slacken with shock and disbelief over the news Blaine presented to him, the report that the bodies of Alwyn Pritchett and Charlotte Davreux were found lying dead in Pritchett's parlor, the woman a murder victim of Pritchett and the man himself a suicide.

"Pritchett? Impossible?" responded Hawkes. "He wouldn't kill himself. Why would he?"

"It has to be" declared Blaine. "Alwyn Pritchett committed suicide, killing himself right in the middle of a séance, shooting himself after putting a bullet in the head of the woman. The evidence says it's so. No other interpretation to be put on it. Cullen is aware that you had a conversation with Pritchett just yesterday. He requests that you come over to the Pritchett house if it's not inconvenient to you. Otherwise he will drop over here later. He'd like to ask you about the man's state of mind. Waste of time, I'd say. On everybody's part. Who cares about the man's state of mind? It's enough to say he pulled the trigger."

Hawkes grunted. "Pritchett's house is not far from here. Give me a minute to get my overcoat."

The glass room sat in Pritchett's parlor, looking like an odd replica of a giant block of ice. There was no obstruction to sight and it was easy enough to see through the glass to the interior of the cube. Two chairs and the séance table, a small round cherrywood table capable of seating only two, were inside. The bodies had long ago been removed by the police. In the center of the séance table sat a small plate on which stood an unlit candle with a rather thick circumference that was burned down an inch or two from the top. On two portions of glass were splashes of blood, indications of the terrible violence that had occurred inside. The glass of the door to the small artificial room was shattered in the middle, near the bolt that held the door shut from the inside. The only side of the cube not glass was the bottom, facing the parlor floor.

The Indian rug that normally covered the living room floor was rolled up and pushed against one wall, making way for the temporary glass room. This same wall against which the rug was pushed also contained the room's lone closet. The bare parquet of the polished floor gleamed marvelously beneath the illumination of the sunlight streaming through the window. Some furniture, a few chairs, and a writing desk, were crammed against another wall, shoved to the side, again to make space for the glass addition. Other furniture, the larger pieces, had been removed from the parlor entirely. The heavy drapes that normally covered the sole window in the room had been pushed aside to let in the sunlight.

Hawkes' sight went about the room as Blaine ordered a patrolman to hunt out Cullen and let him know that Hawkes was now in the Pritchett house. The patrolman went off to retrieve Cullen and then Blaine, disinterested in what Hawkes had to offer the investigation, too left the room, leaving Hawkes alone in the parlor, momentarily granting him the freedom of exploration.

While waiting for Cullen's arrival, Hawkes eyed Pritchett's glass room with great interest, strolling around it and viewing it from all sides. It was sealed tight throughout, the glass held together by its wood frame as tightly as window panes. Wood and glass too heavy to be easily lifted. It seemed to be true that the only way into the cube was through the one door. In no other way was entry possible. If the glass door was bolted, the cube would have been essentially impervious, forbidding entry or exit without breaking the glass.

"Mr. Hawkes," came the voice of Detective Cullen, the call coming from behind Hawkes who turned around immediately in response to it.

"Was this door closed?" Hawkes asked, giving voice to the thought on his mind. "Shut with that bolt on the inside?"

"What? Yes, as a matter of fact, it was," responded Cullen. "We have witnesses attesting to that. Hello, Mr. Hawkes." A smile, or at least as much a smile as Cullen's stern face was capable of producing, came upon his face. "Thank you for coming over."

"It was no inconvenience. I wanted to see this with my own eyes in any case," replied Hawkes. "I understand you want to ask about my small talk with Pritchett yesterday morning in the Rabbits, about Pritchett's state of mind."

"Yes, the facts here are absolutely clear. What's missing is the reason for the suicide. As well as Pritchett's motivation for killing the psychic. Normally suicide is a private affair. Was Pritchett behaving...odd in any way, when he talked to you at the Society?"

"Odd? No, not at all," replied Hawkes. "May I ask how you come to know that Pritchett and I had a talk at the Rabbits?"

In response Cullen reached into the interior pocket of his jacket and produced a small leather bound journal. "He kept this," he told Hawkes. "It says in here he spoke to you of his contraption here. Said you were quite enthusiastic about its success."

Hawkes smiled. "Enthusiastic? Well, I did congratulate him on the quality of his precautions to assure there was no duplicity on the part of his psychic. And I did wish him success, quite sincerely by the way. I suppose he interpreted that as enthusiasm."

"The man was a little...strange, wasn't he?"

"I can only say there was nothing unusual at all about Pritchett when we spoke. His only emotion was his excitement over this experiment. He was looking forward very much to the séance."

"He talked to you about the purpose of this...this...thing...?" returned Cullen, making a motion toward a glass wall of the cube.

"Yes, he had it erected as he believed it would forbid any trickery on the part of the medium."

"Yes, that's what the others said as well. Speaking of mediums. What was his attitude regarding them? Did he...ah, harbor any anger toward them?"

"Anger? Not to my knowledge. Well, no one likes to be made a fool of, of course, or be the subject of a fraud, and he was that more than once, but, if you're asking me if he was irate enough over the false psychics that came his way that he would shoot the very next one he saw, I have to say no. In fact, violence wasn't in his nature at all. He was a very mild person to my knowledge."

"To your knowledge," stated Cullen. "But the fact is, the man *did* shoot Charlotte Davreux right between her arched eyebrows. He then put the gun to his own head. That constitutes a tendency for violence in my book."

"You're certain it was he who pulled the trigger?"

"It cannot be anyone else. Want to hear the facts of it?"

"I'm all ears."

"I'll tell you but first one more question. Are you aware of any troubles Pritchett might have had? Any at all? Money? Relationships?"

"Nothing."

Cullen sighed. "Nothing. That's what everyone says. The man was happy as a pig nosing around in mud, yet…this." He placed Pritchett's diary back in his jacket pocket.

"What exactly did happen here, Cullen? The facts only, if you please."

"Ah, I see you getting that gleam in your eyes, Mr. Hawkes. Let me tell you flat out there is no mystery here except as to why he did what he did. It'll be clear when you know as much as we do. All right, here are the facts." Cullen pulled out his notebook and referred to it. "This…contraption of glass…was the brainchild of Pritchett. We have your statement and others confirming that. Charlotte Davreux arrived here at the Pritchett house around eleven this morning. She and Pritchett had a small lunch together—quite cordial, or so says the servant who gave them their food—and then afterwards they came into this room to begin the séance.

"Before I go on, I should tell you who's in the house. They were in the house at the time of the tragedy as well. There's Pritchett's mother and stepfather, also his stepbrother. That's Mr. and Mrs. William Burgess and their son, Gordon Burgess. Pritchett's mother remarried after Pritchett Senior bit the dust a few years back. With that marriage she became Mrs. Burgess.

"Also in the house are three servants, a butler named Parish, a female cook named Elizabeth Smyth and a maid—Spanish—named Mary Faliciano. All six in the house, family and servants, interviewed separately, have confirmed the general facts as much as each was able. There can be no doubt as to the truth of what they say."

Hawkes grunted. "Pray, continue."

"For some reason," continued Cullen, "it seems seances must be performed in the dark, those drapes over there were pulled across the window to keep the light out of the room. The only light, after the door to the room was closed, was that candle you see in the middle of the séance table."

"I'm told that seances are held in the dark simply because spirits are hard to see in bright light. Who closed the parlor doors?" asked Hawkes, waving a hand to the double doors through which he'd entered the room.

"Here's what happened. Besides Pritchett and the medium, four others were in the room prior to the door being locked. They were: Parish, the butler, Mary the maid, and Pritchett's stepfather and his mother. All four watched while the medium and Pritchett entered the glass contraption here through that door. Once inside, Pritchett himself closed the door shut and bolted it. The candle was then lit and the other lights—this house is one that still has gas lights—here in the room were extinguished. At that point everyone left and Parish rolled the hideaway double doors together and locked them, assuring no one else could enter the parlor."

"So, if I understand correctly," broke in Hawkes, "Pritchett and Charlotte Davreux are then both left alone, sitting within a sealed room of glass that is itself standing *within* a locked room."

"Right," said Cullen. "What's more, after locking the door, while the butler and maid and the stepfather went off, Mrs. Burgess, Pritchett's mother, went directly across the hall into another room to read a novel. From her chair she had a view of the entrance to the parlor the entire time and she is prepared to swear that no one entered the room the entire time, from the moment the doors were locked by Parish until the time the shots were heard from inside."

"What's your impression of...shall we say, her mental keenness?"

"Sharp as a tack. Nothing fuzzy-headed about her," replied Cullen.

"She was reading. Surely there were times when she'd be absorbed in the book and would not be concentrating on the doors of this room," suggested Hawkes.

"I thought the same thing. She is prepared to swear that it is not the case. The book didn't hold her interest. Also she stated that her hearing is very sharp and the sound of someone attempting to unlock the doors would draw her attention in any case. No, she's willing to swear that no one else went into this room."

"Not through the doors in any case. What about the window?"

"Locked throughout. And it locks from the inside. It's locked still."

"If all that is true, then it must follow that no one entered the room after the doors were locked shut."

"Exactly. Five minutes or so after Parish locks up, two shots ring out. Mrs. Burgess is so startled by the sound she drops the book she's reading. She stands and runs straight to the doors, bangs on them, calling to her son. That's all she can do since she doesn't have a key. Parish arrives a minute or so later, the maid is right behind him. He produces the key and opens the doors.

"The three all enter the room together. That's important. The room is dark for the drapes are pulled across the window. The only light comes from the candle on the table burning behind the glass. Through the glass they see the gruesome sight of the murder/suicide. The candlelight is strong enough for all to be immediately clear. Parish said it was an eerie sight, 'ghostly', is what he said. What with the candlelight and the glimmering glass, it looked like something spectral, 'a ghostly scene in the dark of the room' is what he said.

"I can attest myself that it was a gruesome sight. Pritchett's head was bloody from the wound to his temple. He was slumped back in his chair, his head back, his mouth hanging open. Blood had dripped to the floor from the head wound. The gun he'd used was on the floor beside the chair he sat in. That is what the witnesses said they first saw upon entering and that is how we, the police, found him.

"Opposite Pritchett, her head laying on the table facing away from the witnesses, was Charlotte Davreux. No one could see her wound since her head was facing away. It was seen later, by Parish when he examined her, that she received a bullet between the eyes.

"The three, Parish, the maid and the mother, then stand horrified for a few ticks of the clock, then Pritchett's mother screams and she rushes to go to her son. As though her scream was a shouted order to move, Parish and the maid go forward to the glass as well. The mother tries to push the door open, but cannot, *for it remains bolted from the inside*." Cullen's voice emphasized the fact by stressing the last seven words. "It's Parish who ends up breaking the glass of the door. He who then reaches inside and removes the bolt. They all, Parish, the maid and the mother agree on these facts—" Cullen's voice here became deliberate again, once more emphasizing the words, "*—that the door was bolted from the inside when they entered the parlor and that the glass had to be broken in order to get to Pritchett and the medium.*"

Hawkes grunted once more. The keen interest that had first appeared in his eyes upon entering the room was quickly dissipating. There did appear to be no other interpretation that could be placed upon facts such as these except to conclude that it was a murder followed by a suicide. Indeed, what else could it be?

"Parish, after breaking the glass and pulling the bolt aside, enters the cube, telling the women to stay outside," continued Cullen. "He takes a quick look at Pritchett and Davreux and announces them both dead. Both shot to death. At that point Pritchett's mother faints dead away, falling on the floor. Parish exits the cube, picks up the woman and carries her to the sofa in the adjoining room. He tells the maid to let Mr. Burgess know what's happened and himself goes back to again lock the parlor doors, this time to assure nothing is touched until the police arrive. Then he goes off to summon police and a doctor for Pritchett's mother."

"Well, it would then appear that there is no other explanation as to the facts then the one you have reached," said Hawkes, now losing interest entirely. "Pritchett for some unknown reason, entered this room prepared to kill this Davreux woman and then kill himself under some certain conditions. He must have entered the glass room with some intention of violence, since he carried the pistol inside with him at the time. I am aware that it was not the man's normal habit to carry a pistol. I wonder what the medium might have done to drive him to such violence?"

"Precisely. It has to be someone *inside* this contraption who did the shooting. Since the gun was found by Pritchett's side and the wound to his temple is consistent with suicide while the psychic's wound is consistent with—with getting shot right between the eyes—we can say without any doubt that it's Pritchett who did the shooting.

The only real mystery is why he did it, as I said. I was hoping you could help in that regard but unfortunately...."

Hawkes stared through the transparency of the glass, gazing at the pool of blood, now dried, that had collected at the foot of Pritchett's chair. On the table was a stain of blood from the medium's wound. The atmosphere in the cube seemed still to contain a kind of hushed horror, a numbing shock, as though the very air within it was itself jolted by the violent deaths occurring inside. That agitation seemed to be still trapped in the interior, unable to dissipate until all the glass holding it inside was torn down.

"It wouldn't be the first time a man thought to be gentle and incapable of violence proved friends and family wrong," murmured Hawkes. He moved away from Cullen, walking slowly about the glass room. "Yes, it all seems clear, Cullen. You will have no difficulty closing out this case. Well, I will be off—Hello, what's this?" Immediately a change came rushing into Hawkes' passive expression, a new alertness flashing in his keen eyes.

"You see something?"

"When you—the police coroner's people—removed the bodies, did they take them straight out of the room?"

Cullen was surprised by the question. "What? Why? What do you think, we danced a jig with them first?"

"I'm wondering whether there was a reason to bring one or both of the bodies to the rear of the room. Over to the window and the closet back here."

"What? No, there wasn't," replied Cullen.

"You're absolutely certain?"

"I was here when the bodies were removed. They were taken straight out. Why are you asking?"

"I'll show you. Come here"

Hawkes waited for Cullen to come to him and then pointed a finger to a dark spot on the floor near where he stood. The sunlight here poured through the window, bleaching the brown floor golden directly before it. "Look there," said Hawkes, indicating the spot in the midst of the shimmering gold of the sunlit floor.

Cullen's eyes narrowed in scrutiny. "What? What am I looking for?" he asked at last in frustration.

Hawkes moved a foot forward and tapped the floor, directing Cullen's sight to a point just beyond the toe of his shoe. There it was: a small dark blemish on the wood.

Cullen sat on his haunches to get a closer look. "That looks like a drop of blood," he said at last.

"Fresh blood," said Hawkes. "Unless someone else has been bleeding in this room recently, it must be blood from either Pritchett or Davreux."

Cullen stood up and gazed with puzzlement at Hawkes. "Pritchett or Davreux? It can't be the blood of either of them. They died behind the glass."

"Precisely. It cannot be the blood of either of them," responded Hawkes. "Not given the facts as you've stated them. Yet there it is. Blood on the floor where it cannot be."

"That's impossible..." murmured the detective. "It must be someone else's blood."

"I suggest you ask all involved if they suffered a nosebleed or a cut. Ask the police officers who were in here as well. Don't let anyone know why you're asking. Make certain you get the truth from them. Do it right away." The last words were spoken almost as a command and Cullen accepted it as such. He immediately turned and left the room. Hawkes, alone again, opened the closet door near the "impossible" globule of blood and peered inside. There, on the floor of the closet, was another bloodstain, larger than the one outside. Immediately Hawkes produced his lens and began an examination of the interior. Following that, he went about the entire parlor, going down on his haunches in more than one instance to get a closer look at something on the floor. He did the same close examination of all the walls of the glass room erected by Pritchett. The top of the glass room was also composed of glass and it too appeared solid. Except for the bloodstains, Hawkes found nothing of interest.

It was just ten minutes later when a completely befuddled Detective Cullen returned to the room to give Hawkes the results of his interviews. No one, no family member nor servant or police officer, had suffered a nosebleed or injury while inside the Pritchett parlor. The drop of blood on the floor was therefore, without doubt, from the body of one of the deceased.

"I expected as much, once I discovered additional blood within that closet there," said Hawkes.

"The closet?"

"Yes, inside."

"This can't be, Mr. Hawkes," declared a confused Cullen. "How could the blood of one of the victims pass through the glass to end up on the wrong side of that contraption's walls? And then end up in the closet as well?"

Cullen stood motionless staring at Hawkes, his face wearing a perfect mask of pure puzzlement. Hawkes' discovery had thrown the "obvious" facts of his rather straightforward investigation right into the trashcan. "There *can't* be blood there," he repeated. "Not on the floor nor in the closet. It simply doesn't square with the facts."

"The facts include the bloodstains, Cullen. Rather, it is the theory of what occurred here that doesn't sit well with the facts."

"Couldn't she—the psychic—have had a nosebleed or something?" suggested Cullen. "Prior to stepping into this glass room that Pritchett put up?"

Hawkes shook his head. "Unlikely, and why rush into the closet with your nosebleed? Besides, you found no bloodied handkerchiefs, did you? No, yet if one or the other had suffered one you most likely would have had some evidence of an attempt to halt the bleeding. No, the most probable explanation is also the most impossible one. Impossible for the moment, at least. We will assume that the blood *is* that of either Pritchett or Miss Davreux. It *is* outside the glass room although both were shot within that room. That's an anomaly existing in direct conflict with the facts as you have stated them, Cullen. It suggests that *something else* took place here today in Pritchett's parlor."

"But it can't be!" stated Cullen emphatically. "The witnesses all agree as to what happened! The two victims were sealed up! Bolted inside that cube! All the witnesses saw the bolted door when they entered the parlor. They all heard Parish break the glass to make his way inside. It doesn't add up!"

"Still, blood from one of the victims is on the other side of the glass. The *impossibility* of the blood stain must be considered. It's there. It cannot be wished away. It must be explained."

"Wait! Maybe blood got on one of the officers' shoes, when they were inside the cube. Then when he stepped out—"

"No," came back Hawkes. "The blood on the floor is clearly a droplet, rounded at the top. It's not pressed into the wood as it would be if it was first on someone's shoe. The same is true of the larger flow of blood in the closet."

"Cullen lowered his head again, and lifted it again, to gaze at Hawkes with the suffering look of an uncomprehending child being told he must learn and understand complicated mathematical formulas that his mind is incapable of grasping. "I cannot explain it. It makes no sense. None!" he declared. "None whatsoever!"

"Let's talk to your witnesses," said Hawkes, "and see if any sense can be extracted from their words."

Chapter Three

Doctor Watson has said that he considered it a privilege to have been witness to the profound ability of Sherlock Holmes to reason, to *fathom;* to *see and observe* with the amazing faculty of his mind those possibilities that are often concealed beneath the surface of the obvious. Possibilities, hidden from sight and so invisible to others, were often quickly made manifest through Holmes' astounding ability. That amazing capability was swiftly put to work here, and so it was, even as Cullen and Hawkes walked out of the parlor to speak to the witnesses (witnesses not of the crime but of its discovery) and to Pritchett's family members, that Simon Hawkes was already formulating a theory as to what might have actually occurred within the interior of Pritchett's own locked parlor.

Pritchett's mother, Mrs. Eileen Burgess, was haggard with agony when Hawkes and Cullen went to her. She was in a small room on the second floor, seated on a loveseat, wearing a dark navy-blue dressing gown that went up to her chin. Having suffered dreadfully in losing her son (and in viewing his bloodied corpse) she was quite understandably shaken to the foundation by the ordeal. That suffering was apparent in the swelling of her grief-filled eyes and in the dazed anguish that now squatted upon her pale features. She was an elderly woman, a former beauty who still retained in her later years much of that beauty; remaining stately in form and manner. Her shaking hand gripped a handkerchief, damp with her tears. Without the administration of a sedative by her doctor, it was clear she would not have been able to conquer her deep grief and would not have been able to speak to the detectives at all. As it was she was having a difficult time meeting with them.

Hawkes immediately offered his condolences. "I was acquainted with your son," he told her. "He was a fine man."

The words registered but she didn't speak, rather her sad eyes spoke for her, offering him a small light of appreciation, a light that was immediately swallowed up and extinguished by a fresh spasm of sorrow. Her hand went up to her eyes to wipe away additional tears as she fell to weeping once more.

Hawkes and Cullen waited until she once again brought herself under control.

"What do you want of me, gentlemen?" she asked at last, her eyes going straight to Hawkes' face.

"I will be brief," responded Hawkes, placing himself in a chair that he moved so as to sit in front of her. "You were outside the room in which your son met with Miss Davreux, sitting and reading across the hall in another room. Is that correct?"

"Yes."

"The door to the room in which you sat was never closed? You had a continuous unbroken view of the parlor doors?"

"That's so."

"At no time did you see anyone approach the parlor doors?"

"No, no one did."

"Did you hear any unusual sounds from within?"

"Unusual…no, not…not until I heard the…the shots…" Her lips began to quiver, her eyes were once again brimming and overflowing with tears.

"Are you certain the doors to the parlor were locked? Isn't it possible that your man Parish inadvertently failed to lock them properly?"

"What? No, no, I heard the lock click into place. It makes a loud sound. No, he did lock them."

"Did your son request him to do so? Lock the doors?"

"What? Not while I was present. But I assume so."

"One final question. Who else has keys to the parlor? Besides Parish?"

"Keys? Why, my husband has one. I don't bother with keys. I don't know who else actually."

"Thank you, Mrs. Burgess. That will be all, "declared Hawkes, standing. "You've been quite kind to grant us your time. Please, again, accept my condolences for your loss."

* * *

Hawkes and Cullen were well distant from Mrs. Burgess' room before Hawkes spoke again. "I'm inclined to believe her, Cullen," he said. "She appears to be a strong and intelligent woman. There's no reason for her to say so adamantly that she watched the parlor doors throughout if she hadn't done so. So we will say for now that she did precisely what she says she did. Therefore we can conclude that the doors were indeed locked and that no one entered the parlor after the séance began."

"No one without a key could get in even if she wasn't there across the hall. Not with the doors locked," said Cullen.

"Yes, it was locked by Parish, the manservant. And he at least held the key to the room, he and William Burgess, and perhaps others as well, but no one could have unlocked the doors without it making a sound that would draw Mrs. Burgess' attention, even if that attention was first focused on her reading. We will have to test the lock to be certain how loud a noise it makes on the opening and shutting of it but, for now, we will accept Mrs. Burgess' testimony as truth. Therefore the parlor doors were locked when she and the others left the room and remained locked throughout until the shots were heard."

"I never doubted it," stated Cullen. "I don't see how what she said helps us."

"It was necessary to verify the fact," said Hawkes. "Ah, here we are back at the parlor. Can you have someone summon Parish? Make certain he brings his keys with him. We can verify the loudness of the lock mechanism and get his statement at the same time."

Cullen ordered a patrolman to find Parish and he and Hawkes went to wait in the parlor for the manservant's arrival. Had Cullen been closer with Hawkes, and more familiar with the great detective's nature, he would have known that Hawkes was now on a scent and was now more in the process of obtaining data necessary to verify (or disprove) a theory of his rather than in the process of simply gathering additional information in the hope of discovering something of interest. Seeing Cullen's expression of bewilderment as they waited for Parish to arrive, Hawkes took pity on the man and stepped to the closet door. "There is blood on the floor outside this closet, Cullen, and there is blood inside," he said in a rather didactic tone. "We have verified, to the degree possible, that the blood *must* be that of one of the victims. Now, accepting that as a fact for now, what must we conclude but that one of the victims—at least one—was *removed* from the glass chamber at some point *after* their injuries were inflicted, taken to this closet and *placed inside*." He smiled at Cullen. "Once we take that to be true, the rest falls quite nicely into place."

"The rest…?" said Cullen, scratching the top of his head. "Do you think that Parish didn't really lock the door? That someone slipped into the room without Mrs. Burgess seeing?"

"Ah, here is Parish. Let's have him turn the lock."

The manservant was a portly man of medium height with a head of pure white hair and equally white bushy sideburns that crawled down his cheeks, approaching his chin.

There was concern in his light brown eyes as he entered the room and walked its length toward Hawkes and Cullen who stood now near the window. "I was told you wanted to see me," he said to the two detectives, his eyes going from the face of Cullen to Hawkes and back again.

"Yes," responded Hawkes. "Do you have your keys with you?"

Parish seemed surprised by the question. "Keys? Why, yes, of course."

"Let's go to the doors," said Hawkes. "I'd like you to open and close the lock."

The three men stepped to the doors and Parish, producing a key ring, selected a key and turned it in the lock as requested. There was a loud click. Upon turning the key again, another click was heard, although this time it was not as loud as previously.

Hawkes looked at Cullen. "The noise made by the unlocking of the doors is certainly loud enough for Mrs. Burgess to hear, wouldn't you say? Again we must assume the doors remained locked throughout." Then, turning to Parish. "You are certain you locked up after you and the others left Mr. Pritchett and the medium in the room?"

"Why, why of course, sir," responded Parish, gazing at Hawkes as though the detective had just dropped cigar ash on a prized carpet. "Everyone heard it lock as I turned the key."

"And it was you who unlocked the doors after the shots were heard?"

"That's so. When I got here, Mary, that's the housemaid, and Mrs. Burgess were outside the doors. They couldn't get inside since the doors were locked."

"The maid doesn't have the keys to all the rooms of the house?"

"No, sir. Just myself. The rooms are seldom locked. There's no reason for her to have them."

"And Mr. Burgess has keys of course."

"Of course, I meant amongst the servants when I said just myself."

Mr. Burgess' son has the keys as well?"

"Yes."

"Now, being as precise as possible, tell us what happened once the doors were opened. Tell us what you and the others did upon entering the room."

"Well, sir, I pushed the doors wide open. The room was dark and so it took a moment to see inside—"

"The drapes were pulled over the window?"

"Yes, sir. There was only the light of the candle burning. There, on that table inside—"

"It was dark. Did you pull the drapes open?"

"No, I went to the glass here. We could see them inside you see, by the candlelight, and even in that small light it was clear what happened. The sight was terrible. Mrs. Burgess took it in and began to scream. Mary too was shouting. I went to open the door, to see if I could help anyone inside, you see, and found the glass door wouldn't move for me. It was bolted you see. I pushed but the door held fast. I had to break the glass to get inside. Then I examined them for signs of life. But they were both…already gone, sir."

"You're certain of that. Both were dead when you examined them?"

"Absolutely, sir. No doubt about it."

"Hum, and then what did you do?"

"I sought to comfort Mrs. Burgess. Then, after getting her and Mary outside, I locked the room. I thought it best to keep it locked until the police arrived."

"Quite capable of you," said Hawkes. "And unusual, for someone to be so concerned with a crime scene. Quite often the police themselves evidence a lack of such care. Tell me, why were you so concerned?"

"Ah, well, I-I don't know precisely. I just thought it was the right thing to do. To lock the room again, I mean."

Hawkes gazed at him thoughtfully for a time. Then, speaking at last, he said, "Would you be so kind as to ask Mr. Burgess and his son to come here, please? I'd like a word with them. There are a few minor points to be cleared up and perhaps they can help us do so. I'd like you to return with them as well."

Parish nodded his head, turned and left the room.

When the man had gone, Hawkes turned to Cullen. "I think it would be wise if you invite a couple of your officers into the room," he said to him. "Tell them to appear to be busy, pretending to look for evidence will suffice, tell them too to disregard our presence and that of Parish and the Burgesses, but tell them also to be ready for trouble at a moment's notice. Another two officers standing outside will not be unwelcome either."

"What—?"

"Hurry, man. They'll be here momentarily," said Hawkes curtly, and, without further word, Cullen went off to gather his men as Hawkes had requested.

The elder Mr. Burgess was a tall, slim man with deep set eyes sitting in a very angular face. His son, standing at a not insignificant six feet, was a good two inches shorter than his father.

The young man cut a rather dashing figure as he entered the room; clad in an expensive suit and carrying a thick walking cane in his right hand, he looked as though he was prepared to spend the evening at the theater.

Neither man paid more than cursory attention to the uniformed officers who were now in the room, one showing an inordinate interest in the drapes by the window and the other apparently examining for smudges the sheets of glass that made up the walls of Pritchett's glass room.

"Ah, thank you gentlemen, for coming," said Hawkes upon their approach. "This will not take long."

The young Burgess responded with a grunt.

"I hope not," said the elder Burgess, his voice containing some anger. "I would like to be with my wife right now."

"Yes of course, You are Mr. William Burgess, I trust, and this is your son—"

"Gordon," broke in the younger man. "Gordon Burgess. I'll do whatever I can to help you. Although it seems clear what happened here. Poor Alwyn. Wonder what made him snap like that?"

"You have no idea?" asked Hawkes.

"Well, he sorely wanted to *speak* with his wife. Never saw a man so obsessed." He motioned with the cane toward the glass cube. "Well, that is obvious, isn't it? His obsession, I mean. Perhaps, in being disappointed once again…" His voice trailed off, letting the implication hang in the air.

"You have an air gun there, don't you?" said Hawkes, changing the subject and pointing a finger at Gordon Burgess' cane. "A handsome one. May I see it?"

Somewhat reluctantly, the young man surrendered the cane to Hawkes.

"Yes, a breech-loading gun. I see it has the pump attached. I've seen this model previously. American made. You unscrew the upper and lower halves of the gun and thread the pump into the valve end of the air reservoir. The muzzle is hidden and protected while walking by this brass cap. Very nice weapon indeed."

Cullen snorted derisively. "Airgun. I'll take my revolver, if you please."

"No, Cullen, don't dismiss the weapon. It is more than a wealthy man's affectation. Quite a formidable firearm in fact. I was myself the target of a bullet or two from such a gun in the past. Before the perfection of the gun powder cartridge, the air rifle was the weapon of choice for hunting big game such as deer and wild boar. The cane air gun is still a popular weapon in London, for protection while walking the streets, for those able to afford them."

"Is that right?" said Cullen. "Well, shut my mouth. That thing? It looks like nothing more than a regular walking stick."

"May I have my cane back?" requested Gordon Burgess. "I feel quite naked without it."

"No, I'm afraid that is impossible," stated Hawkes sharply. "Here Cullen, hold onto this. Now, Mr. Gordon, at the moment I have only one question for you. If we were to go to your bedroom, and perform a search there, would we find a wig there? *A wig similar in appearance to the long black hair of the psychic, Charlotte Davreux?* Or have you thrown it away?"

The change in Gordon Burgess' demeanor was immediate. A brief instant of surprise, and then his youthful face twisted up into a vision of pure rage. Baring his teeth and snarling like a cornered animal, he thrust his hands forward and leapt for Hawkes' throat. So swift and sudden was the attack that he succeeded in wrapping his fingers around Hawkes' neck before Cullen and the two officers in the room were upon him and pulling him off. In a few seconds they had the man subdued and handcuffed. All the time, the young man's father stood and stared at his son as though the young man had just grown a pair of horns on his forehead. "What—? What is this—?" His eyes, filled with confusion, darted from the hate-filled face of his son to the stern visages of Cullen and Hawkes, seeking an explanation for what was occurring in front of him. "Why are you manhandling my son?" he managed to blurt at last.

"Your son is being arrested," declared Hawkes, "for the murders of Alwyn Pritchett and Charlotte Davreux.

William Burgess stared about in bewilderment. "Oh, come now. That's absurd."

"Look at your son, man!" said Hawkes sharply. "Look at him."

There, in the vehement rage evident upon the face of Gordon Burgess, sat nothing less than a pure confession of his guilt, a better statement than mere words verifying the truth of Hawkes' accusation.

William Burgess could do nothing more than stare in numb disbelief as his son was removed forcefully from the room, his hands handcuffed behind his back and one patrolman on each side of him, each gripping tightly one of his arms, while his screams of fury filled the house.

"We're not done here, Cullen," spoke up Hawkes as the shouts of the young Burgess faded as he was taken outside the house. "Bring a man in here to place cuffs on Parish as well. He is a willing accomplice of the killer."

Unlike Gordon Burgess' violent reaction, Parish responded to arrest by collapsing immediately onto his knees. It looked as if the man had completely deflated upon hearing Hawkes' words. "Please sir, it wasn't my idea, sir. I only did what the man asked me to do. I never did wrong before. Not…not ever in my life! Only…." His voice broke and fell away, stumbling into a flood of sobs. He held his hands before him as though praying in front of a church altar.

"I don't see that you deserve any special consideration," said Hawkes, not hiding his contempt. "But give the police a complete confession and speak against Burgess at his trial and perhaps you will escape with your life. That mercy will be more than you deserve for without your help Burgess could not have done what he did. You plead and beg now but you gave little thought to the lives of others before!"

A patrolman entered upon Cullen's call and, pulling the hands of Parish behind his back, placed the cuffs upon his wrists. The weeping man had to be pulled from the floor and supported in his walk as he was led out of the room to his destiny.

A quick search of Gordon Burgess' bedroom brought forth the wig, hidden in a dresser drawer, just as Hawkes had predicted.

"It was conjecture of course," said Hawkes after the wig was found. "But his own room was the most logical place for him to hide something he didn't want others to see. I mentioned the wig to see if he would react—he had to know then that I saw through his deception—and react he did."

Chapter Four

"Well, it's been an interesting day after all, Cullen. For that I have you to thank," said Hawkes in a rather matter-of-fact tone as he stepped down the steps of the Pritchett/Burgess house and started up the street, going toward the Rabbits Society. "You have questions of course Cullen. Come, I will explain all to you while we walk."

"Mr. Hawkes, I'm in complete astonishment. I don't understand at all how you arranged for all that to occur. It's clear you knew from the start that Gordon Burgess and Parish were behind this crime. Parish was spilling his guts even while being hauled away, confirming your charges against him and the young Burgess, but I still don't see—"

"The accident of the drop of blood was the key. It was the one mistake they made, and it led to the complete unraveling of their schemes. Very cleverly conceived, I must say, and coldly carried out. Cold-blooded murder, Cullen. That's why I asked Burgess for his cane, his air gun. I have no doubt he would have put the weapon to use if I'd accused him of the crime while he still held it."

"Mr. Hawkes, how—?"

"The blood was the first piece of evidence, the other was the presence of the closet in Pritchett's parlor. There was the key to the crime."

"The closet…but…why?" The detective blinked a bewildered eye at Hawkes.

"Don't you see?"

"I see…" replied Cullen, his voice thick with frustration, "…nothing. It's still impossible."

"Pritchett and the psychic were murdered," said Hawkes. "If we accept that as our starting premise then we must ask next: How was that double murder possible? The murder victims were inside a sealed glass room which was in turn located within the dead man's locked parlor. The first question we answered immediately. Did someone enter the room after Pritchett and the psychic were left alone by the family and servants? I thought not, given the evidence of the blood which spoke of something else. Still, it had to be determined. In talking to Mrs. Burgess and then in testing the lock and the noise it created I was reasonably satisfied that no one entered the room after it was locked. Unless Mrs. Burgess was lying to us, and was complicit in the murder of her own son—highly improbable—I saw no reason to think otherwise. No one therefore entered the room after it was locked. Therefore it had to be that the murderer was *already in the room* when the séance began. Where else could he conceal himself except in that closet? The killer, it was obvious, had hidden in the closet before the others had entered the room for the séance."

"Before…yes, I see. But, but, Pritchett and the psychic were dead inside the bolted room! All the witnesses agreed to that. Even Pritchett's mother. How could that be?"

"It is an ingenious crime," said Hawkes. "That much must be acknowledged. Extremely clever. A double-murder by necessity for Charlotte Davreux had to die as well as Pritchett in order for the plan to succeed. But Parish's participation was the key. His assistance had to be obtained by the killer for everything to work. Nothing takes place without Parish."

"How did you know it was Gordon Burgess who did the killing?"

"Elementary, Cullen. Once we determine that the killer was hidden in the closet prior to the séance we see who was physically present at the beginning of it and who was not. Gordon Burgess was the only family member not present with the others at the time. The cook the only servant not present. All things being equal, it stood to reason to consider Burgess as the most likely suspect. In fact, I never seriously considered the cook at all. Of course once Gordon Burgess showed up, having the audacity to be still carrying the murder weapon, it was obvious who the killer was."

"The air gun! He used that to kill—"

"Yes, he used it because of its ability to fire shots *silently*. By the time the shots were fired from the pistol found at Pritchett's feet, the shots that were heard by Pritchett's mother, the murders had already occurred."

"The air gun…" murmured Cullen.

"Precisely. The droplet of blood was found very near the closet, you recall. We must therefore accept as true the fact that a body was at some point *outside* Pritchett's glass room *after* being shot. From that, everything falls into place. Here is how I envision the murders occurring: Gordon Burgess is of course aware of his stepbrother's plans for the séance and sees the construction of the glass room taking place inside the house parlor. He sees, in Pritchett's eccentric behavior, an opportunity to kill the man as a plan forms in his head. Prior to the beginning of the séance, unseen by the others excepting perhaps Parish who is now part of the murderous conspiracy, he conceals himself inside the closet of the room.

"Pritchett's mother and stepfather, the maid and Parish then stand and watch as Pritchett and the psychic both enter the glass construction inside the room. They watch as Pritchett himself bolts the door shut, assuring the cube's total closure, assuring, to Pritchett's mind, that the séance will not be affected by outside forces. Then family and servants exit the room and Parish locks the parlor door. He does so ostensibly to assure privacy for the séance, perhaps Pritchett asked him to lock the doors, perhaps not, but in any case it is necessary they be locked. It's necessary *to make certain that the actions of Gordon Burgess will not be interrupted and witnessed by someone inadvertently entering the room.* Absolute privacy is required of course until the double-murder is completed.

"What are the killer's actions inside the locked room? He exits the closet, his cane perhaps resting casually on his arm, his face disguising his ill intent, and approaches the medium and his step-brother, both of whom are no doubt surprised by his presence. He raps on the glass and so Pritchett rises and unbolts the door, both to ask him why he is in the room and no doubt to ask him to leave. But now, the door unbolted, Burgess enters the glass room and is pointing his weapon at them. Immediately and cold-bloodedly, he gets down to business. He shoots the psychic and then turns on Pritchett, being careful to put the barrel of the air gun close to Pritchett's temple before pulling the trigger as he wants that murder to appear to be a suicide. I'm sure if you examine Pritchett's wounds you will find an absence of gunpowder.

"Now comes the ingenious part of the plan. He then removes the body of Charlotte Davreux from the plastic cube. Perhaps, probably, he is cautious enough to wrap the woman's head in canvas or cloth so as not to trail blood behind him as he moves her, but he's unlucky now, unlucky as a drop of blood *does* escape to fall on the floor just prior to him placing the poor woman's body in the closet. More blood is spilled in the closet.

"He removes the psychic's own colorful robe, places a wig he's purchased that resembles Davreux's own hair onto his head and then returns to the glass room. Inside, he bolts the door and then, using a revolver he has on his person, a pistol loaded with *two blank cartridges* in addition to the other bullets, he fires off two quick shots and lays the fired pistol on the floor at Pritchett's feet. The blanks are necessary so as not to break the glass with the shots. It's done. He slumps over the table, taking the place of the psychic, and waits for Parish and the others to enter the room, drawn there by the shots he's fired. Those shots are also a signal to Parish that all has gone as planned."

"So it was Burgess who was in the glass room with Pritchett's body when the others returned to see the cause for the shots," said Cullen, at last beginning to see the light. "Damn, it must have taken nerves of steel, for him to rest his head down near the spot where Charlotte's own blood stained the tabletop and play dead while the others came into the room."

"Yes, it indicates that our killer is a very capable person. Nerves of steel, as you say, in addition to being quite ingenious. Now you see it all. The two loud shots, the blanks, bring the others running. Parish unlocks the parlor doors and then handles his part perfectly. He allows Pritchett's mother to race to the glass door and try to open it, and in so doing, has her confirm that it has indeed remained closed throughout. He then makes certain that it is he who breaks the glass, unbolts the door and rushes inside to examine the two bodies. It's he who declares them both dead, even while Burgess is staring up at him very much alive, and it's he who again locks the parlor after they all leave. This time it's locked to allow Burgess to move the body of his victim *back* into the glass room. At some point, prior to the police arriving, Burgess leaves the room. Either Parish returns to the room and opens the door, letting Burgess out or else Burgess has his own key and lets himself out. The door is locked again, and all wait for the police to arrive. The crime is complete."

"I'll be...," spoke up Cullen, after sitting in silence for a few seconds. "And it worked. We believed it. A murder and suicide is what we concluded."

"You're not to be faulted," said Hawkes to the dejected detective. "It was an extremely ingenious crime. I believed it to be a murder and a suicide as well. If not for that small droplet of blood on the floor the truth would have been undetectable."

"It was nearly undetectable even with that drop of blood," declared Cullen. "If not for you, Mr. Hawkes, the truth wouldn't have come out. They'd have gotten away with it."

A brief smile appeared on Hawkes' face.

"Why'd he do it?" asked Cullen. "We still don't know that."

"That will come out in their confessions. Or in the confession of Parish if the other stays silent. But if I had to guess, I'd surmise that money is at the root of it—in some manner or another."

"Yes," agreed Cullen. "It usually is."

Hawkes had guessed that money was at the root of Burgess' crime and he was subsequently proven right. Alwyn Pritchett Senior, in his Last Will and Testament, had placed the bulk of his considerable estate into a trust for his son. Under the conditions of the trust the monies therein would become the property of his wife, now remarried, only following the death of his son. Gordon Burgess thought that, in killing his stepbrother and thereby shifting the Pritchett fortune to his stepmother, his own father (and eventually he) would very soon gain control of it. It is entirely possible that, had he gotten away cleanly with the murder of Alwyn Pritchett, his stepmother might very well have been murdered shortly thereafter.

A police investigation did not reveal that the elder Mr. Burgess, Gordon Burgess' father, had any knowledge of his son's plot. Still, the crime of his son now standing firmly between him and Pritchett's mother, the two very soon separated and divorced.

Parish had been promised a sum of twenty thousand dollars for his participation in Pritchett's death. A small fortune. He received instead a sentence of life imprisonment and served out that sentence for a mere two years in a cell within the Tombs before dying of pneumonia.

Charlotte Davreux was not a totally innocent victim. She had been contacted by Gordon Burgess who told her of Pritchett's offer to pay a large amount of money to any psychic willing to prove her talents under his strict conditions. Supplying her with information regarding Pritchett's deceased wife, he told her she could play the role of psychic and together they could share the money Pritchett would pay. Not knowing the true plans of Gordon Burgess she agreed to the fraud and, in doing so, effectively signed her own death warrant. While stating in a letter to Pritchett that she was living in New Orleans, a letter composed by Gordon Burgess, she in fact resided in New York on the Bowery where she earned a living as a palm reader and fortuneteller. The very morning Charlotte had agreed to Burgess's plan, Gordon, leaving her, located a store that sold wigs made of human hair and there purchased one that closely matched Charlotte's own hair.

Three months to the day following the Pritchett murder, Gordon Burgess was found hanging by his neck in his prison cell, an apparent suicide. His body now lies in permanent rest in the Burgess' family plot in Calvary Cemetery.

The Adventure of the Talking Ghost

Chapter One

Sherlock Holmes, strolling alone up Lafayette Street, was deep in thought, considering the contents of the wire he'd just received from England, a telegram sent by his brother Mycroft. It told Hawkes that the criminal empire of Professor Moriarty now lay shattered, a ruin that held little of its former power. Many of the top men of that empire were now either dead or imprisoned. An exception of note was the escape of Colonel Sebastian Moran, a fierce man who desired Holmes' death quite possibly more than did Moriarty himself. It had been as much luck as skill that enabled Holmes to escape Moran after the fall of Moriarty to his death off the Reichenbach ledge. Since that day, Holmes was a hunted man.

Moran was a formidable foe, but he was still only one man. Was the existence of Colonel Moran sufficient to keep Holmes from returning to London, to his old flat on Baker Street? To keep him from enjoying the meals prepared by Mrs. Hudson once more? To deny him the company of his old friend, Watson? Was the continued freedom of Colonel Moran a danger sufficient to keep him a fugitive from his former life?

No, it was not, he decided. He would return to England soon, and, through that return, reclaim his prior life. Wasn't it time to bury Simon Hawkes and resurrect Sherlock Holmes?

It was a bleak December day and the sky above was a leaden gray that seemed to press heavily upon what was left of the daylight, a wan yellow light gleaming weakly from a weary setting sun. A light dusting of snow had come within the last hour, with the end of the day, and the streets were shrouded in a thin white film, a slight covering that was slashed in those parts where the continuous traffic, both horse and pedestrian, had torn their paths through it.

With the setting of the sun, the night was beginning to turn bitterly cold and Simon Hawkes found himself buttoning up his heavy woolen coat against the deepening chill. He took in a deep breath and exhaled a cloud of mist on the air before him. All about him men and women were rushing to get into a place of warmth.

The cold was made even more frigid by an excited breeze that had risen and now twisted and turned down the streets. It brushed against the windows of the houses and the shades of the carriages and grabbed at the gray wool of Hawkes' coat as he walked. Hawkes paid little attention to it.

He turned down Broome Street and walked west, and was soon passing into a series of streets of a less than reputable nature. As was almost always the case when he walked, he carried his revolver with him. It rested now in a pocket of his woolen overcoat. Better safe than sorry.

As he approached Eighth Avenue, he saw a small cluster of police uniforms in front of a three-story brownstone, one of a series of such buildings standing in a line in the middle of the street. The presence of the police piqued Hawkes' interest immediately. As he came to the front of the building he saw a small sign in one of its windows: Madam Tollier, Spiritualist.

All this police activity for the arrest of a fraudulent gypsy? No, if that was all, then there would not be this excess of uniformed men. The door to the brownstone then opened and, at the top of the steps leading up to the entrance, was a face Hawkes recognized: Detective George Blaine.

Blaine's respect for the abilities of Simon Hawkes had risen much since Hawkes' solving of the Pritchett murder just a short while ago. Blaine, like Detective Cullen who was in charge of that case, had believed the Pritchett death to be clear-cut, an obvious suicide. Hawkes had proved both him and Cullen wrong.

Blaine was a broad-shouldered square-faced man with a strong jaw upon which perched a mouth that was almost perpetually pressed into a tight thin line. His eyebrows were usually pulled down upon his eyes so that he appeared to be continually angry at someone or something. He was of medium height, being five feet and nine inches in height from shoe to haircut. The tight, thin line that was his mouth offered a sign of surprise for a moment at seeing Hawkes standing before him at the bottom of the brownstone steps. "Mr. Hawkes," he called down to him. "What are you doing here?" Each word rode upon a white cloud of breath flowing from his mouth onto the cold of the night.

"I'm here quite by chance," replied Hawkes. "I happened to be passing by. May I ask what brings the police here?"

"Murder, or rather an attempted murder and then self-defense on the part of the gypsy woman who lives here." Blaine descended the steps to stand in front of Hawkes, before continuing. "She was attacked. That is the gypsy, Madam Tollier, was. What a piece of work she is. A fortuneteller who presents herself as a connection to the world of ghosts. Imagine believing in that kind of rubbish."

"Many do."

"Yes, like that Pritchett fellow whose murder *we* solved," replied Blaine. "You, me and Cullen, that is. A lot of foolishness, this contacting the dead, if you ask me."

A smile flitted briefly across Hawkes' face upon his hearing the detective's list of names as those who had broken open the Pritchett murder case. He stood silently while Blaine continued to talk of the killing that had occurred inside the brownstone.

"The man the gypsy ended up killing will make this a big story for the news people, let me tell you," he went on. "There'll be an 'extra' for certain. It's Joseph Carter, the Wall Street financier."

"Joseph Carter—" exclaimed Hawkes. "His murder will indeed make news. I'm slightly acquainted with the man. What happened?"

"Are you? Acquainted?" Blaine was surprised.

"Slightly. His wife was the victim of a thief a little while back. She was killed during a robbery attempt. He asked me to look into it, to try to discover the identity of her killer. Unfortunately, I was not able to help him."

"Well, this seems to be a straightforward case of self-defense," said Blaine. "Carter tried to kill her—the gypsy fortuneteller, that is—and she defended herself with a pistol. Two shots in the chest, right in the ticker. But there's an unusual circumstance to it all as well. That is, his rather odd motive for his attacking the gypsy in the first place. That'll catch the attention of the press."

"His motive?"

Blaine smiled, a rather unnatural expression for the man. "It's a motive based on nonsense. But folly, if believed in, can lead people to do some stupid things, isn't that so? It seems Mr. Carter tried to kill the gypsy in order to keep her from talking to a spirit. Or rather to not have the spirit speak through the gypsy to the world. He wanted to silence a ghost and thought by killing the gypsy he could do it."

Chapter Two

"Silence a ghost?" returned a surprised Hawkes, gazing dumfounded at Blaine.

"Astounding isn't it? To kill for such a reason? I'll tell you more but first let me talk to Riley here," said the detective. "I need him to summon the wagon to take Carter's body away. Then we'll go inside the house. Since you're acquainted with Carter you can give me a positive identification of the man. I got his name off some papers in his wallet."

Hawkes welcomed the warmth that engulfed him as he and Blaine went up the brownstone steps and inside the worn building. "I arrived here about a half-hour or so ago," Blaine said to Hawkes. "The man was shot a little before that. I just finished getting the gypsy's statement. It took me ten minutes just to convince her to talk to me and get the story out of her. She obviously doesn't trust the police, like most of her kind. But it seems she's telling the truth of it. It all fits."

The entrance opened into a long, somewhat narrow hall. A series of small gas sconces lined one wall. Only one was lit now and much of the length of the hall remained in shadow. A stairway in front of them, bounded on one side by a wonderfully carved wooden banister and on the other by the rising wall of the corridor, led to the floor above. On the left was the entrance to the parlor, a set of roll-away double doors. It was through these double doors that Blaine walked and Hawkes followed.

The room that the men entered held a patina of age and, with that age, a sense of mystery that struck Hawkes as being perfect for the gypsy's purpose. A set designer for a Bowery play couldn't have done it up better. The walls were wainscoted to the waist with cherrywood, wood darkened over the years to an almost black hue. (The house was almost a half-century old.) On one wall there hung a large zodiac chart. The floor was polished plank and was covered in the center of the room by a good-sized rug that was primarily cerulean blue in color. The blue held within it a design of planets and stars, and a large yellow quarter moon. In the center of this rug stood a large circular table supported by one central post in the center that flared out into three clawed legs on the floor. Hawkes assumed immediately (and correctly) that this was the table at which the gypsy conducted her séances. A thick candle, unlit now and a portion burned away, sat in a glass tub in the middle of the table.

Hawkes, entering the gypsy's parlor, could not help but recall the murder scene behind the unusual glass room that Alwyn Pritchett had erected within his own house just a short time previous. It was apparently becoming a social fad, this notion of talking to the spirits of the dead.

In a chair on the other side of the parlor, sat a woman of no more than thirty years of age, a rather pretty, raven-haired woman with dark brown eyes and mocha-colored skin. Her black hair was tied back from her fiery-eyed countenance with a small piece of red ribbon. She was clad in a long dark-blue dress that covered her entire body, throat to ankle.

Her hands were behind her back and bound by handcuffs. Beside the seated woman stood a uniformed police officer.

"You have her cuffed?" asked Hawkes. As if in response to Hawkes' words, the woman suddenly sprung up out of her chair and began screaming at the top of her lungs, the loud, high-pitched shrieks stopping Blaine and Hawkes dead in their tracks.

"Yiiiiiiiiiiii!!, pigs!!! Pigs! Yiiiiiiiiiii!! Let me go! Let me go or I'll curse you and your miserable ancestry forever! Yiiiiiiiiiii!!! I'll make sure your miserable children die of the plague like rats!!!" The woman was suddenly raging like a shrieking banshee hovering over a row of deathbeds in a hospital. It was fortunate she was handcuffed otherwise she might have been tempted to use the long fingernails she possessed to gouge chunks of flesh from the faces of the men about her.

The officer nearest her, surprised into immobility at first by her sudden rage, quickly recovered enough to grab her, clamping his hands on her shoulders and then holding her at arms length while she twisted to get free. Another uniformed officer ran to his aid and together both men forced the tigress to relative stillness, her lips still curled in a snarl as she cursed them.

"Take her outside!" ordered Blaine. "I won't be listening to her screams. Keep her in the carriage until we go back to the precinct."

"Beasts! Beasts! Beasts!" was the most printable of words she hissed at the police officers as she was taken, feet kicking and swinging, down the hall and out of the building. The last thing Hawkes took notice of was the gypsy's clasping and unclasping of her handcuffed hands behind her back, the long scarlet nails an undeniable threat to the police officers had she not been restrained.

"Madam Tollier, I trust?" spoke up Hawkes after the woman was gone and her screams had faded.

"That's her," replied Blaine. "A handful, isn't she? If not for the cuffs, I'd have feared for the eyes of my men. I wonder what set her off. She seemed calm enough when telling me the facts of the shooting." Then, with a shrug, he provided an answer to his own question. "As I said, it may be just that she doesn't trust the police. There's a whole contingent of gypsies in this city who want nothing to do with us. Perhaps she's convinced that once we take her away, she'll never be heard from again."

"You said she acted in self-defense," said Hawkes. "If that's so, then why put handcuffs on her?"

"She was on her way out of here, running away, when a couple of officers happened to come by and stopped her. We were lucky there. It just chanced that two patrolmen were right outside when the shots were fired. They were on their way to the precinct house. They came running into the house as she was rushing out. Once away from here we'd never have found her. She then resisted the officers', ah…request, that she remain. That's why the cuffs are on her. We don't want her running away."

"Ah…"

"Once she settled down, and I showed up, she told us what happened. Carter's body is in a room near the back. As I said, I've identified him through some papers in his wallet. But now you can verify what those papers say. I don't have any doubt it's him but a positive identification can't hurt."

"The body is in the back?"

"Yes. Plugged with two bullets from the gypsy's pistol. He came at her with his sword. He had one of those concealed swords in a cane, and, as he tried to put the blade through her, she put two holes in him."

"Of course it's only her word for that, isn't that so?"

"Ah, there you go, Mr. Hawkes. No, you're not going to find any hidden truth in this crime. This is not like the Pritchett affair. You were on the money there, that's certain. But there's nothing hidden here. It's clear as to what happened."

"No doubt," replied Hawkes. "Back this way?"

The layout of the brownstone floor was of the kind called "railroad rooms" in the local slang, one room situated directly behind the other, and Hawkes and Blaine passed from the parlor into the adjoining room that clearly was the gypsy's bedroom, then into another smaller room in back of that. This room evidently served both as a large closet of sorts and as a place where the gypsy could dress and put on her makeup. A wooden rack had a few dresses hanging on it and was pushed against one wall. An aged mirrored vanity was placed against another, structured of mahogany. It was at least thirty years old and had spent some of that time at least in being misused. It was well worn and scratched, scarred throughout. Three mirrors stood on it, one larger mirror in the center and two smaller ones on the sides that were capable of being folded over the center glass. An old and equally much blemished wooden chair sat in front of it. Nearby, stood a washstand with ewer and basin. The walls of the room, as was true of all the walls in the house, were unadorned by those female touches which add charm to our lives. The entire place was desperately in need of a fresh coat of paint.

Joseph Julius Carter's body lay in the middle the room. The scent of blood and gunpowder welcomed Hawkes as he and Blaine entered. The dead man lay face up, spread-eagled on his back, his shocked and unseeing eyes staring up at the cracked and grimy ceiling overhead. His ermine-collared overcoat fell open on either side of his prone body displaying the rich fabric of his very expensive tailored suit. The gold chain of his pocket watch sat gleaming across his still-buttoned vest. Stark against the white linen of his shirt were lines of red that crawled from beneath the buttoned vest toward the collar of his shirt, the manifest result of the gypsy's killing shots that had entered the man's chest and ripped away his life.

On the floor by the body was a long thin bladed sword. The blade of the cane-sword Blaine had spoken of. Immediately beside the drawn blade lay the walking stick scabbard. Both sword and scabbard rested on the floor by the dead man's right hand. Hawkes noted that the soles and heels of the dead man's boots were wet with melted snow.

"That's him," declared Hawkes. "That's Joseph Carter."

"Since you're acquainted with the man, can you tell me if you know if it was his normal habit to carry that concealed sword?" asked Blaine.

"He had it with him each time I saw him."

"So it was not unusual for him to be carrying it with him tonight. That seems to fit with the notion that his attack was on the spur of the moment."

"Excellent reasoning, Blaine. Of course its truth is based upon the assumption that he did indeed attack the woman. Did you ask Madam Tollier if she lit a fresh candle for tonight's séance?"

"Fresh candle? What does that—?"

"Was the candle burning when you arrived?"

"What? No, it wasn't. The parlor was dark except for the light from the hall."

"Carter arrived recently. Within the hour. It's not been snowing longer and there is that water on his boots there. Given your statements, and the obvious time of Carter's arrival, there could be hardly more than a few minutes available for a séance. Yet the candle on the table is burned down to the point where it indicates the passage of considerably more time. Certainly more than an hour."

"Wet boots…well, you *are* sharp-eyed, Mr. Hawkes. But you haven't heard the full story yet. What you pointed out, the candle and the wet shoes, doesn't contradict her story. In fact, it's actually very consistent with what the gypsy told us. You see there was a séance, with Carter here and a couple of others. It was begun almost two hours ago and it went on for a time. An hour or so. Then, when it was over, everyone left, except that Carter here then came back at a later time, wanting to kill the gypsy, you see. He came after the snow had started so there's the answer to your wet boots."

"Others? Do you know the names of the others that were here?"

Blaine flipped over a page in his notebook. "Yes, the gypsy told us. Two others. Howard Mendelson and George O'Neil. Mr. Carter is the unlucky third on a match. They left after the séance from what the gypsy told me. Carter left with them but then apparently waited outside, waiting to be certain they'd gone and he would be alone with Madam Tollier. He then returned and subsequently made his attempt on the gypsy's life. I will of course have to talk to both men to verify her story."

"Is that Howard Mendelson, the railroad man? And George O'Neil, the head of The Manhattan Bank?"

"That's my understanding," returned the detective. "A couple of high-rollers. It amazes me how gullible some otherwise sharp men can be. Here they are, two movers and shakers, three counting the dead man, educated at the best schools in the nation, and they still believe in this gypsy's mumbo-jumbo. Still, if something is believed, it's as good as true to the believer—even if it's false. What counts is what Carter believed."

"Yes, that's so," responded Hawkes. "But I must admit, Mr. Blaine, I find this whole situation a little difficult to sort out. Do you think you could you tell me exactly what occurred here this night, and clarify the precise order that events took place?"

"Why not? It'll do me good to state the facts, to get them all straight in my own head. All right…just let me…" Blaine turned a page or two in his notebook, then he looked up again, ready to speak.

As Blaine prepared to speak, Hawkes opened his woolen coat and then placed his back against the wall, leaning his weight on it. "Pray, just state the primary facts as you know them," he said, his keen eyes fixing their sight on some vague spot on the opposite wall.

"This is the gypsy's story," Blaine began. "At or about two hours ago, at ten to four, give or take, Carter, Mendelson and O'Neil arrived at this building. They sit at the table—that's the table outside that we walked past in the parlor—and the gypsy starts her performance. Madam Tollier and the three men are all seated. The only light in the room is from the candle you saw on the table. No other light except that in the hall. They do whatever people do at séances for a time.

And then, after an hour or so, a spirit actually makes contact with them, or so the gypsy says." Here Blaine lifted his head and looked at Hawkes. "Contact with a spirit?" he said in a derisive tone. "Isn't that the most absurd…?"

"Please, continue," requested Hawkes.

"Well, at this point the gypsy starts speaking in a strange voice. 'Other than my own' to quote her precisely. Then she suddenly looks across the table at Carter and says: 'Daddy, is that you?' Carter responds by speaking his dead daughter's name: 'Eleanora?'

"The word 'murder' then is spoken. Then again. 'I was murdered! My killer must be punished. My killer must be punished.' Then, after a minute or so of repeating these words, the spirit leaves the gypsy. As the men sit looking at Madam Tollier, she stands and says she cannot go on. The anger of the spirit has taken too much energy from her, she tells them. The séance is effectively ended. Carter, so Madam Tollier says, is visibly shaken as he leaves the house with the others." The police detective then lifted his face once again from the notebook he held. "Of course, as I said, I'm going to have to speak with Mendelson and O'Neil to confirm the truth of all this," he said to Hawkes.

"Of course. Please go on with your statement of the facts as given to you by Madam Tollier. I find it all very interesting."

"Where was I?" said Blaine. "Yes, the men leave. That can be confirmed easily enough by the other two. However, some minutes later, *after* it had begun to snow, Joseph Carter returns, alone. He rings the bell, insistently, and Madam Tollier, now resting in her bed, is forced to get up and open the door.

"In bursts Carter, furious as all get out. He actually believes his daughter has in fact spoken to him through the gypsy. And so he believes that his daughter will be able to speak through the gypsy again. He is apparently fearful of *what his daughter might say*, for no sooner is he inside then he threatens the gypsy with death. He pulls out his sword and she, seeing his intent, flees for her life, running to the back of the house to this room. She pulls open that center drawer in that vanity where she has a pistol she purchased, she says, for her protection."

"A wise precaution, it would seem," interrupted Hawkes.

"Well, it apparently served its purpose tonight," returned the detective. "He, Carter that is, comes running into the room after her and she has just enough time to take the gun from the drawer, turn and put two bullets into his chest. Then she tries to run away, and dashes into the arms of the two patrolmen, as luck would have it. That's it, the whole story. If it holds up, it's a clear case of self-defense."

"The clear implication here," said Hawkes, "is that Carter was in some manner responsible for his own daughter's death. That, in the daughter speaking of her own murder, she was in fact accusing him—and that his attempt on the gypsy's life was motivated by his desire to silence any further revelations that might be made by his daughter's spirit. To silence a ghost, as you picturesquely phrased it. Is that right?"

"Yes, I don't personally believe in this gypsy's mumbo-jumbo, but as long as Carter believed it, it's motive enough."

"Madam Tollier no doubt considers herself unfortunate due to the presence of the two officers outside."

"Yes, she was fleeing the house, taking her pistol with her, when she was stopped by them. Luck for us there, for it happened that they were walking down the street and were just about standing in front of the house when the shots were fired. They had gone to break up a family brawl just two houses down from this one. Hearing the shots, they rushed up the steps to investigate and she practically ran straight into their arms. If not for that, she'd be long gone and we'd never have gotten her. These gypsies can change their names as easily as their undergarments."

"Are you aware, Blaine, of the circumstances surrounding the death of Carter's daughter?" asked Hawkes shifting his gaze to the face of the detective.

Blaine responded that he was not.

"It happens that I am. He spoke of it at the same time he contacted me regarding the death of his wife. It occurred, if memory serves me, sometime in August of this year. The Carter family have a small house by the shore in Staten Island that they use in the summers. His daughter, Eleanora, had only days earlier celebrated her fifteenth birthday. She was found drowned in the waters, her body washed up onto the beach by the house. A very sad affair. I remember there was some question as to whether the young girl's death was due to a boating accident or whether the girl ended her own life. But I don't believe the thought of murder was contemplated by the police at the time."

"Perhaps it should have been," remarked Blaine.

"It wasn't long after the death of his daughter that the second tragedy struck," stated Hawkes. "That was the killing of his wife that I spoke of."

"What happened there?"

"His wife, Laura Carter, was murdered a month or so following his daughter's death. The victim of a thief in Central Park. She was killed apparently during a robbery attempt. Her assailant was never caught."

"Hmmm. Given the gypsy's story, I wonder if we should take another look at that," considered Blaine. "If there's any truth to the daughter's accusation, then it might be our Mr. Carter has killed, maybe even more than once. Maybe the Carter family life was not all it should have been."

"So then you don't think Madam Tollier's séance was simply mumbo-jumbo, as you say?" declared Hawkes suddenly. "You think enough of the spirit's accusation, the man's deceased daughter's accusation, to open an investigation into her death?"

"Well, not because of the spirit's words. The spirit didn't actually accuse anyone, did it? Rather because of Carter's reaction to what was said. The gypsy talks of murder and he immediately thinks it's him being accused and attempts to silence the voice of that accusation. There's an admission of guilt in that, isn't there? Whether or not the ghost of his daughter was actually speaking through the gypsy or not. She might have been having some fun with the man, for some unknown gypsy reason, and accidentally struck a chord of guilt in him. That fits, doesn't it?"

Hawkes was gazing at the small jars that sat atop the vanity. "What—? Oh, no, Blaine, I do think that is highly unlikely. Rather it is much more probable that everything the gypsy has told you is *not* true," he stated abruptly. "Everything relating to the shooting of Mr. Carter, that is." He held up a small hair brush that was also resting on the vanity. "See that, Blaine?"

"What? See what?" returned Blaine, staring at the brush and then at Hawkes. "Why do you say she's lying?".

"There is blonde hair on the brush," stated Hawkes. He stood thoughtfully for a time. "Hum, could it be…? Yes, I believe it is."

"Could what be?"

"Could you have the woman brought back inside?"

"The gypsy? Why?"

"It'll become clear," returned Hawkes and Blaine, relenting with a shrug of his shoulders, called out to a uniformed officer in the parlor to have Madam Tollier brought back into the house.

"In the meantime, I'll need a little water."

"There's water in the ewer there, on the washstand," said Blaine. "Help yourself."

Hawkes produced a handkerchief and dampened it by dipping some fabric into the ewer. Blaine gazed at him, wondering what was Hawkes purpose in wetting the handkerchief. He didn't bother to give voice to the question.

The gypsy was brought into the room as she'd left the house, kicking and screaming, struggling strenuously against the power of the two police officers on either side of her. They had their work cut out for them just in maintaining control over her. She very clearly was not at all happy over her forced return, although exactly why she should be fighting so vehemently against it, Blaine could not, at the time, even begin to fathom.

It became clear in the next few minutes.

Finally, realizing her struggles were in vain, she ceased her resistance. Still gripped tightly by the police, she stood, breathing hard from her exertions, glaring at the two men in front of her, at Hawkes in particular, her face wearing the expression of a wild animal whose den has just been invaded, ready to kill if only granted the chance. Her eyes contained so much heat, so much anger and hate, it might have been possible that Hawkes himself would burst into flames beneath her gaze.

She stood silently, now waiting, as were all others, to see what would happen next.

Hawkes raised his dampened handkerchief and brought it up to the cheek of the gypsy.

To Blaine's astonishment, and that police officers holding the woman as well, the gypsy reacted as violently as if the handkerchief was a branding iron instead of a wet piece of cloth. Suddenly she was kicking again, twisting and struggling to gain her freedom from the men holding her, fighting like an wild animal resisting the first rope it feels around its neck, the rope of its capture. At last, one of the officers put a large arm around the gypsy's own neck and applied enough pressure against her throat to force her to submission once again.

Her eyes were wide as eggs as Hawkes once again brought the wet cloth up to her twisted face. A few quick rubs and a streak of white appeared in the otherwise brown complexion of her cheek.

"It's been a few weeks, Miss Lametta, since I saw you last," he said, reaching up and pulling away the black wig on her head, revealing the bright blonde hair beneath it. It is a pleasure to see you again." The gypsy's response was one of additional rage. She hissed at him, like a snake at a mongoose, and flung a series of vile curses at him.

"Miss Lametta?" said Blaine, amazed by the white streak that had appeared on the gypsy's brown face and the sudden appearance of blonde hair. "You know this woman?"

:She's Rosemary Lametta, a daughter of Harold Lametta and Rose Carter, Joseph Carter's late sister. She is the dead man's niece."

The detective gazed at the woman in absolute astonishment. "His niece?!" he blurted at last. "What in the world is going on here?"

"Murder, Mr. Blaine. Pure and simple. Although what precisely the motive for it is, I leave for you to determine."

"That's not so," came back Rosemary Lametta, suddenly communicative in her own defense. "I didn't murder anyone. So I'm his niece, so what? It happened like I said. I was playing a prank on him. That's all. How was I to know he'd take it all so seriously? Suddenly he's after me with his sword. I had to shoot him! He wouldn't listen to me! He wouldn't stop!"

"No, Rosemary, it won't do," returned Hawkes. "You murdered your uncle, although why I cannot say. Revenge? Did he ever harm you? Or your mother? Or is there another reason? Money?" She glared at him, clearly wishing him dead.

"How can you be so sure it's murder?" came Blaine's voice between the woman and Hawkes. "It could have happened like she says, couldn't it?"

Hawkes turned and pointed to the sword and cane-scabbard still resting on the floor on one side of the outline of the victim's body. "Not according to that," he said.

"The sword?" asked a puzzled Blaine.

"The sword blade and scabbard *together*," said Hawkes. "It's clear that Carter was shot first and only then was the scabbard removed to reveal the blade. To make it appear as though he was threatening someone. Her mistake was simply laying the scabbard immediately *beside* the blade. If the dead man had done as Ms. Lametta insists, that is, drawn his sword and then attacked her, the blade and scabbard would not then be on the same side of the fallen body. It would be impossible, for he would have wielded the sword in his right hand, but *held the scabbard in his left*. The scabbard, if this was a true attack, would therefore not be on the same side of the man's body as the blade."

Blaine's eyes went to the sword and cane-scabbard lying side by side on the floor.

It was suddenly obvious to him, now that Hawkes had pointed it out, that it had to be as Hawkes said. Like one of those trick drawings for children in which a figure is hidden and difficult to see, until it's seen once, and then it's so obvious you wonder how you could fail to pick it out immediately, the truth of Hawkes' words were immediately evident and irrefutable.

"Damn you, Simon Hawkes!" hissed Rosemary Lametta. "Damn you all the way to hell! I wish you dead! You should die! Damn you! Damn you!"

"Take her out of here," ordered Blaine. "She's being arrested for the murder of Joseph Carter. Premeditated murder. Go on, get her out of here."

"That explains why she acted as she did when we first arrived," spoke up Hawkes once the women had been taken away. "She knew who I was and was afraid I'd recognize her if I got a good look at her. She wanted to get out of the room as quickly as possible. To get away from me."

"Before you could get a good look at her," said Blaine. "So that's why she started going crazy."

"Yes, and her fear was justified," said Hawkes. "I have a good memory for faces, although, due to her disguise it took the blonde hairs on that brush there to trigger the memory. She wore the wig for this charade."

"Good thing you were here. I think she'd have pulled it off, the charade I mean."

"I doubt her intention was ever to fool the police with it. You said that two officers, those who happened to be passing by, heard the shots and stopped her as she was running away. It's clear her original intention was to kill Carter and then flee, leaving the police with the idea that the man had been killed by a mysterious gypsy named Madam Tollier. A gypsy that no doubt would have subsequently disappeared forever as though she never existed. After shooting the man, she removed the scabbard to reveal the sword blade, perhaps on the spur of the moment, in order to suggest he'd been killed due to an altercation or disagreement of some sort. She knew her uncle never went anywhere without it. It was her bad luck that the police stopped her from leaving. If not for that she'd be long gone."

"Bad luck too that you happened by."

"Yes, fortune wasn't on her side tonight. That's certain," responded Hawkes.

"If you recognized her, how come her uncle didn't?" asked Blaine.

"Carter and his sister, Rosemary's mother, had a falling out many years ago. They didn't speak. He hasn't seen his niece since she was nine or ten. I met her a few weeks back because I went to the Lametta house to interview the family. I was attempting to find if they could tell me anything, anything at all, that might help me learn who had killed Carter's wife. Rosemary was there at the time. I talked to her as well. Now that I think of it, from that interview, from what I saw while in the Lametta house, I concluded that family had come upon hard times financially. The house had fallen into some disrepair, and the state of their clothes and shoes indicated a similar need for repair that was not being filled. There might be motive in that. That is, if Joseph refused to help his sister out when she needed his help, it might produce some hard feelings. Check into that, Blaine, find out everything you can about Rosemary Lametta and her family. It's possible that the reason for this murder plot against her uncle will manifest itself if you do."

"You astound me, Mr. Hawkes," stated Blaine. "I said there was nothing hidden in this case before, and it's clear now that everything that was true was being concealed. She might very well have been released if not for you."

"It was an elementary case. Don't be too hard on yourself. I did have the advantage of meeting the woman previously. I leave it to you to discover the full truth as to why she did what she did. Good night, Blaine."

Chapter Three

As was widely publicized afterwards, the crimes of Rosemary Lametta were broader in scope than at first suspected by the police. Some may recall the facts which follow, facts made public through the media accounts of the crimes of "The Heinous Heiress" (as a New York City daily dubbed her). Ms. Lametta's mother did not possess the many millions of dollars her brother, her uncle, had accumulated and Rosemary had begun to cast an envious and greedy eye toward that wealth. It was hers by right, or at least a large portion of it, she determined. Like the bard's Macbeth, who saw only a few lives standing between him and the harvest of his life's desire, she decided to eliminate those few living human barriers to her own ambition.

She resolved to leave herself as the only living heir to her uncle's fortune, to eliminate those legal beneficiaries standing between her and the money she coveted. There was little to stop her, certainly there was no sense of familial connection or love inside her. Her uncle moved within his own sphere of existence, financially far removed from her own. She hadn't even seen him, or his family, for more than a decade. He was little more than a stranger to her.

But she was nothing if not clever. She reasoned that she couldn't kill off the members of her uncle's family in a series of unexplained murders. That would create a circumstance that would scream for resolution by the police. No, best if each died accidentally, or at least under circumstances that carried within them their own explanation for death. Each murder had to contain within it its own clarification, each had to be marked "closed" on the records of the police. No killing should point toward her.

Unbeknownst to her family, she rented a small apartment on the West Side of Manhattan. There, she obtained the ability to plan and execute her plans of murder free from interference. There were three deaths required, her Aunt Laura, her uncle and their daughter, Eleanora. Carter's fortune would then pass to his sister, Rosemary's own mother, who would then be her uncle's only living relative. Then, of course, upon her parents' deaths, to Rosemary herself.

Whether she was willing to wait for her parents to die of natural causes is not entirely clear.

Eleanora was first.

Rosemary took a ferry to the Carter summer home. The young girl was easy to approach, easy to befriend and, being so much smaller than she was, easy to hold beneath the ocean waters until her young life bubbled out of her and was gone.

For a couple of weeks, she followed her aunt, Laura Carter, about, studying the woman's patterns of daily life. From that knowledge, she quickly developed a plan for her murder. The woman took a walk in Central Park almost every evening and always along the same paths. That made it easy.

Laura Carter's death due to a robbery attempt in the park was well publicized at the time. She was found shot through the heart lying in a thicket of bushes very near the bridal path. Her money and jewelry had been taken from her, and she was viewed by the police as another unfortunate victim of a violent crime.

Only her uncle remained.

How to kill him? After the deaths of his wife and daughter, the man, in his sorrow, became a virtual recluse, rarely leaving his home. Where was she to get her opportunity to kill? Here, more subtlety was called for.

She began to write notes of consolation to him, in hopes of learning something that would grant her the chance she wanted, and, in his short thankful replies, she thought she found what she wanted. He wrote more than once of his wish to be able to talk to his "darling baby" again. Out of this small seed grew her cunning plan of murder, and from that plan came the creation of Madam Tollier.

She wrote to him, suggesting it might be possible for him to talk to his Eleanora once again as he wanted to do, through the use of a spiritualist she was acquainted with, a woman with a superlative reputation. His reply was one of doubt. At first. Another letter and he was convinced. Indeed, as she told him in that second letter, what did he have to lose by trying?

She held every confidence in her acting ability. She purchased a black wig, darkened her skin to a mocha tan, and became her creation, the gypsy spiritualist, Madam Tollier.

To her surprise, the first time her uncle came to her, he was accompanied by friends. Unexpected as this was, she had little choice but to perform her little séance for them. Her brief conversation with Eleanora just prior to her drowning the girl gave her the necessary knowledge to allow her to ably imitate the dead girl's voice. Just a few words. The right words. She was familiar with him and his family and knew what to say. Enough to convince her uncle to return for a second seance.

The second time, when her uncle arrived with his friends, she was better prepared.

She performed for them, and shocked them all with a vague accusation of murder. "My killer must be punished." Then, as they were leaving, she whispered a private message to her visibly shaken uncle. "Your daughter has more to say to you, but she must speak to you alone. Let the others leave, return in a few minutes if you want to learn who killed your Eleanora."

In this at least she was truthful. The man did, moments before the bullets entered his chest, learn the true identity of the gypsy and, with only seconds of life left to him, was told by his giggling niece that it was she who murdered his wife and daughter and it was she who was about to murder him. The last sight he carried with him as he abandoned this world for the next was that of his niece's gleeful face as she, twice in quick succession, pulled the trigger of the pistol that she pointed toward his heart.

If not for a bit of bad luck in running into the police as she fled the last of the three crime scenes, and her mistake of placing the cane scabbard beside her uncle's drawn sword, she might very well have succeeded in achieving her intentions and escaped punishment entirely.

In fact, except for her being imprisoned for her crimes, it is a sad fact that Ms. Lametta has indeed succeeded just as she intended. Investigations by the police revealed that her parents were not involved at all in her foul plans. Being innocent of any involvement, and despite some legal protests and the contesting of Carter's last will and testament, the bulk of his fortune did indeed pass to Rosemary's mother, Carter's sister and (now) closest living relative. There exists no legal reason that would forbid that fortune from eventually passing from parents to child, to the young woman now serving three concurrent life sentences for murder.

In the meantime, her victim's fortune is currently being used to her benefit. It is common knowledge that her mother has hired some of the country's top attorneys to do all that legally can be done to have her daughter's sentence lessened and have her released from prison.

Until that eventuality, should it ever occur, Rosemary Lametta has found religion, or at least it is so declared in the media. Sitting in her prison cell, she reads from the Bible every day, a leather bound volume embossed in twenty-four carat gold. A gift from her mother.

Simon Hawkes, at the time he was putting dampened handkerchief to the cheek of Rosemary Lametta, could not help but recall the image of Hugh Boone, the professional beggar whose story had been chronicled by Dr. Watson years earlier. The orange hair, the pale disfigured face, all were as false as was the disguise of Rosemary Lametta.

London and his previous life beckoned to him.

After a week of contemplation following his successful unraveling of the events surrounding the murder of Joseph Julius Carter, a week in which he read and reread the wire he'd received from his brother, he at last finalized his decision. He would send a message to Mycroft telling him to prepare for his return to England. The restoration of his former life would not be immediate but certainly would occur within the next few months.

It was time to be Sherlock Holmes again.

About the Author

Philip Carraher was born in Manhattan and continues to live in New York City, now residing in the borough of Brooklyn with his wife, Ann. His philosophy regarding his books is threefold: first, they should be entertaining, second, they should strive to rise above simple entertainment, i.e., be thought provoking, and, lastly, each new book should not merely be a practiced variation of the previous one.

Printed in the United States
22685LVS00005B/259-264

9 781403 369925